MARGRET HOWTH

A Story of To-day

By Rebecca Harding Davis

Afterword by Jean Fagan Yellin

"My matter hath no voice to alien ears."

THE FEMINIST PRESS
at The City University of New York
New York

Afterword © 1990 by Jean Fagan Yellin
Published 1990 by The Feminist Press at The City
University of New York, 311 East 94 Street, New York,
N.Y. 10128
Distributed by The Talman Company, Inc., 150 Fifth
Avenue, New York, N.Y. 10011

Margret Howth: A Story of To-day was originally
published in 1862.

93 92 91 90 6 5 4 3 2 1

Library of Congress Cataloging-in-Publication Data

Davis, Rebecca Harding, 1831–1910.
    Margret Howth: a story of to-day / by Rebecca Harding
Davis; afterword by Jean Fagan Yellin.
        p. cm.
    Originally published: Boston: Ticknor and Fields, 1862.
    ISBN 1-55861-030-8 (alk. paper): $35.00. —
ISBN 1-55861-036-7 (pbk.: alk. paper): $11.95
    I. Title.
PS1517.M37   1990
813'.4—dc20   90-3684
                                                      CIP

This publication is made possible, in part, by public funds
from the New York State Council on the Arts.

Cover design: Paula Martinac
Cover art: Eastman Johnson, *A Day Dream,* © 1877.
    Private collection. Reproduced by permission.
Back cover photo: From *The Richard Harding Davis
    Years* by Gerald Langford. Copyright © 1961 by Gerald
    Langford. Photograph from the collection of Mrs. Hope
    Davis Kehrig. Reprinted by permission of Henry Holt
    and Company, Inc.

Printed in the United States of America on acid-free
paper by McNaughton & Gunn, Inc.

MARGRET HOWTH

CONTENTS

MARGRET HOWTH

MARGRET HOWTH.

A STORY OF TO-DAY.

CHAPTER I.

LET me tell you a story of To-Day, — very homely and narrow in its scope and aim. Not of the To-Day whose significance in the history of humanity only those shall read who will live when you and I are dead. We can bear the pain in silence, if our hearts are strong enough, while the nations of the earth stand afar off. I have no word of this To-Day to speak. I write from the border of the battle-field, and I find in it no theme for shallow argument or flimsy rhymes. The shadow of death has fallen on us; it chills the very heaven. No child laughs in my face as I pass down the street. Men have forgotten to hope, forgotten to pray; only in the bitterness of endurance, they say "in the morning, ' Would God it were even!' and in the evening, ' Would God it were morning!'" Neither I nor you have the prophet's vision to see the age as its meaning stands

written before God. Those who shall live when
we are dead may tell their children, perhaps,
how, out of anguish and darkness such as the
world seldom has borne, the enduring morning
evolved of the true world and the true man.
It is not clear to us. Hands wet with a brother's blood for the Right, a slavery of intoler-
ance, the hackneyed cant of men, or the blood-
thirstiness of women, utter no prophecy to us
of the great To-Morrow of content and right
that holds the world. Yet the To-Morrow is
there; if God lives, it is there. The voice of
the meek Nazarene, which we have deafened
down as ill-timed, unfit to teach the watchword
of the hour, renews the quiet promise of its
coming in simple, humble things. Let us go
down and look for it. There is no need that
we should feebly vaunt and madden ourselves
over our self-seen rights, whatever they may
be, forgetting what broken shadows they are
of eternal truths in that calm where He sits
and with His quiet hand controls us.

Patriotism and Chivalry are powers in the
tranquil, unlimited lives to come, as well as
here, I know; but there are less partial truths,
higher hierarchies who serve the God-man, that
do not speak to us in bayonets and victories, —
Mercy and Love. Let us not quite neglect
them, unpopular angels though they be. Very

humble their voices are, just now : yet not altogether dead, I think.   Why, the very low glow
of the fire upon the hearth tells me something
of recompense coming in the hereafter, —
Christmas-days, and heartsome warmth ; in
these bare hills trampled down by armed men,
the yellow clay is quick with pulsing fibres,
hints of the great heart of life and love throbbing within ; slanted sunlight would show me,
in these sullen smoke-clouds from the camp,
walls of amethyst and jasper, outer ramparts
of the Promised Land.   Do not call us trait-
ors, then, who choose to be cool and silent
through the fever of the hour, — who choose to
search in common things for auguries of the
hopeful, helpful calm to come, finding even in
these poor sweet-peas, thrusting their tendrils
through the brown mould, a deeper, more
healthful lesson for the eye and soul than
warring truths.   Do not call me a traitor, if
I dare weakly to hint that there are yet other
characters besides that of Patriot in which a
man may appear creditably in the great masquerade, and not blush when it is over ; or if
I tell you a story of To-Day, in which there
shall be no bloody glare, — only those home-
lier, subtiler lights which we have overlooked.
If it prove to you that the sun of old times still
shines, and the God of old times still lives, is not
that enough ?

My story is very crude and homely, as I said,
— only a rough sketch of one or two of those
people whom you see every day, and call
" dregs," sometimes, — a dull, plain bit of
prose, such as you might pick for yourself out
of any of these warehouses or back-streets. I
expect you to call it stale and plebeian, for I
know the glimpses of life it pleases you best
to find; idyls delicately tinted; passion-veined
hearts, cut bare for curious eyes; prophetic
utterances, concrete and clear; or some word
of pathos or fun from the old friends who have
endenizened themselves in everybody's home.
You want something, in fact, to lift you out
of this crowded, tobacco-stained commonplace,
to kindle and chafe and glow in you. I want
you to dig into this commonplace, this vulgar
American life, and see what is in it. Sometimes I think it has a new and awful significance that we do not see.

Your ears are openest to the war-trumpet
now. Ha! that is spirit-stirring! — that wakes
up the old Revolutionary blood! Your man-
lier nature had been smothered under drudgery,
the poor daily necessity for bread and butter.
I want you to go down into this common,
every-day drudgery, and consider if there might
not be in it also a great warfare. Not a serfish
war; not altogether ignoble, though even its

only end may appear to be your daily food. A great warfare, I think, with a history as old as the world, and not without its pathos. It has its slain. Men and women, lean-jawed, crippled in the slow, silent battle, are in your alleys, sit beside you at your table; its martyrs sleep under every green hill-side.

You must fight in it; money will buy you no discharge from that war. There is room in it, believe me, whether your post be on a judge's bench, or over a wash-tub, for heroism, for knightly honour, for purer triumph than his who falls foremost in the breach. Your enemy, Self, goes with you from the cradle to the coffin; it is a hand-to-hand struggle all the sad, slow way, fought in solitude, — a battle that began with the first heart-beat, and whose victory will come only when the drops ooze out, and suddenly halt in the veins, — a victory, if you can gain it, that will drift you not a little way upon the coasts of the wider, stronger range of being, beyond death.

Let me roughly outline for you one or two lives that I have known, and how they conquered or were worsted in the fight. Very common lives, I know, — such as are swarming in yonder market-place; yet I dare to call them voices of God, — all!

My reason for choosing this story to tell you is simple enough. 1*

An old book, which I happened to find to-day,
recalled it. It was a ledger, iron-bound, with
the name of the firm on the outside, — Knowles
& Co. You may have heard of the firm : they
were large woollen manufacturers : supplied the
home market in Indiana for several years. This
ledger, you see by the writing, has been kept by
a woman. That is not unusual in Western
trading towns, especially in factories where the
operatives are chiefly women. In such establish-
ments, they can fill every post successfully, but
that of overseer : they are too hard with the
hands for that.

The writing here is curious : concise, square,
not flowing, — very legible, however, exactly
suited to its purpose. People who profess to
read character in chirography would decipher
but little from these cramped, quiet lines. Only
this, probably : that the woman, whoever she
was, had not the usual fancy of her sex for
dramatizing her soul in her writing, her dress,
her face, — kept it locked up instead, intact ;
that her words and looks, like her writing, were
most likely simple, mere absorbents by which
she drew what she needed of the outer world
to her, not flaunting helps to fling herself, or
the tragedy or comedy that lay within, before
careless passers-by. The first page has the
date, in red letters, *October* 2, 1860, largely and

clearly written. I am sure the woman's hand
trembled a little when she took up the pen; but
there is no sign of it here; for it was a new,
desperate adventure to her, and she was young,
with no faith in herself. She did not look desperate, at all, — a quiet, dark girl, coarsely
dressed in brown.

There was not much light in the office where
she sat; for the factory was in one of the close
by-streets of the town, and the office they gave
her was only a small square closet in the sev-
enth story. It had but one window, which
overlooked a back-yard full of dyeing vats. The
sunlight that did contrive to struggle in ob-
liquely through the dusty panes and cobwebs
of the window, had a sleepy odour of copperas
latent in it. You smelt it when you stirred.
The manager, Pike, who brought her up, had
laid the day-books and this ledger open on the
desk for her. As soon as he was gone, she shut
the door, listening until his heavy boots had
thumped creaking down the rickety ladder leading to the frame-rooms. Then she climbed up
on the high office-stool (climbed, I said, for she
was a little, lithe thing) and went to work,
opening the books, and copying from one to
the other as steadily, monotonously, as if she
had been used to it all her life. Here are the
first pages : see how sharp the angles are of the

blue and black lines, how even the long col-
umns : one would not think, that, as the steel
pen traced them out, it seemed to be lining out
her life, narrow and black.   If any such morbid
fancy were in the girl's head, there was no tear
to betray it.   The sordid, hard figures seemed
to her types of the years coming, but she wrote
them down unflinchingly : perhaps life had nothing better for her, so she did not care.   She finished soon : they had given her only an hour or
two's work for the first day.   She closed the
books, wiped the pens in a quaint, mechanical
fashion, then got down and examined her new
home.

It was soon understood.   There were the
walls with their broken plaster, showing the
laths underneath, with here and there, over
them, sketches with burnt coal, showing that
her predecessor had been an artist in his way,
— his name, P. Teagarden, emblazoned on the
ceiling with the smoke of a candle ; heaps of
hanks of yarn in the dusty corners ; a half-used
broom ; other heaps of yarn on the old toppling
desk covered with dust ; a raisin-box, with P.
Teagarden done on the lid in bas-relief, half
full of ends of cigars, a pack of cards, and a rot-
ten apple.   That was all, except an impalpable
sense of dust and worn-outness pervading the
whole.   One thing more, odd enough there : a

wire cage, hung on the wall, and in it a miserable pecking chicken, peering dolefully with
suspicious eyes out at her, and then down at
the mouldy bit of bread on the floor of his cage,
— left there, I suppose, by the departed Teagarden. That was all, inside. She looked out
of the window. In it, as if set in a square black
frame, was the dead brick wall, and the oppo-
site roof, with a cat sitting on the scuttle. Going closer, two or three feet of sky appeared. It
looked as if it smelt of copperas, and she· drew
suddenly back.

She sat down, waiting until it was time to
go; quietly taking the dull picture into her slow,
unrevealing eyes ; a sluggish, hackneyed weariness creeping into her brain; a curious feeling,
that all her life before had been a silly dream,
and this dust, these desks and ledgers, were
real, — all that was real. It was her birthday;
she was twenty. As she happened to remember that, another fancy floated up before her,
oddly life-like : of the old seat she made under
the currant-bushes at home when she was a
child, and the plans she laid for herself, when
she should be a woman, sitting there, — how
she would dig down into the middle of the
world, and find the kingdom of the griffins, or
would go after Mercy and Christiana in their
pilgrimage. It was only a little while ago

since these things were more alive to her than
anything else in the world. The seat was
under the currant-bushes still. Very little time
ago; but she was a woman now, — and, look
here! A chance ray of sunlight slanted in,
falling barely on the dust, the hot heaps of
wool, waking a stronger smell of copperas; the
chicken saw it, and began to chirp a weak, dismal joy, more sorrowful than tears. She went
to the cage, and put her finger in for it to peck
at. Standing there, if the vacant life coming
rose up before her in that hard blare of sunlight, she looked at it with the same still, waiting eyes, that told nothing.

The door opened at last, and a man came in,
— Dr. Knowles, the principal owner of the factory. He nodded shortly to her, and, going to
the desk, turned over the books, peering suspi-
ciously at her work. An old man, overgrown,
looking like a huge misshapen mass of flesh, as
he stood erect, facing her.

"You can go now," he said, gruffly. "To-
morrow you must wait for the bell to ring, and
go — with the rest of the hands."

A curious smile flickered over her face like a
shadow; but she said nothing. He waited a
moment.

"So!" he growled, "the Howth blood does
not blush to go down into the slime of the gutter? is sufficient to itself?"

A cool, attentive motion, — that was all.
Then she stooped to tie her sandals. The old
man watched her, irritated. She had been used
to the keen scrutiny of his eyes since she was
a baby, so was cool under it always. The face
watching her was one that repelled most men :
dominant, restless, flushing into red gusts of
passion, a small, intolerant eye, half hidden in
folds of yellow fat, — the eye of a man who
would give to his master (whether God or Sa-
tan) the last drop of his own blood, and exact
the same of other men.

She had tied her bonnet and fastened her
shawl, and stood ready to go.

" Is that all you want ? " he demanded.
" Are you waiting to hear that your work is
well done ? Women go through life as babies
learn to walk, — a mouthful of pap every step,
only they take it in praise or love. Pap is better. Which do you want ? Praise, I fancy."

" Neither," she said, quietly brushing her
shawl. " The work is well done, I know."

The old man's eye glittered for an instant,
satisfied ; then he turned to the books. He
thought she had gone, but, hearing a slight
clicking sound, turned round. She was taking
the chicken out of the cage.

" Let it alone ! " he broke out, sharply.
" Where are you going with it ? "

"Home," she said, with a queer, quizzical face. "Let it smell the green fields, Doctor. Ledgers and copperas are not good food for a chicken's soul, or body either."

"Let it alone!" he growled. "You take it for a type of yourself, eh? It has another work to do than to grow fat and sleep about the barnyard."

She opened the cage.

"I think I will take it."

"No," he said, quietly. "It has a master here. Not P. Teagarden. Why, Margret," pushing his stubby finger between the tin bars, "do you think the God you believe in would have sent it here without a work to do?"

She looked up; there was a curious tremour in his flabby face, a shadow in his rough voice.

"If it dies here, its life won't have been lost. Nothing is lost. Let it alone."

"Not lost?" she said, slowly, refastening the cage. "Only I think" ——

"What, child?"

She glanced furtively at him.

"It's a hard, scraping world where such a thing as that has work to do!"

He vouchsafed no answer. She waited to see his lip curl bitterly, and then, amused, went down the stairs. She had paid him for his sneer.

The steps were but a long ladder set in the wall, not the great staircase used by the hands : that was on the other side of the factory. It was a huge, unwieldy building, such as crowd the suburbs of trading towns. This one went round the four sides of a square, with the yard for the vats in the middle. The ladders and passages she passed down were on the inside, narrow and dimly lighted: she had to grope her way sometimes. The floors shook constantly with the incessant thud of the great looms that filled each story, like heavy, monotonous thunder. It deafened her, made her dizzy, as she went down slowly. It was no short walk to reach the lower hall, but she was down at last. Doors opened from it into the ground-floor ware-rooms; glancing in, she saw vast, dingy recesses of boxes piled up to the dark ceilings. There was a crowd of porters and draymen cracking their whips, and lounging on the trucks by the door, waiting for loads, talking politics, and smoking. The smell of tobacco, copperas, and burning logwood was heavy to clamminess here. She stopped, uncertain. One of the porters, a short, sickly man, who stood aloof from the rest, pushed open a door for her with his staff. Margret had a quick memory for faces ; she thought she had seen this one before as she passed, — a dark face, sullen, heavy-lipped, the hair cut con-

vict-fashion, close to the head. She thought
too, one of the men muttered "jail-bird," jeering him for his forwardness. "Load for Clin-
ton! Western Railroad!" sung out a sharp
voice behind her, and, as she went into the
street, a train of cars rushed into the hall to
be loaded, and men swarmed out of every corner, — red-faced and pale, whiskey-bloated and
heavy-brained, Irish, Dutch, black, with souls
half asleep somewhere, and the destiny of a
nation in their grasp, — hands, like herself, going through the slow, heavy work, for, as Pike
the manager would have told you, "three dollars a week, — good wages these tight times."
For nothing more ? Some other meaning may
have fallen from their faces into this girl's subtile
intuition in the instant's glance, — cheerfuller,
remoter aims, hidden in the most sensual face, —
homeliest home-scenes, low climbing ambitions,
some delirium of pleasure to come, — whiskey,
if nothing better: aims in life like yours differing in degree. Needing only to make them the
same —— did you say what ?

She had reached the street now, — a back-
street, a crooked sort of lane rather, running
between endless piles of warehouses. She hurried down it to gain the suburbs, for she lived
out in the country. It was a long, tiresome
walk through the outskirts of the town, where

the dwelling-houses were, — long rows of two-story bricks drabbled with soot-stains. It was two years since she had been in the town. Remembering this, and the reason why she had shunned it, she quickened her pace, her face growing stiller than before. One might have fancied her a slave putting on a mask, fearing to meet her master. The town, being unfamiliar to her, struck her newly. She saw the expression on its face better. It was a large trading city, compactly built, shut in by hills. It had an anxious, harassed look, like a speculator concluding a keen bargain; the very dwelling-houses smelt of trade, having shops in the lower stories; in the outskirts, where there are cottages in other cities, there were mills here; the trees, which some deluded dreamer had planted on the flat pavements, had all grown up into abrupt Lombardy poplars, knowing their best policy was to keep out of the way; the boys, playing marbles under them, played sharply " for keeps; " the bony old dray-horses, plodding through the dusty crowds, had speculative eyes, that measured their oats at night with a " you-don't-cheat-me " look. Even the churches had not the grave repose of the old brown house yonder in the hills, where the few field-people — Arians, Calvinists, Churchmen — gathered every Sunday, and air and sunshine

and God's charity made the day holy. These
churches lifted their hard stone faces insolent-
ly, registering their yearly alms in the morning
journals. To be sure the back-seats were free
for the poor; but the emblazoned crimson of
the windows, the carving of the arches, the very
purity of the preacher's style, said plainly that
it was easier for a camel to go through the eye
of a needle than for a man in a red *wam-us* to
enter the kingdom of heaven through that gate.

Nature itself had turned her back on the
town: the river turned aside, and but half a
river crept reluctantly by; the hills were but
bare banks of yellow clay. There was a cinder-
road leading through these. Margret climbed
it slowly. The low town-hills, as I said, were
bare, covered at their bases with dingy stubble-
fields. In the sides bordering the road gaped
the black mouths of the coal-pits that burrowed
under the hills, under the town. Trade everywhere, — on the earth and under it. No wonder the girl called it a hard, scraping world.
But when the road had crept through these
hills, it suddenly shook off the cinders, and
turned into the brown mould of the meadows, — turned its back on trade and the smoky
town, and speedily left it out of sight contemptuously, never looking back once. This was the
country now in earnest.

Margret slackened her step, drawing long
breaths of the fresh cold air. Far behind her,
panting and puffing along, came a black, burly
figure, Dr. Knowles. She had seen him behind
her all the way, but they did not speak. Between the two there lay that repellent resem-
blance which made them like close relations, —
closer when they were silent. You know such
people? When you speak to them, the little
sharp points clash. Yet they are the few whom
you surely know you will meet in the life beyond death, " saved " or not. The Doctor came
slowly along the quiet country-road, watching
the woman's figure going as slowly before him.
He had a curious interest in the girl, — a secret
reason for the interest, which as yet he kept
darkly to himself. For this reason he tried to
fancy how her new life would seem to her. It
should be hard enough, her work, — he was determined on that; her strength and endurance
must be tested to the uttermost. He must
know what stuff was in the weapon before he
used it. He had been reading the slow, cold
thing for years, — had not got into its secret
yet. But there was power there, and it was
the power he wanted. Her history was simple
enough : she was going into the mill to support
a helpless father and mother ; it was a common
story ; she had given up much for them ; — other

women did the same.   He gave her scanty praise.
Two years ago (he had keen, watchful eyes, this
man) he had fancied that the homely girl had a
dream, as most women have, of love and marriage : she had put it aside, he thought, forever;
it was too expensive a luxury; she had to begin
the life-long battle for bread and butter.   Her
dream had been real and pure, perhaps ; for she
accepted no sham love in its place : if it had left
an empty hunger in her heart, she had not tried
to fill it.   Well, well, it was the old story.   Yet
he looked after her kindly as he thought of it;
as some people look sorrowfully at children, going back to their own childhood.   For a moment he half relented in his purpose, thinking,
perhaps, her work for life was hard enough.
But no: this woman had been planned and
kept by God for higher uses than daughter or
wife or mother.   It was his part to put her work
into her hands.

The road was creeping drowsily now between
high grass-banks, out through the hills. A sleepy,
quiet road.   The restless dust of the town never
had been heard of out there.   It went wandering lazily through the corn-fields, down by
the river, into the very depths of the woods, —
the low October sunshine slanting warmly down
it all the way, touching the grass-banks and the
corn-fields with patches of russet gold.   Nobody

in such a road could be in a hurry. The quiet
was so deep, the free air, the heavy trees, the
sunshine, all so full and certain and fixed, one
could be sure of finding them the same a hundred years from now. Nobody ever was in a
hurry. The brown bees came along there, when
their work was over, and hummed into the great
purple thistles on the roadside in a voluptuous
stupor of delight. The cows sauntered through
the clover by the fences, until they wound up by
lying down in it and sleeping outright. The coun-
try-people, jogging along to the mill, walked their
fat old nags through the stillness and warmth
so slowly that even Margret left them far behind. As the road went deeper into the hills,
the quiet grew even more penetrating and certain, — so certain in these grand old mountains
that one called it eternal, and, looking up to the
peaks fixed in the clear blue, grew surer of a
world beyond this where there is neither change
nor death.

It was growing late ; the evening air more
motionless and cool ; the russet gold of the sunshine mottled only the hill-tops now ; in the
valleys there was a duskier brown, deepening
every moment. Margret turned from the road,
and went down the fields. One did not wonder, feeling the silence of these hills and broad
sweeps of meadow, that this woman, coming

down from among them, should be strangely
still, with dark questioning eyes dumb to their
own secrets.

Looking into her face now, you could be sure
of one thing: that she had left the town, the
factory, the dust far away, shaken the thought
of them off her brain.   No miles could measure
the distance between her home and them.   At
a stile across the field an old man sat waiting.   She hurried now, her cheek colouring.   Dr.
Knowles could see them going to the house beyond, talking earnestly.   He sat down in the
darkening twilight on the stile, and waited half
an hour.   He did not care to hear the story of
Margret's first day at the mill, knowing how her
father and mother would writhe under it, soften
it as she would.   It was nothing to her, he
knew.   So he waited.   After a while he heard
the old man's laugh, like that of a pleased child,
and then went in and took her place beside him.
She went out, but came back presently, every
grain of dust gone, in her clear dress of pearl
gray.   The neutral tint suited her well.   As she
stood by the window, listening gravely to them,
the homely face and waiting figure came into
full relief.   Nature had made the woman in a
freak of rare sincerity.   There were no reflected
lights about her; no gloss on her skin, no glitter
in her eyes, no varnish on her soul.   Simple

and dark and pure, there she was, for God and
her master to conquer and understand. Her
flesh was cold and colourless, — there were no
surface tints on it, — it warmed sometimes
slowly from far within; her voice, quiet, — out
of her heart; her hair, the only beauty of the
woman, was lustreless brown, lay in unpolished
folds of dark shadow. I saw such hair once,
only once. It had been cut from the head of a
man, who, unconscious, simple as a child, lived
out the law of his nature, and set the world at
defiance, — Bysshe Shelley.

The Doctor, talking to her father, watched the
girl furtively, took in every point, as one might
critically survey a Damascus blade which he
was going to carry into battle. There was neither love nor scorn in his look, — a mere fixedness of purpose to make use of her some day.
He talked, meanwhile, glancing at her now and
then, as if the subject they discussed were indi-
rectly linked with his plan for her. If it were,
she was unconscious of it. She sat on the
wooden step of the porch, looking out on the
melancholy sweep of meadow and hill range
growing cool and dimmer in the dun twilight,
not hearing what they said, until the sharpened,
earnest tones roused her.

" You will fail, Knowles."

It was her father who spoke.

" Nothing can save such a scheme from fail-

ure.   Neither the French nor German Socialists
attempted to base their systems on the lowest
class, as you design."

"I know," said Knowles. "That accounts
for their partial success."

"Let me understand your plan practically,"
eagerly demanded her father.

She thought Knowles evaded the question, —
wished to leave the subject. Perhaps he did
not regard the poor old school-master as a practical judge of practical matters. All his life he
had called him thriftless and unready.

"It never will do, Knowles," he went on in
his slow way. "Any plan, Phalanstery or Community, call it what you please, founded on self-
government, is based on a sham, the tawdriest
of shams."

The old school-master shook his head as one
who knows, and tried to push the thin gray
hairs out of his eyes in a groping way. Margret lifted them back, so quietly that he did not
feel her.

"You'll call the Republic a sham next!" said
the Doctor, coolly aggravating.

"The Republic!" The old man quickened
his tone, like a war-horse scenting the battle
near at hand. "There never was a thinner-
crusted Devil's egg in the world than democracy. I think I've told you that before?"

"I think you have," said the other, dryly.

" You always were a Tory, Mr. Howth," said his wife, in her placid, creamy way. " It is in the blood, I think, Doctor. The Howths fought under Cornwallis, you know."

The school-master waited until his wife had ended.

" Very true, Mrs. Howth," he said, with a grave smile. Then his thin face grew hot again.

" No, Dr. Knowles. Your scheme is but a sign of the mad age we live in. Since the thirteenth century, when the anarchic element sprang full-grown into the history of humanity, that history has been chaos. And this republic is the culmination of chaos."

" Out of chaos came the new-born earth," suggested the Doctor.

" But its foundations were granite," rejoined the old man with nervous eagerness, — " granite, not the slime of yesterday. When you found empires, go to work as God worked."

The Doctor did not answer; sat looking, instead, out into the dark indifferently, as if the heresies which the old man hurled at him were some old worn-out song. Seeing, however, that the school-master's flush of enthusiasm seemed on the point of dying out, he roused himself to gibe it into life.

" Well, Mr. Howth, what will you have? If the trodden rights of the human soul are the slime of yesterday, how shall we found our empire to last? On despotism? Civil or theocratic ? "

" Any despotism is better than that of newly enfranchised serfs," replied the school-master.

The Doctor laughed.

" What a successful politician you would have made? You would have had such a winning way to the hearts of the great unwashed ! "

Mrs. Howth laid down her knitting.

" My dear," she said, timidly, " I think that is treason."

The angry heat died out of his face instantly, as he turned to her, without the glimmer of a covert smile at her simplicity. She was a woman ; and when he spoke to the Doctor, it was in a tone less sharp.

" What is it the boys used to declaim, their Yankee hearts throbbing under their roundabouts ? ' Happy, proud America ! ' Somehow in that way. ' Cursed, abased America !' better if they had said. Look at her, in the warm vigour of her youth, most vigorous in decay ! Look at the germs and dregs of nations, creeds, religions, fermenting together ! As for the theory of self-government, it will muddle down here, as in the three great archetypes of the experiment, into a puling, miserable failure ! "

The Doctor did not hear. Some sharper shadow seemed to haunt him than the downfall of the Republic. What help did he seek in this girl? His keen, deep eyes never left her unconscious face.

"No," Mr. Howth went on, having the field to himself, — "we left Order back there in the ages you call dark, and Progress will trumpet the world into the ditch."

"Comte!" growled the Doctor.

The school-master's cane beat an angry tattoo on the hearth.

"You sneer at Comte? Because, having the clearest eye, the widest sweeping eye ever given to man, he had no more? It was to show how far flesh can go alone. Could he help it, if God refused the prophet's vision?"

"I'm sure, Samuel," interrupted his wife with a sorrowful earnestness, "your own eyes were as strong as a man's could be. It was ten years after I wore spectacles that you began. Only for that miserable fever, you could read short-hand now."

Her own blue eyes filled with tears. There was a sudden silence. Margret shivered, as if some pain stung her. Holding her father's bony hand in hers, she patted it on her knee. The hand trembled a little. Knowles's sharp eyes darted from one to the other; then, with a smothered growl, he shook himself, and rushed headlong into the old battle which he and the school-master had been waging now, off and on, some six years. That was a fight, I can tell you! None of your shallow, polite clashing of modern theories, — no talk of your Jeffersonian Democracy, your high-bred Federalism! They took hold of the matter by the roots, clear at the beginning.

Mrs. Howth's breath fairly left her, they went into the soul of the matter in such a dangerous way. What if Joel should hear? No doubt he would report that his master was an infidel, — that would be the next thing they would hear. He was in the kitchen now: he finished his wood-chopping an hour ago. Asleep, doubtless; that was one comfort. Well, if he were awake, he could not understand. That class of people —— And Mrs. Howth (into whose kindly brain just enough of her husband's creed had glimmered to make her say, "that class of people," in the tone with which Abraham would *not* have spoken of Dives over the gulf) went tranquilly back to her knitting, wondering why Dr. Knowles should come ten times now where he used to come once, to provoke Samuel into these wearisome arguments. Ever since their misfortune came on them, he had been there every night, always at it. She should think he might be a little more considerate. Mr. Howth surely had enough to think of, what with his — his misfortune, and the starvation waiting for them, and poor Margret's degradation, (she sighed here,) without bothering his head about the theocratic principle, or the Battle of Armageddon. She had hinted as much to Dr. Knowles one day, and he had muttered out something about its being "the life of the dog, Ma'am." She wondered what he meant by that! She looked over at his bearish figure, snuff-drabbled waistcoat, and shock of black hair. Well, poor man, he could not help it, if he were coarse, and an Abolitionist, and a Fourierite, and —— She was getting a little muddy now, she was conscious, so turned her mind back to the repose of her stocking. Margret took it very quietly, seeing her father flaming so. But Margret never had any opinions to express. She was not like the Parnells: they were noted for their clear judgment. Mrs. Howth was a Parnell.

"The combat deepens, — on, ye brave!"

The Doctor's fat, leathery face was quite red now, and his sentences were hurled out in a sarcastic bass, enough to wither the marrow of a weak man. But the school-master was no weak man. His foot was entirely on his native heath, I assure you. He knew every inch of

the ground, from the domination of the absolute
faith in the ages of Fetichism, to its pseudo-
presentment in the tenth century, and its actual
subversion in the nineteenth. Every step. Our
politicians might have picked up an idea or two
there, I should think! Then he was so cool
about it, so skilful! He fairly rubbed his hands
with glee, enjoying the combat. And he was so
sure that the Doctor was savagely in earnest:
why, any one with half an ear could hear that!
He did not see how, in the very heat of the fray,
his eyes would wander off listlessly. But Mr.
Howth did not wander; there was nothing careless or two-sided in the making of this man, —
no sham about him, or borrowing. They came
down gradually, or out, — for, as I told you,
they dug into the very heart of the matter at
first, — they came out gradually to modern
times. Things began to assume a more fa-
miliar aspect. Spinoza, Fichte, Saint Simon,
— one heard about them now. If you could
but have heard the school-master deal with these
his enemies! With what tender charity for the
man, what relentless vengeance for the belief,
he pounced on them, dragging the soul out of
their systems, holding it up for slow slaughter!
As for Humanity, (how Knowles lingered on
that word, with a tenderness curious in so uncouth a mass of flesh!) — as for Humanity, it

was a study to see it stripped and flouted and
thrown out of doors like a filthy rag by this
poor old Howth, a man too child-hearted to kill
a spider. It was pleasanter to hear him when
he defended the great Past in which his ideal
truth had been faintly shadowed. How he
caught the salient tints of the feudal life!
How the fine womanly nature of the man rose
exulting in the free picturesque glow of the day
of crusader and heroic deed! How he crowded
in traits of perfected manhood in the conqueror,
simple trust in the serf, to colour and weaken
his argument, not seeing that he weakened it!
How, when he thought he had cornered the
Doctor, he would colour and laugh like a boy,
then suddenly check himself, lest he might
wound him! A curious laugh, genial, cheery,
— bubbling out of his weak voice in a way
that put you in mind of some old and rare
wine. When he would check himself in one
of these triumphant glows, he would turn to
the Doctor with a deprecatory gravity, and for
a few moments be almost submissive in his
reply. So earnest and worn it looked then,
the poor old face, in the dim light! The black
clothes he wore were so threadbare and shining
at the knees and elbows, the coarse leather shoes
brought to so fine a polish! The Doctor idly
wondered who had blacked them, glancing at
Margret's fingers.

2 *

There was a flower stuck in the button-hole
of the school-master's coat, a pale tea-rose.   If
Dr. Knowles had been a man of fine instincts,
(which his opaque shining eyes would seem to
deny,) he might have thought it was not unapt
or ill-placed even in the shabby, scuffed coat.   A
scholar, a gentleman, though in patched shoes
and trousers a world too short.   Old and gaunt,
hunger-bitten even it may be, with loose-jointed,
bony limbs, and yellow face; clinging, loyal and
brave, to the quaint, delicate fancies of his
youth, that were dust and ashes to other men.
In the very haggard face you could find the
quiet purity of the child he had been, and the
old child's smile, fresh and credulous, on the
mouth.

The Doctor had not spoken for a moment.
It might be that he was careless of the poetic
lights with which Mr. Howth tenderly decorated
his old faith, or it might be, that even he, with
the terrible intentness of a real life-purpose in
his brain, was touched by the picture of the far
old chivalry, dead long ago.   The master's voice
grew low and lingering now.   It was a labour
of love, this.   Oh, it is so easy to go back out
of the broil of dust and meanness and barter
into the clear shadow of that old life where love
and bravery stand eternal verities, — never to be
bought and sold in that dusty town yonder!   To
go back?   To dream back, rather.   To drag out

of our own hearts, as the hungry old master did, whatever is truest and highest there, and clothe it with name and deed in the dim days of chivalry. Make a poem of it, — so much easier than to make a life!

Knowles shuffled uneasily, watching the girl keenly, to know how the picture touched her. Was, then, she thought, this grand, dead Past so shallow to him? These knights, pure, unstained, searching until death for the Holy Greal, could he understand the life-long agony, the triumph of their conflict over Self? These women, content to live in solitude forever because they once had loved, could any man understand that? Or the dead queen, dead that the man she loved might be free and happy, — why, this *was* life, — this death! But did pain, and martyrdom, and victory lie back in the days of Galahad and Arthur alone? The homely face grew stiller than before, looking out into the dun sweep of moorland, — cold, unrevealing. It baffled the man that looked at it. He shuffled, chewed tobacco vehemently, tilted his chair on two legs, broke out in a thunder-gust at last.

" Dead days for dead men! The world hears a bugle-call to-day more noble than any of your piping troubadours. We have something better to fight for than a vacant tomb."

The old man drew himself up haughtily.

" I know what you would say, — Liberty for the low and vile. It is a good word. That was a better which they hid in their hearts in the old time, — Honour ! "

Honour! I think, Calvinist though he was, that word was his religion. Men have had worse. Perhaps the Doctor thought this ; for he rose abruptly, and, leaning on the old man's chair, said, gently, —

" It is better, even here. Yet you poison this child's mind. You make her despise To-Day ; make honour live for her now."

" It does not," the school-master said, bitterly. " The world's a failure. All the great old dreams are dead. Your own phantom, your Republic, your experiment to prove that all men are born free and equal, — what is it to-day ? "

Knowles lifted his head, looking out into the brown twilight. Some word of pregnant meaning flashed in his eye and trembled on his lip ; but he kept it back. His face glowed, though, and the glow and strength gave to the huge misshapen features a grand repose.

" You talk of To-Day," the old man continued, querulously. " I am tired of it. Here is its type and history," touching a county newspaper, — "a fair type, with its cant, and bigotry, and weight of uncomprehended fact. Bargain

and sale, — it taints our religion, our brains, our
flags, — yours and mine, Knowles, with the rest.
Did you never hear of those abject spirits who
entered neither heaven nor hell, who were neither faithful to God nor rebellious, caring only
for themselves ? "

He paused, fairly out of breath. Margret
looked up. Knowles was silent. There was
a smothered look of pain on the coarse face ;
the school-master's words were sinking deeper
than he knew.

"No, father," said Margret, hastily ending his
quotation, "'io non averei creduto, che [vita]
tanta n' avesse disfatta.'"

Skilful Margret! The broil must have been
turbid in the old man's brain which the grand,
slow-stepping music of the Florentine could not
calm. She had learned that long ago, and used
it as a nurse does some old song to quiet her
pettish infant. His face brightened instantly.

"Do not believe, then, child," he said, after a
pause. "It is a noble doubt, in Dante or in
you."

The Doctor had turned away; she could not
see his face. The angry scorn was gone from
the old master's countenance ; it was bent with
its usual wistful eagerness on the floor. A moment after he looked up with a flickering smile.

"' Onorate l' altissimo poeta!'" he said, gen-

tly lifting his finger to his forehead in a military
fashion. " Where is my cane, Margret ?   The
Doctor and I will go and walk on the porch before it grows dark."

The sun had gone down long before, and
the stars were out; but no one spoke of this.
Knowles lighted the school-master's pipe and his
own cigar, and then moved the chairs out of
their way, stepping softly that the old man
might not hear him.   Margret, in the room,
watched them as they went, seeing how gentle
the rough, burly man was with her father, and
how, every time they passed the sweet-brier, he
bent the branches aside, that they might not
touch his face.   Slow, childish tears came into
her eyes as she saw it ; for the school-master
was blind.   This had been their regular walk
every evening, since it grew too cold for them
to go down under the lindens.   The Doctor had
not missed a night since her father gave up the
school, a month ago : at first, under pretence of
attending to his eyes ; but since the day he had
told them there was no hope of cure, he had
never spoken of it again.   Only, since then,
he had grown doubly quarrelsome, — standing
ready armed to dispute with the old man every
inch of every subject in earth or air, keeping
the old man in a state of boyish excitement during the long, idle days, looking forward to this
nightly battle.

It was very still ; for the house, with its half-dozen acres, lay in an angle of the hills, looking out on the river, which shut out all distant noises. Only the men's footsteps broke the silence, passing and repassing the window. Without, the October starlight lay white and frosty on the moors, the old barn, the sharp, dark hills, and the river, which was half hidden by the orchard. One could hear it, like some huge giant moaning in his sleep, at times, and see broad patches of steel blue glittering through the thick apple-trees and the bushes. Her mother had fallen into a doze. Margret looked at her, thinking how sallow the plump, fair face had grown, and how faded the kindly blue eyes were now. Dim with crying, — she knew that, though she never saw her shed a tear. Always cheery, going placidly about the house in her gray dress and Quaker cap, as if there were no such things in the world as debt or blindness. But Margret knew, though she said nothing. When her mother came in from those wonderful foraging expeditions in search of late pease or corn, she could see the swollen circle round the eyes, and hear her breath like that of a child which has sobbed itself tired. Then, one night, when she had gone into her mother's room, after she was in bed, the blue eyes were set in a wild, hopeless way, as if staring down into years of

starvation and misery. The fire on the hearth
burned low and clear; the old worn furniture
stood out cheerfully in the red glow, and threw
a maze of twisted shadow on the floor. But the
glow was all that was cheerful. To-morrow,
when the hard daylight should jeer away the
screening shadows, it would unbare a desolate,
shabby home. She knew; struck with the white
leprosy of poverty; the blank walls, the faded
hangings, the old stone house itself, looking
vacantly out on the fields with a pitiful significance of loss. Upon the mantel-shelf there was
a small marble figure, one of the Dancing Graces:
the other two were gone, gone in pledge. This
one was left, twirling her foot, and stretching
out her hands in a dreary sort of ecstasy, with
no one to respond. For a moment, so empty
and bitter seemed her home and her life, that
she thought the lonely dancer with her flaunting
joy mocked her, — taunted them with the slow,
gray desolation that had been creeping on them
for years. Only for a moment the morbid fancy
hurt her.

The red glow was healthier, suited her temperament better. She chose to fancy the house
as it had been once, — should be again, please
God. She chose to see the old comfort and the
old beauty which the poor school-master had
gathered about their home. Gone now. But

it should return. It was well, perhaps, that he
was blind, he knew so little of what had come
on them. There, where the black marks were
on the wall, there had hung two pictures.
Margret and her father religiously believed them
to be a Tintoret and Copley. Well, they were
gone now. He had been used to dust them
with a light brush every morning, himself, but
now he said, —

"You can clean the pictures to-day, Margret.
Be careful, my child."

And Margret would remember the greasy
Irishman who had tucked them under his arm,
and flung them into a cart, her blood growing
hotter in her veins.

It was the same through all the house; there
was not a niche in the bare rooms that did not
recall a something gone, — something that should
return. She willed that, that evening, standing
by the dim fire. What women will, whose eyes
are slow, attentive, still, as this Margret's, usually
comes to pass.

The red fire-glow suited her; another glow,
warming her floating fancy, mingled with it,
giving her every-day purpose the trait of heroism. The old spirit of the dead chivalry, of
succour to the weak, life-long self-denial, — did
it need the sand waste of Palestine or a tour-
nament to call it into life? Down in that

trading town, in the thick of its mills and
drays, it could live, she thought.   That very
night, perhaps, in some of those fetid cellars or
sunken shanties, there were vigils kept of purpose as unselfish, prayer as heaven-command-
ing, as that of the old aspirants for knighthood.
She, too, — her quiet face stirred with a simple,
childish smile, like her father's.

"Why, mother!" she said, stroking down the
gray hair under the cap, "shall you sleep here
all night?" laughing.

A cheery, tender laugh, this woman's was, —
seldom heard, — not far from tears.

Mrs. Howth roused herself.   Just then, a
broad, high-shouldered man, in a gray flannel
shirt, and shoes redolent of the stable, appeared
at the door.   Margret looked at him as if he
were an accusing spirit, — coming down, as
woman must, from heights of self-renunciation
or bold resolve, to an undarned stocking or an
uncooked meal.

"Kittle 's b'ilin'," he announced, flinging in
the information as a general gratuity.

"That will do, Joel," said Mrs. Howth.

The tone of stately blandness which Mrs.
Howth erected as a shield between herself and
"that class of people" was a study: a success;
the *résumé* of her experience in the combat that
had devoured half her life, like that of other

American house-keepers. " Be gentle, but let
them know their place, my dear!" The class
having its type and exponent in Joel, stopped
at the door, and hitched up its suspenders.

" That will *do,* Joel," with a stern suavity.

Some idea was in Joel's head under the brush
of red hair, — probably the " anarchic element."

" Uh was wishin' toh read the G'zette."
Whereupon he advanced into the teeth of the
enemy and bore off the newspaper, going before Margret, as she went to the kitchen, and
seating himself beside a flaring tallow-candle
on the table.

Reading, with Joel, was not the idle pas-
time that more trivial minds find it ; a thing,
on the contrary, to be gone into with slow
spelling, and face knitted up into savage stern-
ness, especially now, when, as he gravely explained to Margret, " in *his* opinion the crissis
was jest at hand, and ev'ry man must be seein'
ef the gover'ment was carryin' out the views of
the people."

With which intent, Joel, in company with
five thousand other sovereigns, consulted, as
definitive oracle, " The Daily Gazette " of Tow-
bridge. The school-master need not have grumbled for the old time : feodality in the days of
Warwick and of " The Daily Gazette " was not
so widely different as he and Joel thought.

Now and then, partly as an escape-valve for his overcharged conviction, partly in compassion to the ignorance of women in political economics, he threw off to Margret divers commentaries on the text, as she passed in and out.

If she had risen to the full level of Joel's views, she might have considered these views tinctured with radicalism, as they consisted in the propriety of the immediate " impinging of the President." Besides, (Joel was a good-natured man, too, merciful to his beast,) Nero-like, he wished, with the tiger drop of blood that lies hid in everybody's heart, that the few millions who differed with himself and the " Gazette " had but one neck for their more convenient hanging, " It's all that 'll save the kentry," he said, and believed it, too.

If Margret fell suddenly from the peak of out-look on life to the homely labor of cooking supper, some of the healthy heroic flush of the knightly days and the hearth-fire went down with her, I think. It brightened and reddened the square kitchen with its cracked stove and meagre array of tins ; she bustled about in her quaint way, as if it had been filled up and running over with comforts. It brightened and reddened her face when she came in to put the last dish on the table, — a cosey, snug table, set

for four. Heroic dreams with poets, I suppose,
make them unfit for food other than some feast
such as Eve set for the angel. But then Margret was no poet. So, with the kindling of her
hope, its healthful light struck out, and warmed
and glorified these common things. Such common things! Only a coarse white cloth, re-
deemed by neither silver nor china, the amber
coffee, (some that Knowles had brought out to
her father, — " thrown on his hands; he could
n't use it, — product of slave-labour! — never,
Sir!") the delicate brown fish that Joel· had
caught, the bread her mother had made, the
golden butter, — all of them touched her nerves
with a quick sense of beauty and pleasure.
And more, the gaunt face of the blind old man,
his bony hand trembling as he raised the cup to
his lips, her mother and the Doctor managing
silently to place everything he liked best near
his plate. Was n't it all part of the fresh,
hopeful glow burning in her consciousness ?
It brightened and deepened. It blotted out the
hard, dusty path of the future, and showed
warm and clear the success at the end. Not
much to show, you think. Only the old home
as it once was, full of quiet laughter and content; only her mother's eyes clear shining again;
only that gaunt old head raised proudly, owing
no man anything but courtesy. The glow deep-

ened, as she thought of it. It was strange, too,
that, with the deep, slow-moving nature of this
girl, she should have striven so eagerly to throw
this light over the future. Commoner natures
have done more and hoped less. It was a poor
gift, you think, this of the labour of a life for
so plain a duty ; hardly heroic. She knew it.
Yet, if there lay in this coming labour any pain,
any wearing effort, she clung to it desperately,
as if this should banish, it might be, worse loss.
She tried desperately, I say, to clutch the far,
uncertain hope at the end, to make happiness
out of it, to give it to her silent gnawing heart
to feed on. She thrust out of sight all possible
life that might have called her true self into being, and clung to this present shallow duty and
shallow reward. Pitiful and vain so to cling!
It is the way of women. As if any human
soul could bury that which might have been,
in that which is!

The Doctor, peering into her thought with
sharp, suspicious eyes, heeded the transient
flush of enthusiasm but little. Even the pleasant cheery talk that pleased her father so was
but surface-deep, he knew. The woman he
must conquer for his great end lay beneath,
dark and cold. It was only for that end he
cared for her. Through what cold depths of
solitude her soul breathed faintly mattered lit-

tle. Yet an idle fancy touched him, what a triumph the man had gained, whoever he might be, who had held the master-key to a nature so rare as this, who had the kingly power in his hand to break its silence into electric shivers of laughter and tears, — terrible subtile pain, or joy as terrible. Did he hold the power still? he wondered. Meanwhile she sat there, unread.

CHAPTER II.

THE evening came on, slow and cold. Life
itself, the Doctor thought, impatiently, was cool
and tardy here among the hills. Even he fell
into the tranquil tone, and chafed under it.
Nowhere else did the evening gray and sombre
into the mysterious night impalpably as here.
The quiet, wide and deep, folded him in, forced
his trivial heat into silence and thought. The
world seemed to think there. Quiet in the
dead seas of fog, that filled the valleys like
restless vapour curdled into silence; quiet in the
listening air, stretching gray up to the stars, —
in the solemn mountains, that stood motionless,
like hoary-headed prophets, waiting with uplifted
hands, day and night, to hear the Voice, silent
now for centuries; the very air, heavy with the
breath of the sleeping pine-forests, moved slowly
and cold, like some human voice weary with
preaching to unbelieving hearts of a peace on
earth. This man's heart was unbelieving; he
chafed in the oppressive quiet; it was unfeeling
mockery to a sick and hungry world, — a dead
torpor of indifference. Years of hot and turbid

pain had dulled his eyes to the eternal secret of the night; his soul was too sore with stumbling, stung, inflamed with the needs and suffering of the countless lives that hemmed him in, to accept the great prophetic calm. He was blind to the prophecy written on the earth since the day God first bade it tell thwarted man of the great To-Morrow.

He turned from the night in-doors. Human hearts were his proper study. The old house, he thought, slept with the rest. One did not wonder that the pendulum of the clock swung long and slow. The frantic, nervous haste of town-clocks chorded better with the pulse of human life. Yet life in the veins of these people flowed slow and cool; their sorrows and joys were few and life-long. The enduring air suited this woman, Margret Howth. Her blood could never ebb or flow with sudden gusts of passion, like his own, throbbing, heating continually: one current, absorbing, deep, would carry its tide from one eternity to the other, one love or one hate. Whatever power was in the tide should be his, in its entirety. It was his right. Was not his aim high, the highest? It was his right.

Margret, looking up, saw the man's eye fixed on her. She met it coolly. All her short life, this strange man, so tender to the weak, had

3

watched her with a sort of savage scorn, sneer-
ing at her childish, dreamy apathy, driving her
from effort to effort with a scourge of contempt.
What did he want now with her? Her duty
was light; she took it up, — she was glad to
take it up; what more would he have? She
put the whole matter away from her.

It grew late. She sat down by the lamp and
began to read to her father, as usual. Her
mother put away her knitting; Joel came in
half-asleep; the Doctor put out his everlasting
cigar, and listened, as he did everything else,
intently. It was an old story that she read, —
the story of a man who walked the fields and
crowded streets of Galilee eighteen hundred
years ago. Knowles, with his heated brain,
fancied that the silence without in the night
grew deeper, that the slow-moving air stopped
in its course to listen. Perhaps the simple story
carried a deeper meaning to these brooding
mountains and solemn sky than to the purblind
hearts within. It was a far-off story to them, —
very far off. The old school-master heard it with
a lowered head, with the proud obedience with
which a cavalier would receive his leader's orders. Was not the leader a knight, the knight
of truest courage? All that was high, chivalric
in the old man sprang up to own him Lord.
That he not only preached to, but ate and

drank with publicans and sinners, was a re-
quirement of his mission; nowadays ————.
Joel heard the " good word" with a bewildered
consciousness of certain rules of honesty to be
observed next day, and a maze of crowns and
harps shining somewhere beyond. As for any
immediate connection between the teachings of
this book and " The Daily Gazette," it was
pure blasphemy to think of it. The Lord held
those old Jews in His hand, of course; but as
for the election next month, that was quite
another thing. If Joel thrust the history out
of the touch of common life, the Doctor brought
it down, and held it there on trial. To him it
was the story of a Reformer who, eighteen centuries ago, had served his day. Could he serve
this day? Could he? The need was desperate.
Was there anything in this Christianity, freed
from bigotry, to work out the awful problem
which the ages had left for America to solve?
He doubted it. People called this old Knowles
an infidel, said his brain was as unnatural and
distorted as his body. God, looking down into
his heart that night, saw the savage wrestling
there, and judged him with other eyes than
theirs.

The story stood alive in his throbbing brain,
demanding hearing. All things were real to
this man, this uncouth mass of flesh that his

companions sneered at; most real of all, the
unhelped pain of life, the great seething mire
of dumb wretchedness in streets and alleys, the
cry for aid from the starved souls of the world.
You and I have other work to do than to listen,
— pleasanter. But he, coming out of the mire,
his veins thick with the blood of a despised race,
had carried up their pain and hunger with him :
it was the most real thing on earth to him, —
more real than his own share in the unseen
heaven or hell. By the reality, the peril of the
world's instant need, he tried the offered help
from Calvary. It was the work of years, not
of this night. Perhaps, if they who preach
Christ crucified had doubted him as this man
did, their work in the coming heaven might be
higher, — and ours, who hear them. When the
girl had finished reading, she went out into the
cool air. The Doctor passed her without notice. He went, in his lumbering way, down the
hill into the city; glad to go ; the trustful, waiting quiet oppressed, taunted him. It sent him
back more mad against Destiny, his heart more
bitter in its great pity. Let him go to the great
city, with its stifling gambling-hells, its negro-
pens, its foul cellars ; — his place and work. If
he stumble blindly against unconquerable ills,
and die, others have so stumbled and so died.
Do you think their work is lost ?

Margret stood looking down at the sloping
moors and fog. She, too, had her place and
work. She thought that night she saw it
clearly, and kept her eyes fixed on it, as I said.
They plodded steadily down the wide years
opening before her. Whatever slow, unending
toil lay in them, whatever hungry loneliness, or
coarseness of deed, she saw it all, shrinking
from nothing. She looked at the big blue-corded
veins in her wrist, full of untainted blood, —
gauged herself coolly, her lease of life, her
power of endurance, — measurèd it out against
the work waiting for her. No short task, she
knew that. She would be old before it was finished, quite an old woman, hard, mechanical,
worn out. But the day would be so bright, when
it came, it would atone for all: the day would
be bright, the home warm again ; it would
hold all that life had promised her of good.

All? Oh, Margret, Margret! Was there no
sullen doubt in the brave resolve? Was there
no shadow just then, dark, ironical, blotting out
father and mother and home, creeping nearer,
less alien to your soul than these, than even
your God?

If any such cold, masterful shadow rose out
of years gone, and clutched at the truest life
of her heart, she stifled it, and thrust it down.
And yet, leaning on the gate, and thinking va-

cantly, she remembered a time when through
that shadow, she believed more in a God than
she did now. When, by the help of that very
dead hope, He of whom she read to-night stood
close, an infinitely tender Helper, that with
the differing human loves she knew, had loved
His mother and Mary. Therefore, a Helper.
Now, struggle as she would for warmth or
healthy hopes, the world was gray and silent.
Her defeated woman's nature called it so, bitterly. Christ was a dim, ideal power, heaven
far-off. She doubted if it held anything as real
as that which she had lost.

As if to bring back the old times more vividly
to her, there happened one of those curious little
coincidences with which Fate, we think, has
nothing to do. She heard a quick step along
the clay road, and a muddy little terrier jumped
up, barking, beside her. She stopped with a
suddenness strange in her slow movements.
" *Tiger !* " she said, stroking its head with passionate eagerness. The dog licked her hand,
smelt her clothes to know if she were the same :
it was two years since he had seen her. She sat
there, softly stroking him. Presently there was
a sound of wheels jogging down the road, and
a voice singing snatches of some song, one of
those cheery street-songs that the boys whistle.
It was a low, weak voice, but very pleasant.

Margret heard it through the dark : she kissed
the dog with a strange paleness on her face, and
stood up, quiet, attentive as before. Tiger still
kept licking her hand, as it hung by her side : it
was cold, and trembled as he touched it. She
waited a moment, then pushed him from her, as
if his touch, even, caused her to break some vow.
He whined, but she hurried away, not waiting
to know how he came, or with whom. Perhaps,
if Dr. Knowles had seen her face as she looked
back at him, he would have thought there were
depths in her nature which his probing eyes had
never reached.

The wheels came close, and directly a cart
stopped at the gate. It was one of those little
wagons that hucksters drive ; only this seemed
to be a home-made affair, patched up with
wicker-work and bits of board. It was piled up
with baskets of vegetables, eggs, and chickens,
and on a broken bench in the middle sat the
driver, a woman. You could not help laughing,
when you looked at the whole turn-out, it had
such a make-shift look altogether. The reins
were twisted rope, the wheels uneven. It went
jolting along in such a careless, jolly way, as if
it would not care in the least, should it go to
pieces any minute just there in the road. The
donkey that drew it was bony and blind of one
eye ; but he winked the other knowingly at you,

to ask if you saw the joke of the thing. Even
the voice of the owner of the establishment,
chirruping some idle song, as I told you, was
one of the cheeriest sounds you ever heard.
Joel, up at the barn, forgot his dignity to salute
it with a prolonged " Hillo ! " and presently appeared at the gate.

" I 'm late, Joel," said the weak voice. It
sounded like a child's, near at hand.

" We can trade in the dark, Lois, both bein'
honest," he responded, graciously, hoisting a
basket of tomatoes into the cart, and taking out
a jug of vinegar.

" Is that Lois ? " said Mrs. Howth, coming to
the gate. " Sit still, child. Don't get down."

But the child, as she called her, had scrambled
off the cart, and stood beside her, leaning on the
wheel, for she was helplessly crippled.

" I thought you would be down to-night. I
put some coffee on the stove. Bring it out,
Joel."

Mrs. Howth never put up the shield between
herself and this member of " the class," — because, perhaps, she was so wretchedly low in
the social scale. However, I suppose she never
gave a reason for it even to herself. Nobody
could help being kind to Lois, even if he tried.
Joel brought the coffee with more readiness than
he would have waited on Mrs. Howth.

" Barney will be jealous," he said, patting the bare ribs of the old donkey, and glancing wistfully at his mistress.

" Give him his supper, surely," she said, taking the hint.

It was a real treat to see how Lois enjoyed her supper, sipping and tasting the warm coffee, her face in a glow, like an epicure over some rare Falernian. You would be sure, from just that little thing, that no sparkle of warmth or pleasure in the world slipped by her which she did not catch and enjoy and be thankful for to the uttermost. You would think, perhaps, pitifully, that not much pleasure or warmth would ever go down so low, within her reach. Now that she stood on the ground, she scarcely came up to the level of the wheel ; some deformity of her legs made her walk with a curious rolling jerk, very comical to see. She laughed at it, when other people did ; if it vexed her at all, she never showed it. She had turned back her calico sun-bonnet, and stood looking up at Mrs. Howth and Joel, laughing as they talked with her. The face would have startled you on so old and stunted a body. It was a child's face, quick, eager, with that pitiful beauty you always see in deformed people. Her eyes, I think, were the kindliest, the hopefullest I ever saw. Nothing but the livid thickness of her

3 *

skin betrayed the fact that set Lois apart from
even the poorest poor, — the taint in her veins
of black blood.

" Whoy! be n't this Tiger ? " said Joel, as the
dog ran yelping about him. " How comed yoh
with him, Lois ? "

" Tiger an' his master 's good friends o' mine,
— you remember they allus was. An' he 's
back now, Mr. Holmes, — been back for a
month."

Margret, walking in the porch with her father,
stopped.

" Are you tired, father ?   It is late."

" And you are worn out, poor child !   It was
selfish in me to forget.   Good-night, dear ! "

Margret kissed him, laughing cheerfully, as
she led him to his room-door.   He lingered,
holding her dress.

" Perhaps it will be easier for you to-morrow
than it was to-day ? " hesitating.

" I am sure it will.   To-morrow will be sure
to be better than to-day."

She left him, and went away with a step that
did not echo the promise of her words.

Joel, meanwhile, consulted apart with his mistress.

" Of course," she said, emphatically. — " You
must stay until morning, Lois.   It is too late.
Joel will toss you up a bed in the loft."

The queer little body hesitated.

" I can stay," she said, at last. " It's his watch at the mill to-night."

" Whose watch ? " demanded Joel.

Her face brightened.

" Father's. He's back, mum."

Joel caught himself in a whistle.

" He's very stiddy, Joel, — as stiddy as yoh."

" I am very glad he has come back,• Lois," said Mrs. Howth, gravely.

At every place where Lois had been that day she had told her bit of good news, and at every place it had been met with the same kindly smile and " I'm glad he's back, Lois."

Yet Joe Yare, fresh from two years in the penitentiary, was not exactly the person whom society usually welcomes with open arms. Lois had a vague suspicion of this, perhaps ; for, as she hobbled along the path, she added to her own assurance of his " stiddiness" earnest explanations to Joel of how he had a place in the Croft Street woollen-mills, and how Dr. Knowles had said he was as ready a stoker as any in the furnace-rooms.

The sound of her weak, eager voice was silent presently, and nothing broke the solitary cold of the night.

CHAPTER III.

THE morning, when it came long after, came
quiet and cool, — the warm red dawn helplessly
smothered under great waves of gray cloud.
Margret, looking out into the thick fog, lay
down wearily again, closing her eyes. What
was the day to her?

Very slowly the night was driven back. An
hour after, when she lifted her head again, the
stars were still glittering through the foggy arch,
like sparks of brassy blue, and hills and valleys
were one drifting, slow-heaving mass of ashy
damp. Off in the east a stifled red film groped
through. It was another day coming; she
might as well get up, and live the rest of her
life out; — what else had she to do?

Whatever this night had been to the girl, it
left one thought sharp, alive, in the exhausted
quiet of her brain: a cowardly dread of the
trial of the day, when she would see him again.
Was the old struggle of years before coming
back? Was it all to go over again? She was
worn out. She had been quiet in these two
years: what had gone before she never looked

back upon; but it made her thankful for even
this stupid quiet. And now, when she had
planned her life, busy, useful, contented, why
need God have sent the old thought to taunt
her? A wild, sickening sense of what might
have been struggled up: she thrust it down, —
she had kept it down all night; the old pain
should not come back, — it should not. She
did not think of the love she had given up as a
dream, as verse-makers or sham people do; she
knew it to be the quick seed of her soul. She
cried for it even now, with all the fierce strength
of her nature ; it was the best she knew ;
through it she came nearest to God. Thinking
of the day when she had given it up, she remembered it with a vague consciousness of
having fought a deadly struggle with her fate,
and that she had been conquered, — never had
lived again. Let it be ; she could not bear the
struggle again.

She went on dressing herself in a dreary,
mechanical way. Once, a bitter laugh came on
her face, as she looked into the glass, and saw
the dead, dull eyes, and the wrinkle on her forehead. Was that the face to be crowned with
delicate caresses and love ? She scorned herself for the moment, grew sick of herself, balked,
thwarted in her true life as she was. Other
women whom God has loved enough to probe

to the depths of their nature have done the
same, — saw themselves as others saw them :
their strength drying up within them, jeered at,
utterly alone. It is a trial we laugh at. I think
the quick fagots at the stake were fitter subjects
for laughter than the slow gnawing hunger in
the heart of many a slighted woman or a selfish
man. They come out of the trial as out of
martyrdom, according to their faith : you see its
marks sometimes in a frivolous old age going
down with tawdry hopes and starved eyes to
the grave; you see its victory in the freshest,
fullest lives in the earth. This woman had
accepted her trial, but she took it up as an in-
flexible fate which she did not understand; it
was new to her; its solitude, its hopeless thirst
were freshly bitter. She loathed herself as one
whom God had thought unworthy of every
woman's right, — to love and be loved.

She went to the window, looking blankly
out into the gray cold. Any one with keen
analytic eye, noting the thin muscles of this
woman, the protruding brain, the eyes deep,
concealing, would have foretold that she would
conquer in the fight; force her soul down, —
but that the forcing down would leave the
weak, flaccid body spent and dead. One thing
was certain : no curious eyes would see the
struggle; the body might be nerveless or sickly,

but it had the great power of reticence; the
calm with which she faced the closest gaze was
natural to her, — no mask. When she left her
room and went down, the same unaltered quiet
that had baffled Knowles steadied her step and
cooled her eyes.

After you have made a sacrifice of yourself
for others, did you ever notice how apt you
were to doubt, as soon as the deed was irrev-
ocable, whether, after all, it were worth while
to have done it? How mean seems the good
gained! How new and unimagined the agony
of empty hands and stifled wish! Very slow
the angels are, sometimes, that are sent to
minister!

Margret, going down the stairs that morning, found none of the chivalric unselfish glow
of the night before in her home. It was an old,
bare house in the midst of dreary stubble fields,
in which her life was slowly to be worn out:
working for those who did not comprehend her;
thanked her little, — that was all. It did not
matter; life was short: she could thank God
for that at least.

She opened the house-door. A draught of
cold morning air struck her face, sweeping from
the west; it had driven the fog in great gray
banks upon the hills, or in shimmering swamps
into the cleft hollows: a vague twilight filled

the space left bare. Tiger, asleep in the hall, rushed out into the meadow, barking, wild with the freshness and cold, then back again to tear round her for a noisy good-morning. The touch of the dog seemed to bring her closer to his master; she put him away; she dared not suffer even that treachery to her purpose: the very circumstances that had forced her to give him up made it weak cowardice to turn again. It was a simple story, yet one which she dared not tell to herself; for it was not altogether for her father's sake she had made the sacrifice. She knew, that, though she might be near to this man Holmes as his own soul, she was a clog on him, — stood in his way, — kept him back. So she had quietly stood aside, taken up her own solitary burden, and left him with his clear self-reliant life, — with his Self, dearer to him than she had ever been. Why should it not be dearer? she thought, — remembering the man as he was, a master among men: fit to be a master. She, — what was she compared to him? He was back again; she must see him. So she stood there with this persistent dread running through her brain.

Suddenly, in the lane by the house, she heard a voice talking to Joel, — the huckster-girl. What a weak, cheery sound it was in the cold and fog! It touched her curiously:

broke through her morbid thought as anything
true and healthy should have done. " Poor
Lois!" she thought, with an eager pity, forgetting her own intolerable future for the moment,
as she gathered up some breakfast and went
with it down the lane. Morning had come;
great heavy bars of light fell from behind the
hills athwart the banks of gray and black fog;
there was shifting, uneasy, obstinate tumult
among the shadows; they did not mean to
yield to the coming dawn. The hills, the
massed woods, the mist opposed their immovable front, scornfully. Margret did not notice
the silent contest until she reached the lane.
The girl Lois, sitting in her cart, was looking,
attentive, at the slow surge of the shadows,
and the slower lifting of the slanted rays.

" T' mornin' comes grand here, Miss Mar-
g'et!" she said, lowering her voice.

Margret said nothing in reply; the morning,
she thought, was gray and cold, like her own
life. She stood leaning on the low cart; some
strange sympathy drew her to this poor wretch,
dwarfed, alone in the world, — some tie of
equality, which the odd childish face, nor the
quaint air of content about the creature, did
not lessen. Even when Lois shook down the
patched skirt of her flannel frock straight, and
settled the heaps of corn and tomatoes about

her, preparatory for a start, Margret kept her hand on the side of the cart, and walked slowly by it down the road. Once, looking at the girl, she thought with a half smile how oddly clean she was. The flannel skirt she arranged so complacently had been washed until the colours had run madly into each other in sheer desperation; her hair was knotted with relentless tightness into a comb such as old women wear. The very cart, patched as it was, had a snug, cosey look; the masses of vegetables, green and crimson and scarlet, were heaped with a certain reference to the glow of colour, Margret noticed, wondering if it were accidental. Looking up, she saw the girl's brown eyes fixed on her face. They were singularly soft, brooding brown.

" Ye 'r' goin' to th' mill, Miss Marg'et ? " she asked, in a half whisper.

" Yes. You never go there now, Lois ? "

" No, 'm."

The girl shuddered, and then tried to hide it in a laugh. Margret walked on beside her, her hand on the cart's edge. Somehow this creature, that Nature had thrown impatiently aside as a failure, so marred, imperfect, that even the dogs were kind to her, came strangely near to her, claimed recognition by some subtle instinct.

Partly for this, and partly striving to forget herself, she glanced furtively at the childish face of the distorted little body, wondering what impression the shifting dawn made on the unfinished soul that was looking out so intently through the brown eyes. What artist sense had she, — what could she know — the ignorant huckster — of the eternal laws of beauty or grandeur? Nothing. Yet something in the girl's face made her think that these hills, this air and sky, were in fact alive to her, — real; that her soul, being lower, it might be, than ours, lay closer to Nature, knew the language of the changing day, of these earnest-faced hills, of the very worms crawling through the brown mould. It was an idle fancy; Margret laughed at herself for it, and turned to watch the slow morning-struggle which Lois followed with such eager eyes.

The light was conquering. Up the gray arch the soft, dewy blue crept gently, deepening, broadening; below it, the level bars of light struck full on the sullen black of the west, and worked there undaunted, tinging it with crimson and imperial purple. Two or three coy mist-clouds, soon converted to the new allegiance, drifted giddily about, mere flakes of rosy blushes. The victory of the day came slowly, but sure, and then the full morning flushed out, fresh with moisture and light and delicate perfume. The bars of sunlight fell on the lower earth from the steep hills like pointed swords; the foggy swamp of wet vapour trembled and broke, so touched, rose at last, leaving patches of damp brilliance on the fields, and floated majestically up in radiant victor clouds, led by the conquering wind. Victory: it was in the cold, pure ether filling the heavens, in the solemn gladness of the hills. The great forests thrilling in the soft light, the very sleepy river wakening under the mist, chorded with a grave bass in the rising anthem of welcome to the new life which God had freshly given to the world. From the sun himself, come forth as a bridegroom from his chamber, to the flickering raindrops on the road-side mullein, the world seemed to rejoice, exultant in victory. Homely, cheerier sounds broke the outlined grandeur of the morning, on which Margret looked wearily. Lois lost none of them; no morbid shadow of her own balked life kept their meaning from her.

The light played on the heaped vegetables in the old cart; the bony legs of the donkey trotted on with fresh vigour. There was not a lowing cow in the distant barns, nor a chirping swallow on the fence-bushes, that did not seem to include the eager face of the little huckster in

their morning greetings. Not a golden dande-
lion on the road-side, not a gurgle of the plash-
ing brown water from the well-troughs, which
did not give a quicker pleasure to the glowing
face. Its curious content stung the woman
walking by her side. What secret of recompense had the poor wretch found?

"Your father is here, Lois," she said carelessly, to break the silence. "I saw him at the mill
yesterday."

Her face kindled instantly.

"He's home, Miss Marg'et, — yes. An' it's
all right wid him. Things allus do come right,
some time," she added, in a reflective tone,
brushing a fly off Barney's ear.

Margret smiled.

"Always? Who brings them right for you,
Lois?"

"The Master," she said, turning with an answering smile.

Margret was touched. The owner of the mill
was not a more real verity to this girl than the
Master of whom she spoke with such quiet
knowledge.

"Are things right in the mill?" she said, testing her.

A shadow came on her face; her eyes wandered uncertainly, as if her weak brain were
confused, — only for a moment.

"They 'll come right!" she said, bravely.
"The Master 'll see to it!"

But the light was gone from her eyes; some
old pain seemed to be surging through her narrow thought; and when she began to talk, it
was in a bewildered, doubtful way.

"It's a black place, th' mill," she said, in a
low voice. "It was a good while I was there :
frum seven year old till sixteen. 'T seemed
longer t' me 'n 't was. 'T seemed as if I'd been
there allus, — jes' forever, yoh know. 'Fore I
went in, I had the rickets, they say : that's what
ails me. 'T hurt my head, they 've told me, —
made me different frum other folks."

She stopped a moment, with a dumb, hungry
look in her eyes. After a while she looked at
Margret furtively, with a pitiful eagerness.

"Miss Marg'et, I think there *be* something
wrong in my head. Did *yoh* ever notice it?"

Margret put her hand kindly on the broad,
misshapen forehead.

"Something is wrong everywhere, Lois," she
said, absently.

She did not see the slow sigh with which the
girl smothered down whatever hope had risen
just then, listened half-attentive as the huckster
maundered on.

"It was th' mill," she said at last. "I kind
o' grew into that place in them years : seemed

to me like as I was part o' th' engines, somehow. Th' air used to be thick in my mouth,
black wi' smoke 'n' wool 'n' smells.

"In them years I got dazed in my head, I
think. 'T was th' air 'n' th' work. I was weak
allus. 'T got so that th' noise o' th' looms went
on in my head night 'n' day, — allus thud, thud.
'N' hot days, when th' hands was chaffin' 'n'
singin', th' black wheels 'n' rollers was alive,
starin' down at me, 'n' th' shadders o' th' looms
was like snakes creepin', — creepin' anear all th'
time. They was very good to me, th' hands
was, — very good. Ther' 's lots o' th' Master's
people down there, though they never heard His
name : preachers don't go there. But He 'll
see to 't. He 'll not min' their cursin' o' Him,
seein' they don't know His face, 'n' thinkin' He
belongs to th' gentry. I knew it wud come
right wi' me, when times was th' most bad. I
knew " ——

The girl's hands were working together, her
eyes set, all the slow years of ruin that had eaten
into her brain rising before her, all the tainted
blood in her veins of centuries of slavery and
heathenism struggling to drag her down. But
above all, the Hope rose clear, simple : the trust
in the Master : and shone in her scarred face, —
through her marred senses.

"I knew it wud come right, allus. I was

alone then : mother was dead, and father was
gone, 'n' th' Lord thought 't was time to see
to me, — special as th' overseer was gettin' me
an enter to th' poor-house. So He sent Mr.
Holmes along. Then it come right!"

Margret did not speak. Even this mill-girl
could talk of him, pray for him ; but she never
must take his name on her lips!

"He got th' cart fur me, 'n' this blessed old
donkey, 'n' my room. Did yoh ever see my
room, Miss Marg'et?"

Her face lighted suddenly with its peculiar
childlike smile.

"No? Yoh 'll come some day, surely? It 's
a pore place, yoh 'll think ; but it 's got th' air,
— th' air."

She stopped to breathe the cold morning
wind, as if she thought to find in its fierce
freshness the life and brains she had lost.

"Ther' 's places in them alleys 'n' dark holes,
Miss Marg'et, like th' openin's to hell, with th'
thick smells 'n' th' sights yoh 'd see."

She went back with a terrible clinging pity to
the Gehenna from which she had escaped. The
ill of life was real enough to her, — a hungry
devil down in those alleys and dens. Margret
listened, waked reluctantly to the sense of a
different pain in the world from her own, —
lower deeps from which women like herself

draw delicately back, lifting their gauzy dresses.

" Miss Marg'et ! "

Her face flashed.

" Well, Lois ? "

" Th' Master has His people 'mong them very lowest, that 's not for such as yoh to speak to. He knows 'em : men 'n' women starved 'n' drunk into jails 'n' work-houses, that 'd scorn to be cowardly or mean, — that shows God's kindness, through th' whiskey 'n' thievin', to th' orphints or — such as me. Ther' 's things th' Master likes in them, 'n' it 'll come right, it 'll come right at last; they 'll have a chance — somewhere."

Margret did not speak; let the poor girl sob herself into quiet. What had she to do with this gulf of pain and wrong ? Her own higher life was starved, thwarted. Could it be that the blood of these her brothers called against *her* from the ground ? No wonder that the huckster-girl sobbed, she thought, or talked heresy. It was not an easy thing to see a mother drink herself into the grave. And yet — was she to blame ? Her Virginian blood was cool, high-bred ; she had learned conservatism in her cradle. Her life in the West had not yet quickened her pulse. So she put aside whatever social mystery or wrong faced her in this girl, just

4

as you or I would have done. She had her own
pain to bear. Was she her brother's keeper?
It was true, there was wrong; this woman's
soul lay shattered by it; it was the fault of her
blood, of her birth, and Society had finished the
work. Where was the help? She was free, —
and liberty, Dr. Knowles said, was the cure for
all the soul's diseases, and ——

Well, Lois was quiet now, — ready to be
drawn into a dissertation on Barney's vices and
virtues, or her room, where " th' air was so strong,
'n' the fruit 'n' vegetables allus stayed fresh, —
best in *this* town," she said, with a bustling pride.

They went on down the road, through the
corn-fields sometimes, or on the river-bank, or
sometimes skirting the orchards or barn-yards
of the farms. The fences were well built, she
noticed, — the barns wide and snug-looking:
for this county in Indiana is settled by New
England people, as a general thing, or Penn-
sylvanians. They both leave their mark on
barns or fields, I can tell you! The two wom-
en were talking all the way. In all his life Dr.
Knowles had never heard from this silent girl
words as open and eager as she gave to the
huckster about paltry, common things, — partly,
as I said, from a hope to forget herself, and
partly from a vague curiosity to know the
strange world which opened before her in this

disjointed talk. There were no morbid shadows
in this Lois's life, she saw. Her pains and
pleasures were intensely real, like those of her
class. If there were latent powers in her distorted brain, smothered by hereditary vice of
blood, or foul air and life, she knew nothing
of it. She never probed her own soul with
fierce self-scorn, as this quiet woman by her
side did ; — accepted, instead, the passing moment, with keen enjoyment. For the rest,
childishly trusted " the Master."

This very drive, now, for instance, — although
she and the cart and Barney went through the
same routine every day, you would have thought
it was a new treat for a special holiday, if you
had seen the perfect *abandon* with which they
all threw themselves into the fun of the thing.
Not only did the very heaps of ruby tomatoes,
and corn in delicate green casings, tremble and
shine as though they enjoyed the fresh light and
dew, but the old donkey cocked his ears, and
curved his scraggy neck, and tried to look as
like a high-spirited charger as he could. Then
everybody along the road knew Lois, and she
knew everybody, and there was a mutual liking
and perpetual joking, not very refined, perhaps,
but hearty and kind. It was a new side of life
for Margret. She had no time for thoughts
of self-sacrifice, or chivalry, ancient or modern,

watching it. It was a very busy ride, — something to do at every farm-house: a basket of eggs to be taken in, or some egg-plants, maybe, which Lois laid side by side, Margret noticed, — the pearly white balls close to the heap of royal purple. No matter how small the basket was that she stopped for, it brought out two or three to put it in; for Lois and her cart were the event of the day for the lonely farm-houses. The wife would come out, her face ablaze from the oven, with an anxious charge about that butter; the old man would hail her from the barn to know "ef she'd thought toh look in th' mail yes'rday;" and one or the other was sure to add, "Jes' time for breakfast, Lois." If she had no baskets to stop for, she had "a bit o' business," which turned out to be a paper she had brought for the grandfather, or some fresh mint for the baby, or "jes' to inquire fur th' fam'ly."

As to the amount that cart carried, it was a perpetual mystery to Lois. Every day since she and the cart went into partnership, she had gone into town with a dead certainty in the minds of lookers-on that it would break down in five minutes, and a triumphant faith in hers in its unlimited endurance. "This cart 'll be right side up fur years to come," she would assert, shaking her head. "It 's got no

more notion o' givin' up than me nor Barney, —
not a bit." Margret had her doubts, — and so
would you, if you had heard how it creaked
under the load, — how they piled in great
straw panniers of apples: black apples with
yellow hearts, — scarlet veined, golden pippin
apples, that held the warmth and light longest,
— russet apples with a hot blush on their rough
brown skins, — plums shining coldly in their
delicate purple bloom, — peaches with the crimson velvet of their cheeks aglow with the pris-
oned heat of a hundred summer days.

I wish with all my heart somebody would
paint me Lois and her cart! Mr. Kitts, the
artist in the city then, used to see it going past
his room out by the coal-pits every day, and
thought about it seriously. But he had his
grand battle-piece on hand then, — and after
that he went the way of all geniuses, and died
down into colourer for a photographer. He met
them, that day, out by the stone quarry, and
touched his hat as he returned Lois's " Good-
morning," and took a couple of great papaws
from her. She was a woman, you see, and he
had some of the school-master's old-fashioned
notions about women. He was a sickly-look-
ing soul. One day Lois had heard him say
that there were papaws on his mother's place
in Ohio; so after that she always brought him

some every day. She was one of those people
who must give, if it is nothing better than a
Kentucky banana.

After they passed the stone quarry, they left
the country behind them, going down the stub-
ble-covered hills that fenced in the town. Even
in the narrow streets, and through the ware-
houses, the strong, dewy air had quite blown
down and off the fog and dust. Morning (town
morning, to be sure, but still morning) was shining in the red window-panes, in the tossing smoke
up in the frosty air, in the very glowing faces
of people hurrying from market with their noses
nipped blue and their eyes watering with cold.
Lois and her cart, fresh with country breath hanging about them, were not so out of place, after
all. House-maids left the steps half-scrubbed,
and helped her measure out the corn and beans,
gossiping eagerly; the newsboys " Hi-d! " at
her in a friendly, patronizing way ; women in
rusty black, with sharp, pale faces, hoisted their
baskets, in which usually lay a scraggy bit of
flitch, on to the wheel, their whispered bargain-
ing ending oftenest in a low " Thank ye, Lois! "
— for she sold cheaper to some people than they
did in the market.

Lois was Lois in town or country. Some
subtile power lay in the coarse, distorted body,
in the pleading child's face, to rouse, wherever

they went, the same curious, kindly smile. Not,
I think, that dumb, pathetic eye, common to deformity, that cries, " Have mercy upon me, O
my friend, for the hand of God hath touched
me!" — a deeper, mightier charm, rather: a trust
down in the fouled fragments of her brain, even
in the bitterest hour of her bare life, — a faith,
faith in God, faith in her fellow-man, faith in
herself. No human soul refused to answer its
summons. Down in the dark alleys, in the
very vilest of the black and white wretches
that crowded sometimes about her cart, there
was an undefined sense of pride in protecting
this wretch whose portion of life was more
meagre and low than theirs. Something in
them struggled up to meet the trust in the
pitiful eyes, — something which scorned to betray the trust, — some Christ-like power in their
souls, smothered, dying, under the filth of their
life and the terror of hell. A something in them
never to be lost. If the Great Spirit of love and
trust lives, not lost!

Even in the cold and quiet of the woman
walking by her side the homely power of the
poor huckster was wholesome to strengthen.
Margret left her, turning into the crowded
street leading to the part of the town where
the factories lay. The throng of anxious-faced
men and women jostled and pushed, but she

passed through them with a different heart from
yesterday's. Somehow, the morbid fancies were
gone ; she was keenly alive ; the coarse real life
of this huckster fired her, touched her blood with
a more vital stimulus than any tale of crusader.
As she went down the crooked maze of dingy
lanes, she could hear Lois's little cracked bell far
off: it sounded like a Christmas song to her. She
half smiled, remembering how sometimes in her
distempered brain the world had seemed a gray,
dismal Dance of Death. How actual it was
to-day, — hearty, vigorous, alive with honest
work and tears and pleasure! A broad, good
world to live and work in, to suffer or die, if
God so willed it, — God, the good!

CHAPTER IV.

She entered the vast, dingy factory; the woollen dust, the clammy air of copperas were easier to breathe in; the cramped, sordid office, the work, mere trifles to laugh at; and she bent over the ledger with its hard lines in earnest good-will, through the slow creeping hours of the long day. She noticed that the unfortunate chicken was making its heart glad over a piece of fresh earth covered with damp moss. Dr. Knowles stopped to look at it when he came, passing her with a surly nod.

"So your master 's not forgotten you," he snarled, while the blind old hen cocked her one eye up at him.

Pike, the manager, had brought in some bills.

"Who 's its master?" he said, curiously, stopping by the door.

"Holmes, — he feeds it every morning."

The Doctor drawled out the words with a covert sneer, watching the cold face bending over the desk, meantime.

Pike laughed.

"Bah! it 's the first thing he ever fed, then,

4 *

besides himself. Chickens must lie nearer his heart than men."

Knowles scowled at him; he had no fancy for Pike's scurrilous gossip.

The quiet face was unmoved. When he heard the manager's foot on the ladder without, he tested it again. He had a vague suspicion which he was determined to verify.

" Holmes," he said, carelessly, " has an affinity for animals. No wonder. Adam must have been some such man as he, when the Lord gave him ' dominion over the fish of the sea, and over the fowl of the air.' "

The hand paused courteously a moment, then resumed its quick, cool movement over the page. He was not baffled.

" If there were such a reality as mastership, that man was born to rule. Pike will find him harder to cheat than me, when he takes possession here."

She looked up now.

" He came here to take my place in the mills, — buy me out, — articles will be signed in a day or two. I know what you think, — no, — not worth a dollar. Only brains and a soul, and he 's sold them at a high figure, — threw his heart in, — the purchaser being a lady. It was light, I fancy, — starved out, long ago."

The old man's words were spurted out in the

bitterness of scorn. The girl listened with a cool incredulity in her eyes, and went back to her work.

" Miss Herne is the lady, — my partner's daughter. Herne and Holmes they 'll call the firm. He is here every day, counting future profit."

Nothing could be read on the face; so he left her, cursing, as he went, men who put themselves up at auction, — worse than Orleans slaves. Margret laughed to herself at his passion; as for the story he hinted, it was absurd. She forgot it in a moment.

Two or three gentlemen down in one of the counting-rooms, just then, looked at the story from another point of view. They were talking low, out of hearing from the clerks.

" It 's a good thing for Holmes," said one, a burly, farmer-like man, who was choosing specimens of wool.

" Cheap. And long credit. Just half the concern he takes."

" There is a lady in the case?" suggested a young doctor, who, by virtue of having spent six months in the South, dropped his *r*-s, and talked of " niggahs " in a way to make a Georgian's hair stand on end.

" A lady in the case?"

" O-f course. Only child of Herne's. *He*

comes down with the dust as dowry. Good thing for Holmes. 'Stonishin' how he 's made his way up. If money 's what he wants in this world, he 's making a long stride now to 't."

The young doctor lighted his cigar, asserting that —

"Ba George, some low people did get on, re-markably! Mary Herne, now, was best catch in town."

"Do you think money is what he wants?" said a quiet little man, sitting lazily on a barrel, — a clergyman, Vandyke; whom his clerical brothers shook their heads when they named, but never argued with, and bowed to with uncommon deference.

The wool-buyer hesitated with a puzzled look.

"No," he said, slowly; "Stephen Holmes is not miserly. I 've knowed him since a boy. To buy place, power, perhaps, eh.? Yet not that, neither," he added, hastily. "We think a sight of him out our way, (self-made, you see,) and would have had him the best office in the State before this, only he was so cursedly indifferent."

"Indifferent, yes. No man cares much for stepping-stones in themselves," said Vandyke, half to himself.

"Great fault of American society, especially

in the West," said the young aristocrat. " Stepping-stones lie low, as my reverend friend suggests; impudence ascends; merit and refinement scorn such dirty paths," — with a mournful remembrance of the last dime in his waistcoat-pocket.

" But do you," exclaimed the farmer, with sudden solemnity, " do you understand this scheme of Knowles's? Every dollar he owns is in this mill, and every dollar of it is going into some castle in the air that no sane man can comprehend."

" Mad as a March hare," contemptuously muttered the doctor.

His reverend friend gave him a look, — after which he was silent.

" I wish to the Lord some one would persuade him out of it," persisted the wool-man, earnestly looking at the attentive face of his listener. " We can't spare old Knowles's brain or heart while he ruins himself. It 's something of a Communist fraternity : I don't know the name, but I know the thing."

Very hard common-sense shone out of his eyes just then at the clergyman, whom he suspected of being one of Knowles's abettors.

" There 's two ways for 'em to end. If they 're made out of the top of society, they get so refined, so idealized, that every particle

flies off on its own special path to the sun, and
the Community 's broke; and if they 're made
of the lower mud, they keep going down, down
together, — they live to drink and eat, and make
themselves as near the brutes as they can.   It
is n't easy to believe, Sir, but it 's true.   I have
seen it.   I 've seen every one of them the United
States can produce.   It 's *facts*, Sir; and facts,
as Lord Bacon says, 'are the basis of every
sound speculation.' "

The last sentence was slowly brought out, as
quotations were not exactly his *forte*, but, as he
said afterwards, — " You see, that nailed the
parson."

The parson nodded gravely.

" You 'll find no such experiment in the
Bible," threw in the young doctor, alluding to
" serious things " as a peace-offering to his
reverend friend.

" One, I believe," dryly.

" Well," broke in the farmer, folding up his
wool, " that 's neither here nor there.   This experiment of Knowles's is like nothing known
since the Creation.   Plan of his own.   He
spends his days now hunting out the gallows-
birds out of the dens in town here, and they
're all to be transported into the country to
start a new Arcadia.   A few men and women
like himself, but the bulk is from the dens, I

tell you. All start fair, level ground, perpetual celibacy, mutual trust, honour, rise according to the stuff that 's in them, — pah! it makes me sick!"

" Knowles's inclination to that sort of people is easily explained," spitefully lisped the doctor. " Blood, Sir. His mother was a half-breed Creek, with all the propensities of the redskins to fire-water and ' itching palms.' Blood will out."

" Here he is," maliciously whispered the wool-man. " No, it 's Holmes," he added, after the doctor had started into a more respectful posture, and glanced around frightened.

He, the doctor, rose to meet Holmes's coming footstep, — " a low fellah, but always sure to be the upper dog in the fight, goin' to marry the best catch," etc., etc. The others, on the contrary, put on their hats and sauntered away into the street.

The day broadencd hotly ; the shadows of the Lombardy poplars curdling up into a sluggish pool of black at their roots along the dry gutters. The old school-master in the shade of the great horse-chestnuts (brought from the homestead in the Piedmont country, every one) husked corn for his wife, composing, meanwhile, a page of his essay on the " Sirventes de Bertrand de Born." Joel, up in the barn by him-

self, worked through the long day in the old
fashion, — pondering gravely (being of a religious turn) upon a sermon by the Reverend Mr.
Clinche, reported in the " Gazette ; " wherein
that disciple of the meek Teacher invoked, as
he did once a week, the curses of the law upon
slaveholders, praying the Lord to sweep them
immediately from the face of the earth. Which
rendering of Christian doctrine was so much rel-
ished by Joel, and the other leading members of
Mr. Clinche's church, that they hinted to him it
might be as well to continue choosing his texts
from Moses and the Prophets until the excitement of the day was over. The New Testament was, — well, — hardly suited for the
emergency ; did not, somehow, chime in with
the lesson of the hour. I may remark, in passing, that this course of conduct so disgusted the
High-Church rector of the parish, that he not
only ignored all new devils, (as Mr. Carlyle
might have called them,) but talked as if the
millennium were *un fait accompli*, and he had
leisure to go and hammer at the poor dead old
troubles of Luther's time. One thing, though,
about Joel : while he was joining in Mr.
Clinche's petition for the " wiping out " of some
few thousands, he was using up all the fragments of the hot day in fixing a stall for a half-
dead old horse he had found by the road-side.

Perhaps, even if the listening angel did not grant the prayer, he marked down the stall at least, as a something done for eternity.

Margret, through the stifling air, worked steadily alone in the dusty office, her face bent over the books, never changing but once. It was a trifle then; yet, when she looked back afterwards, the trifle was all that gave the day a name. The room shook, as I said, with the thunderous, incessant sound of the engines and the looms; she scarcely heard it, being used to it. Once, however, another sound came between, — an iron tread, passing through the long wooden corridor, — so firm and measured that it sounded like the monotonous beatings of a clock. She heard it through the noise in the far distance; it came slowly nearer, up to the door without, — passed it, going down the echoing plank walk. The girl sat quietly, looking out at the dead brick wall. The slow step fell on her brain like the sceptre of her master; if Knowles had looked in her face then, he would have seen bared the secret of her life. Holmes had gone by, unconscious of who was within the door. She had not seen him; it was nothing but a step she heard. Yet a power, the power of the girl's life, shook off all outward masks, all surface cloudy fancies, and stood up in her with a terrible passion at the sound; her

blood burned fiercely; her soul looked out, her
soul as it was, as God knew it, — God and this
man.   No longer a cold, clear face; you would
have thought, looking at it, what a strong spirit
the soul of this woman would be, if set free in
heaven or in hell.   The man who held it in his
grasp went on carelessly, not knowing that the
mere sound of his step had raised it as from the
dead.   She, and her right, and her pain, were
nothing to him now, she remembered, staring
out at the taunting hot sky.   Yet so vacant was
the sudden life opened before her when he was
gone, that, in the desperation of her weakness,
her mad longing to see him but once again, she
would have thrown herself at his feet, and let
the cold, heavy step crush her life out, — as he
would have done, she thought, choking down
the icy smother in her throat, if it had served
his purpose, though it cost his own heart's life
to do it.   He would trample her down, if she
kept him back from his end; but be false to her,
false to himself, that he would never be!

The red bricks, the dusty desk covered with
wool, the miserable chicken peering out, grew
sharper and more real.   Life was no morbid
nightmare now; her weak woman's heart found
it near, cruel.   There was not a pain nor a
want, from the dumb question in the dog's eyes
that passed her on the street, to her father's

hopeless fancies, that did not touch her sharply
through her own loss, with a keen pity, a wild
wish to help to do something to save others
with this poor life left in her hands.

So the day wore on in the town and country;
the old sun glaring down like some fierce old
judge, intolerant of weakness or shams, — bak-
ing the hard earth in the streets harder for the
horses' feet, drying up the bits of grass that
grew between the boulders of the gutter, scaling
off the paint from the brazen faces of the interminable brick houses. He looked down in that
city as in every American town, as in these
where you and I live, on the same countless
maze of human faces going day by day through
the same monotonous routine. Knowles, passing through the restless crowds, read with keen
eye among them strange meanings by this common light of the sun, — meanings such as you
and I might read, if our eyes were clear as his,
— or morbid, it may be, you think? A commonplace crowd like this in the street without:
women with cold, fastidious faces, heavy-brained,
bilious men, dapper 'prentices, draymen, prize-
fighters, negroes. Knowles looked about him
as into a seething caldron, in which the people I
tell you of were atoms, where the blood of un-
counted races was fused, but not mingled, —
where creeds, philosophies, centuries old, grap-

pled hand to hand in their death-struggle, —
where innumerable aims and beliefs and powers of intellect, smothered rights and triumphant wrongs, warred together, struggling for
victory.

Vulgar American life? He thought it a life
more potent, more tragic in its history and
prophecy, than any that has gone before. People called him a fanatic. It may be that he was
one: yet the uncouth old man, sick in soul from
some pain that I dare not tell you of, in his own
life, looked into the depths of human loss with a
mad desire to set it right. On the very faces of
those who sneered at him he found some trace
of failure, something that his heart carried up to
God with a loud and exceeding bitter cry. The
voice of the world, he thought, went up to
heaven a discord, unintelligible, hopeless, — the
great blind world, astray since the first ages!
Was there no hope, no help?

The sun shone down, as it had done for six
thousand years; it shone on open problems in
the lives of these men and women, these dogs
and horses who walked the streets, problems
whose end and beginning no eye could read.
There were places where it did not shine: down
in the fetid cellars, in the slimy cells of the
prison yonder: what riddles of life lay there he
dared not think of. God knows how the man

groped for the light, — for any voice to make earth and heaven clear to him.

There was another light by which the world was seen that day, rarer than the sunshine, and purer. It fell on the dense crowds, upon the just and the unjust. It went into the fogs of the fetid dens from which the coarser light was barred, into the deepest mires of body where a soul could wallow, and made them clear. It lighted the depths of the hearts whose outer pain and passion men were keen to read in the unpitying sunshine, and bared in those depths the feeble gropings for the right, the loving hope, the unuttered prayer. No kind thought, no pure desire, no weakest faith in a God and heaven somewhere, could be so smothered under guilt that this subtile light did not search it out, glow about it, shine under it, hold it up in full view of God and the angels, — lighting the world other than the sun had done for six thousand years. I have no name for the light: it has a name, — yonder. Not many eyes were clear to see its shining that day; and if they did, it was as through a glass, darkly. Yet it belonged to us also, in the old time, the time when men could " hear the voice of the Lord God in the garden in the cool of the day." It is God's light now alone.

Yet Lois caught faint glimpses, I think, sometimes, of its heavenly clearness. I think it was this light that made the burning of Christmas fires warmer for her than for others, that showed her all the love and outspoken honesty and hearty frolic which her eyes saw perpetually in the old warm-hearted world. That evening, as she sat on the step of her frame-shanty, knitting at a great blue stocking, her scarred face and misshapen body very pitiful to the passers-by, it was this that gave to her face its homely, cheery smile. It made her eyes quick to know the message in the depths of colour in the evening sky, or even the flickering tints of the green creeper on the wall with its crimson cornuco-pias filled with hot shining. She liked clear, vital colours, this girl, — the crimsons and blues. They answered her, somehow. They could speak. There were things in the world that like herself were marred, — did not understand, — were hungry to know : the gray sky, the mud streets, the tawny lichens. She cried sometimes, looking at them, hardly knowing why : she could not help it, with a vague sense of loss. It seemed at those times so dreary for them to be alive, — or for her. Other things her eyes were quicker to see than ours : delicate or grand lines, which she perpetually sought for unconsciously, — in the homeliest things, the very soft curling of the woollen yarn in her

fingers, as in the eternal sculpture of the mountains. Was it the disease of her injured brain
that made all things alive to her, — that made
her watch, in her ignorant way, the grave hills,
the flashing, victorious rivers, look pitifully into
the face of some starved hound, or dingy mush-
room trodden in the mud before it scarce had
lived, just as we should look into human faces
to know what they would say to us? Was it
weakness and ignorance that made everything
she saw or touched nearer, more human to her
than to you or me? She never got used to
living as other people do; these sights and
sounds did not come to her common, hackneyed. Why, sometimes, out in the hills, in the
torrid quiet of summer noons, she had knelt by
the shaded pools, and buried her hands in the
great slumberous beds of water-lilies, her blood
curdling in a feverish languor, a passioned trance,
from which she roused herself, weak and tired.

She had no self-poised artist sense, this Lois,
— knew nothing of Nature's laws, as you do.
Yet sometimes, watching the dun sea of the
prairie rise and fall in the crimson light of
early morning, or, in the farms, breathing the
blue air trembling up to heaven exultant with
the life of bird and forest, she forgot the poor
vile thing she was, some coarse weight fell off,
and something within, not the sickly Lois of

the mill, went out, free, like an exile dreaming
of home.

You tell me, that, doubtless, in the wreck of
the creature's brain, there were fragments of
some artistic insight that made her thus rise
above the level of her daily life, drunk with
the mere beauty of form and colour. I do not
know, — not knowing how sham or real a thing
you mean by artistic insight. But I do know
that the clear light I told you of shone for this
girl dimly through this beauty of form and
colour; alive. The Life, rather; and ignorant,
with no words for her thoughts, she believed in
it as the Highest that she knew. I think it
came to her thus in imperfect language, (not an
outward show of tints and lines, as to artists,)
— a language, the same that Moses heard when
he stood alone, with nothing between his naked
soul and God, but the desert and the mountain
and the bush that burned with fire. I think the
weak soul of the girl staggered from its dun-
geon, and groped through these heavy-browed
hills, these colour-dreams, through the faces of
dog or man upon the street, to find the God
that lay behind. So she saw the world, and its
beauty and warmth being divine as near to her,
the warmth and beauty became real in her,
found their homely reflection in her daily life.
So she knew, too, the Master in whom she be-

lieved, saw Him in everything that lived, more
real than all beside.   The waiting earth, the
prophetic sky, the very worm in the gutter was
but a part of this man, something come to tell
her of Him, — she dimly felt; though, as I said,
she had no words for such a thought.   Yet even
more real than this.   There was no pain nor
temptation down in those dark cellars where
she went that He had not borne, — not one.
Nor was there the least pleasure came to her
or the others, not even a cheerful fire, or kind
words, or a warm, hearty laugh, that she did
not know He sent it and was glad to do it.
She knew that well!   So it was that He took
part in her humble daily life, and became more
real to her day by day.   Very homely shadows
her life gave of His light, for it was His: homely, because of her poor way of living, and of
the depth to which the heavy foot of the world
had crushed her.   Yet they were there all the
time, in her cheery patience, if nothing more.
To-night, for instance, how differently the surging crowd seemed to her from what it did to
Knowles!   She looked down on it from her
high wood-steps with an eager interest, ready
with her weak, timid laugh to answer every
friendly call from below.   She had no power
to see them as types of great classes; they
were just so many living people, whom she

5

knew, and who, most of them, had been kind
to her.   Whatever good there was in the vilest
face, (and there was always something,) she
was sure to see it.   The light made her poor
eyes strong for that.

She liked to sit there in the evenings, being
alone, yet never growing lonesome ; there was
so much that was pleasant to watch and listen
to, as the cool brown twilight came on.   If, as
Knowles thought, the world was a dreary discord, she knew nothing of it.   People were
going from their work now, — they had time
to talk and joke by the way, — stopping, or
walking slowly down the cool shadows of the
pavement ; while here and there a lingering red
sunbeam burnished a window, or struck athwart
the gray boulder-paved street.   From the houses
near you could catch a faint smell of supper :
very friendly people those were in these houses ;
she knew them all well.   The children came
out with their faces washed, to play, now the
sun was down : the oldest of them generally
came to sit with her and hear a story.

After it grew darker, you would see the girls
in their neat blue calicoes go sauntering down
the street with their sweethearts for a walk.
There was old Polston and his son Sam coming home from the coal-pits, as black as ink,
with their little tin lanterns on their caps.   After

a while Sam would come out in his suit of
Kentucky jean, his face shining with the soap,
and go sheepishly down to Jenny Ball's, and
the old man would bring his pipe and chair out
on the pavement, and his wife would sit on the
steps.   Most likely they would call Lois down,
or come over themselves, for they were the most
sociable, coseyest old couple you ever knew.
There was a great stopping at Lois's door, as
the girls walked past, for a bunch of the flowers
she brought from the country, or posies, as they
called them, (Sam never would take any to
Jenny but "old man" and pinks,) and she always had them ready in broken jugs inside.
They were good, kind girls, every one of them,
— had taken it in turn to sit up with Lois last
winter all the time she had the rheumatism.
She never forgot that time, — never once.

Later in the evening you would see a man
coming along, close by the wall, with his head
down, the same Margret had seen in the mill, —
a dark man, with gray, thin hair, — Joe Yare,
Lois's old father.   No one spoke to him, —
people always were looking away as he passed;
and if old Mr. or Mrs. Polston were on the
steps when he came up, they would say, "Good-
evening, Mr. Yare," very formally, and go away
presently.   It hurt Lois more than anything
else they could have done.   But she bustled

about noisily, so that he would not notice it.
If they saw the marks of the ill life he had
lived on his old face, she did not; his sad, uncertain eyes may have been dishonest to them,
but they were nothing but kind to the misshapen little soul that he kissed so warmly with
a " Why, Lo, my little girl!" Nobody else in
the world ever called her by a pet name.

Sometimes he was gloomy and silent, but
generally he told her of all that had happened
in the mill, particularly any little word of notice or praise he might have received, watching
her anxiously until she laughed at it, and then
rubbing his hands cheerfully. He need not
have doubted Lois's faith in him. Whatever
the rest did, she believed in him; she always
had believed in him, through all the dark years,
when he was at home, and in the penitentiary.
They were gone now, never to come back. It
had come right. If the others wronged him,
and it hurt her bitterly that they did, that would
come right some day too, she would think, as
she looked at the tired, sullen face of the old
man bent to the window-pane, afraid to go out.
But they had very cheerful little suppers there
by themselves in the odd, bare little room, as
homely and clean as Lois herself.

Sometimes, late at night, when he had gone
to bed, she sat alone in the door, while the

moonlight fell in broad patches over the square, and the great poplars stood like giants whispering together. Still the far sounds of the town came up cheerfully, while she folded up her knitting, it being dark, thinking how happy an ending this was to a happy day. When it grew quiet, she could hear the solemn whisper of the poplars, and sometimes broken strains of music from the cathedral in the city floated through the cold and moonlight past her, far off into the blue beyond the hills. All the keen pleasure of the day, the warm, bright sights and sounds, coarse and homely though they were, seemed to fade into the deep music, and make a part of it.

Yet, sitting there, looking out into the listening night, the poor child's face grew slowly pale as she heard it. It humbled her. It made her meanness, her low, weak life so plain to her! There was no pain nor hunger she had known that did not find a voice in its articulate cry. *She!* what was she? The pain and wants of the world must be going up to God in that sound, she thought. There was something more in it, — an unknown meaning of a great content that her shattered brain struggled to grasp. She could not. Her heart ached with a wild, restless longing. She had no words for the vague, insatiate hunger to understand. It

was because she was ignorant and low, perhaps; others could know. She thought her
Master was speaking. She thought that unknown Joy linked all earth and heaven together, and made it plain. So she hid her
face in her hands, and listened, while the low
harmony shivered through the air, unheeded by
others, with the message of God to man. Not
comprehending, it may be, — the poor girl, —
hungry still to know. Yet, when she looked
up, there were warm tears in her eyes, and her
scarred face was bright with a sad, deep content and love.

So the hot, long day was over for them all,
— passed as thousands of days have done for
us, gone down, forgotten: as that long, hot day
we call life will be over some time, and go
down into the gray and cold. Surely, whatever of sorrow or pain may have made darkness in that day for you or me, there were
countless openings where we might have seen
glimpses of that other light than sunshine: the
light of that great To-Morrow, of the land
where all wrongs shall be righted. If we had
but chosen to see it, — if we only had chosen!

CHAPTER V.

Now that I have come to the love part of my story, I am suddenly conscious of dingy common colors on the palette with which I have been painting. I wish I had some brilliant dyes. I wish, with all my heart, I could take you back to that " Once upon a time " in which the souls of our grandmothers delighted, — the time which Dr. Johnson sat up all night to read about in " Evelina," — the time when all the celestial virtues, all the earthly graces were revealed in a condensed state to man through the blue eyes and sumptuous linens of some Belinda Portman or Lord Mortimer. None of your good-hearted, sorely-tempted villains then! It made your hair stand on end only to read of them, — going about perpetually seeking innocent maidens and unsophisticated old men to devour. That was the time for holding up virtue and vice; no trouble then in seeing which were sheep and which were goats! A person could write a story with a moral to it, then, I should hope! People that were born in those days had no fancy for going through the world with half-

and-half characters, such as we put up with; so
Nature turned out complete specimens of each
class, with all the appendages of dress, fortune,
et cetera, chording decently. The heroine glides
into life full-charged with rank, virtues, a name
three-syllabled, and a white dress that never
needs washing, ready to sail through dangers
dire into a triumphant haven of matrimony; —
all the aristocrats have high foreheads and cold
blue eyes; all the peasants are old women, mi-
raculously grateful, in neat check aprons, or
sullen-browed insurgents planning revolts in
caves.

Of course, I do not mean that these times are
gone : they are alive (in a modern fashion) in
many places in the world; some of my friends
have described them in prose and verse. I only
mean to say that I never was there ; I was born
unlucky. I am willing to do my best, but I
live in the commonplace. Once or twice I have
rashly tried my hand at dark conspiracies, and
women rare and radiant in Italian bowers; but
I have a friend who is sure to say, " Try and
tell us about the butcher next door, my dear."
If I look up from my paper now, I shall be just
as apt to see our dog and his kennel as the
white sky stained with blood and Tyrian purple.
I never saw a full-blooded saint or sinner in my
life. The coldest villain I ever knew was the

only son of his mother, and she a widow, — and
a kinder son never lived. Doubtless there are
people capable of a love terrible in its strength;
but I never knew such a case that some one did
not consider its expediency as "a match" in
the light of dollars and cents. As for heroines,
of course I have seen beautiful women, and good
as fair. The most beautiful is delicate and pure
enough for a type of the Madonna, and has a
heart almost as warm and holy. (Very pure blood
is in her veins, too, if you care about blood.)
But at home they call her Tode for a nickname;
all we can do, she will sing, and sing through
her nose; and on washing-days she often cooks
the dinner, and scolds wholesomely, if the tea-
napkins are not in order. Now, what is anybody to do with a heroine like that? I have
known old maids in abundance, with pathos
and sunshine in their lives; but the old maid
of novels I never have met, who abandoned her
soul to gossip, — nor yet the other type, a life-
long martyr of unselfishness. They are mixed
generally, and not unlike their married sisters,
so far as I can see. Then as to men, certainly
I know heroes. One man, I knew, as high a
chevalier in heart as any Bayard of them all;
one of those souls simple and gentle as a woman, tender in knightly honour. He was an
old man, with a rusty brown coat and rustier

5 *

wig, who spent his life in a dingy village office. You poets would have laughed at him. Well, well, his history never will be written. The kind, sad, blue eyes are shut now. There is a little farm-graveyard overgrown with privet and wild grape-vines, and a flattened grave where he was laid to rest; and only a few who knew him when they were children care to go there, and think of what he was to them. But it was not in the far days of Chivalry alone, I think, that true and proud souls have stood in the world unwelcome, and, hurt to the quick, have turned away and dumbly died. Let it be. Their lives are not lost, thank God!

I meant only to ask you, How can I help it, if the people in my story seem coarse to you, — if the hero, unlike all other heroes, stopped to count the cost before he fell in love, — if it made his fingers thrill with pleasure to touch a full pocket-book as well as his mistress's hand, — not being withal, this Stephen Holmes, a man to be despised? A hero, rather, of a peculiar type, — a man, more than other men : the very mould of man, doubt it who will, that women love longest and most madly. Of course, if I could, I would have blotted out every meanness before I showed him to you; I would have told you Margret was an impetuous, whole-souled woman, glad to throw her life down for her

father, without one bitter thought of the wife
and mother she might have been ; I would have
painted her mother tender, (as she was,) forgetting how pettish she grew on busy days : but
what can I do ? I must show you men and
women as they are in that especial State of the
Union where I live. In all the others, of course,
it is very different. Now, being prepared for
disappointment, will you see my hero ?

He had sauntered out from the city for a
morning walk, — not through the hills, as Margret went, going home, but on the other side,
to the river, over which you could see the Prairie. We are in Indiana, remember. The sunlight was pure that morning, powerful, tintless,
the true wine of life for body or spirit. Stephen
Holmes knew that, being a man of delicate
animal instincts, and so used it, just as he had
used the dumb-bells in the morning. All things
were made for man, were n't they ? He was
leaning against the door of the school-house, —
a red, flaunting house, the daub on the landscape : but, having his back to it, he could not
see it, so through his half-shut eyes he suffered
the beauty of the scene to act on him. Suffered :
in a man, according to his creed, the will being
dominant, and all influences,. such as beauty,
pain, religion, permitted to act under orders.
Of course.

It was a peculiar landscape, — like the man
who looked at it, of a thoroughly American
type. A range of sharp, dark hills, with a
sombre depth of green shadow in the clefts,
and on the sides massed forests of scarlet and
flame and crimson. Above, the sharp peaks of
stone rose into the wan blue, wan and pale
themselves, and wearing a certain air of fixed
calm, the type of an eternal quiet. At the base
of the hills lay the city, a dirty mass of bricks
and smoke and dust, and at its far edge flowed
the Wabash, — deep here, tinted with green,
writhing and gurgling and curdling on the banks
over shelving ledges of lichen and mud-covered
rock. Beyond it yawned the opening to the
great West, — the Prairies. Not the dreary
deadness here, as farther west. A plain, dark
russet in hue, — for the grass was sun-scorched,
— stretching away into the vague distance, intolerable, silent, broken by hillocks and puny
streams that only made the vastness and silence
more wide and heavy. Its limitless torpor
weighed on the brain; the eyes ached, stretching to find some break before the dull russet
faded into the amber of the horizon and was
lost. An American landscape : of few features,
simple, grand in outline as a face of one of the
early gods. It lay utterly motionless before
him, not a fleck of cloud in the pure blue above,

even where the mist rose from the river; it only
had glorified the clear blue into clearer violet.

Holmes stood quietly looking; he could have
created a picture like this, if he never had seen
one; therefore he was able to recognize it, accepted it into his soul, and let it do what it
would there.

Suddenly a low wind from the far Pacific
coast struck from the amber line where the
sun went down. A faint tremble passed over
the great hills, the broad sweeps of colour darkened from base to summit, then flashed again,
— while below, the prairie rose and fell like
a dun sea, and rolled in long, slow, solemn
waves.

The wind struck so broad and fiercely in
Holmes's face that he caught his breath. It
was a savage freedom, he thought, in the West
there, whose breath blew on him, — the freedom
of the primitive man, the untamed animal man,
self-reliant and self-assertant, having conquered
Nature. Well, this fierce, masterful freedom
was good for the soul, sometimes, doubtless.
It was old Knowles's vital air. He wondered
if the old man would succeed in his hobby,
if he could make the slavish beggars and
thieves in the alleys yonder comprehend this
fierce freedom. They craved leave to live on
sufferance now, not knowing their possible di-

vinity. It was a desperate remedy, this sense of
unchecked liberty; but their disease was desperate. As for himself, he did not need it; that
element was not lacking. In a mere bodily
sense, to be sure. He felt his arm. Yes, the
cold rigor of this new life had already worn off
much of the clogging weight of flesh, strengthened the muscles. Six months more in the
West would toughen the fibres to iron. He
raised an iron weight that lay on the steps,
carelessly testing them. For the rest, he was
going back here; something of the cold, loose
freshness got into his brain, he believed. In
the two years of absence his power of con-
centration had been stronger, his perceptions
more free from prejudice, gaining every day
delicate point, acuteness of analysis. He drew
a long breath of the icy air, coarse with the wild
perfume of the prairie. No, his temperament
needed a subtiler atmosphere than this, rarer
essence than mere brutal freedom The East,
the Old World, was his proper sphere for self-
development. He would go as soon as he could
command the means, leaving all clogs behind.
All? His idle thought balked here, suddenly;
the sallow forehead contracted sharply, and his
gray eyes grew in an instant shallow, careless,
formal, as a man who holds back his thought.
There was a fierce warring in his brain for a

moment. Then he brushed his Kossuth hat
with his arm, and put it on, looking out at the
landscape again. Somehow its meaning was
dulled to him. Just then a muddy terrier came
up, and rubbed itself against his knee. "Why,
Tige, old boy!" he said, stooping to pat it
kindly. The hard, shallow look faded out; he
half smiled, looking in the dog's eyes. A curious smile, unspeakably tender and sad. It was
the idiosyncrasy of the man's face, rarely seen
there. He might have looked with it at a criminal, condemning him to death. But he would
have condemned him, and, if no hangman could
be found, would have put the rope on with his
own hands, and then most probably would have
sat down pale and trembling, and analyzed his
sensations on paper, — being sincere in all.

He sat down on the school-house step, which
the boys had hacked and whittled rough, and
waited; for he was there by appointment, to
meet Dr. Knowles.

Knowles had gone out early in the morning
to look at the ground he was going to buy for
his Phalanstery, or whatever he chose to call it.
He was to bring the deed of sale of the mill out
with him for Holmes. The next day it was to
be signed. Holmes saw him at last lumbering
across the prairie, wiping the perspiration from
his forehead. Summer or winter, he contrived

to be always hot   There was a cart drawn by
an old donkey coming along beside him. Knowles
was talking to the driver. The old man clapped
his hands as stage-coachmen do, and drew in
long draughts of air, as if there were keen life and
promise in every breath.   They came up at last,
the cart empty, and drying for the day's work
after its morning's scrubbing, Lois's pock-marked
face all in a glow with trying to keep Barney
awake.   She grew quite red with pleasure at
seeing Holmes, but went on quickly as the men
began to talk.   Tige followed her, of course ;
but when she had gone a little way across the
prairie, they saw her stop, and presently the dog
came back with something in his mouth, which
he laid down beside his master, and bolted off.
It was only a rough wicker-basket which she
had filled with damp plushy moss, and half-bur-
ied in it clusters of plumy fern, delicate brown
and ashen lichens, masses of forest-leaves all
shaded green with a few crimson tints.   It had
a clear woody smell, like far-off myrrh.   The
Doctor laughed as Holmes took it up.

" An artist's gift, if it is from a mulatto," he
said.   " A born colourist."

The men were not at ease, for some reason ;
they seized on every trifle to keep off the subject
which had brought them together.

" That girl's artist-sense is pure, and her religion, down under the perversion and ignorance of her brain. Curious, eh ? "

" Look at the top of her head, when you see her," said Holmes. " It is necessity for such brains to worship. They let the fire lick their blood, if they happen to be born Parsees. This girl, if she had been a Jew when Christ was born, would have known him as Simeon did."

Knowles said nothing, — only glanced at the massive head of the speaker, with its overhanging brow, square development at the sides, and lowered crown, and smiled significantly.

" Exactly," laughed Holmes, putting his hand on his head. " Crippled there by my Yorkshire blood, — my mother. Never mind ; outside of this life, blood or circumstance matters nothing."

They walked on slowly towards town. Surely there was nothing in the bill-of-sale which the old man had in his pocket but a mere matter of business ; yet they were strangely silent about it, as if it brought shame to some one. There was an embarrassed pause. The Doctor went back to Lois for relief.

" I think it is the pain and want of such as she that makes them susceptible to religion. The self in them is so starved and humbled that it cannot obscure their eyes ; they see God clearly."

" Say rather," said Holmes, " that the soul is

so starved and blind that it cannot recognize
itself as God."

The Doctor's intolerant eye kindled.

" Humph! So that 's your creed! Not Pan-
theism. *Ego sum.* Of course you go on with
the conjugation: *I have been, I shall be. I,* —
that covers the whole ground, creation, redemp-
tion, and commands the hereafter? "

" It does so," said Holmes, coolly.

" And this wretched huckster carries her deity
about her, — her self-existent soul? How, in
God's name, is her life to set it free? "

Holmes said nothing. The coarse sneer could
not be answered. Men with pale faces and
heavy jaws like his do not carry their religion
on their tongue's end; their creeds leave them
only in the slow oozing life-blood, false as the
creeds may be.

Knowles went on hotly, half to himself, seiz-
ing on the new idea fiercely, as men and women
do who are yet groping for the truth of life.

" What is it your Novalis says? ' The true
Shechinah is man.' You know no higher God?
Pooh! the idea is old enough; it began with
Eve. It works slowly, Holmes. In six thousand years, taking humanity as one, this self-
existent soul should have clothed itself with a
freer, royaller garment than poor Lois's body, —
or mine," he added, bitterly.

"It works slowly," said the other, quietly. "Faster soon, in America. There are yet many ills of life for the divinity within to conquer."

"And Lois and the swarming mass yonder in those dens? It is late for them to begin the fight?"

"Endurance is enough for them here, and their religions teach them that. They could not bear the truth. One does not put a weapon into the hands of a man dying of the fetor and hunger of the siege."

"But what will this life, or the lives to come, give to you, champions who know the truth?"

"Nothing but victory," he said, in a low tone, looking away.

Knowles looked at the pale strength of the iron face.

"God help you, Stephen!" he broke out, his shallow jeering falling off. "For there *is* a God higher than we. The ills of life you mean to conquer will teach it to you, Holmes. You'll find the Something above yourself, if it's only to curse Him and die."

Holmes did not smile at the old man's heat, — walked gravely, steadily.

There was a short silence. Knowles put his hand gently on the other's arm.

"Stephen," he hesitated, "you're a stronger man than I. I know what you are; I've

watched you from a boy. But you 're wrong
here. I 'm an old man. There 's not much I
know in life, — enough to madden me. But I
do know there 's something stronger, — some
God outside of the mean devil they call ' Me.'
You 'll learn it, boy. There 's an old story of a
man like you and the rest of your sect, and of
the vile, mean, crawling things that God sent to
bring him down. There are such things yet.
Mean passions in your divine soul, low, selfish
things, that will get the better of you, show you
what you are. You 'll do all that man can do.
But they are coming, Stephen Holmes! they
're coming!"

He stopped, startled. For Holmes had turned
abruptly, glancing over at the city with a strange
wistfulness. It was over in a moment. He resumed the slow, controlling walk beside him.
They went on in silence into town, and when
they did speak, it was on indifferent subjects,
not referring to the last. The Doctor's heat, as
it usually did, boiled out in spasms on trifles.
Once he stumped his toe, and, I am sorry to
say, swore roundly about it, just as he would
have done in the new Arcadia, if one of the
jail-birds comprising that colony had been ungrateful for his advantages. Philanthropists, for
some curious reason, are not the most amiable
members of small families.

He gave Holmes the roll of parchment he had
in his pocket, looking keenly at him, as he did
so, but only saying, that, if he meant to sign it,
it would be done to-morrow. As Holmes took
it, they stopped at the great door of the factory.
He went in alone, Knowles going down the
street. One trifle, strange in its way, he remembered afterwards. Holding the roll of paper in his hand that would make the mill his,
he went, in his slow, grave way, down the long
passage to the loom-rooms. There was a crowd
of porters and firemen there, as usual, and he
thought one of them hastily passed him in the
dark passage, hiding behind an engine. As the
shadow fell on him, his teeth chattered with a
chilly shudder. He smiled, thinking how super-
stitious people would say that some one trod on
his grave just then, or that Death looked at him,
and went on. Afterwards he thought of it.
Going through the office, the fat old book-
keeper, Huff, stopped him with a story he had
been keeping for him all day. He liked to tell
a story to Holmes; he could see into a joke; it
did a man good to hear a fellow laugh like that.
Holmes did laugh, for the story was a good one,
and stood a moment, then went in, leaving the
old fellow chuckling over his desk. Huff did
not know how, lately, after every laugh, this
man felt a vague scorn of himself, as if jokes

and laughter belonged to a self that ought to
have been dead long ago. Perhaps, if the fat
old book-keeper had known it, he would have
said that the man was better than he knew.
But then, — poor Huff! He passed slowly
through the alleys between the great looms.
Overhead the ceiling looked like a heavy maze
of iron cylinders and black swinging bars and
wheels, all in swift, ponderous motion. It was
enough to make a brain dizzy with the clanging
thunder of the engines, the whizzing spindles of
red and yellow, and the hot daylight glaring
over all. The looms were watched by women,
most of them bold, tawdry girls of fifteen or
sixteen, or lean-jawed women from the hills,
wives of the coal-diggers. There was a breathless odour of copperas. As he went from one
room to another up through the ascending stories, he had a vague sensation of being followed.
Some shadow lurked at times behind the engines, or stole after him in the dark entries.
Were there ghosts, then, in mills in broad daylight? None but the ghosts of Want and Hunger and Crime, he might have known, that do
not wait for night to walk our streets: the
ghosts that poor old Knowles hoped to lay
forever.

Holmes had a room fitted up in the mill,
where he slept. He went up to it slowly, hold-

ing the paper tightly in one hand, glancing at the operatives, the work, through his furtive half-shut eye. Nothing escaped him. Passing the windows, he did not once look out at the prophetic dream of beauty he had left without. In the mill he was of the mill. Yet he went slowly, as if he shrank from the task waiting for him. Why should he? It was a simple matter of business, this transfer of Knowles's share in the mill to himself; to-day he was to decide whether he would conclude the bargain. If any dark history of wrong lay underneath, if this simple decision of his was to be the struggle for life and death with him, his cold, firm face told nothing of it. Let us be just to him, stand by him, if we can, in the midst of his desolate home and desolate life, and look through his cold, sorrowful eyes at the deed he was going to do. Dreary enough he looked, going through the great mill, despite the power in his quiet face. A man who had strength for solitude; yet, I think, with all his strength, his mother could not have borne to look back from the dead that day, to see her boy so utterly alone. The day was the crisis of his life, looked forward to for years; he held in his hand a sure passport to fortune. Yet he thrust the hour off, perversely, trifling with idle fancies, pushing from him the one question which all the years past and to come had left for this day to decide.

Some such idle fancy it may have been that
made the man turn from the usual way down
a narrow passage into which opened doors from
small offices. Margret Howth, he had learned
to-day, was in the first one. He hesitated before he did it, his sallow face turning a trifle
paler; then he went on in his hard, grave way,
wondering dimly if she remembered his step,
if she cared to see him now. She used to
know it, — she was the only one in the world
who ever had cared to know it, — silly child!
Doubtless she was wiser now. He remembered he used to think, that, when this woman
loved, it would be as he himself would, with a
simple trust which the wrong of years could
not touch.   And once he had thought ——
Well, well, he was mistaken. Poor Margret!
Better as it was. They were nothing to each
other. She had put him from her, and he had
suffered himself to be put away. Why, he
would have given up every prospect of life, if
he had done otherwise! Yet he wondered
bitterly if she had thought him selfish, — if she
thought it was money he cared for, as the
others did. It mattered nothing what they
thought, but it wounded him intolerably that
she should wrong him.   Yet, with all this,
whenever he looked forward to death, it was
with the certainty that he should find her there
beyond. There would be no secrets then; she

would know then how he had loved her always. Loved her? Yes; he need not hide it from himself, surely.

He was now by the door of the office; — she was within. Little Margret, poor little Margret! struggling there day after day for the old father and mother. What a pale, cold little child she used to be! such a child! yet kindling at his look or touch, as if her veins were filled with subtile flame. Her soul was — like his own, he thought. He knew what it was, — he only. Even now he glowed with a man's triumph to know he held the secret life of this woman bare in his hand. No other human power could ever come near her; he was secure in possession. She had put him from her; — it was better for both, perhaps. Their paths were separate here; for she had some unreal notions of duty, and he had too much to do in the world to clog himself with cares, or to idle an hour in the rare ecstasy of even love like this.

He passed the office, not pausing in his slow step. Some sudden impulse made him put his hand on the door as he brushed against it: just a quick, light touch; but it had all the fierce passion of a caress. He drew it back as quickly, and went on, wiping a clammy sweat from his face.

6

The room he had fitted up for himself was whitewashed and barely furnished; it made one's bones ache to look at the iron bedstead and chairs. Holmes's natural taste was more glowing, however smothered, than that of any saffron-robed Sybarite. It needed correction, he knew; here was discipline. Besides, he had set apart the coming three or four years of his life to make money in, enough for the time to come. He would devote his whole strength to that work, and so be sooner done with it. Money, or place, or even power, was nothing but a means to him: other men valued them because of their influence on others. As his work in the world was only the development of himself, it was different, of course. What would it matter to his soul the day after death, if millions called his name aloud in blame or praise? Would he hear or answer then? What would it matter to him then, if he had starved with them, or ruled over them? People talked of benevolence. What would it matter to him then, the misery or happiness of those yet working in this paltry life of ours? In so far as the exercise of kindly emotions or self-denial developed the higher part of his nature, it was to be commended; as for its effect on others, that he had nothing to do with. He practised self-denial constantly to strengthen the benevolent instincts. That very morning he had given his last dollar to Joe Byers, a half-starved cripple. "Chucked it at me," Joe said, "like as he 'd give a bone to a dog, and be damned to him! Who thanks him?" To tell the truth, you will find no fairer exponent than this Stephen Holmes of the great idea of American sociology, — that the object of life is *to grow*. Circumstances had forced it on him, partly. Sitting now in his room, where he was counting the cost of becoming a merchant prince, he could look back to the time of a boyhood passed in the depths of ignorance and vice. He knew what this Self within him was; he knew how it had forced him to grope his way up, to give this hungry, insatiate soul air and freedom and knowledge. All men around him were doing the same, — thrusting and jostling and struggling, up, up. It was the American motto, Go ahead; mothers taught it to their children; the whole system was a scale of glittering prizes. He at least saw the higher meaning of the truth; he had no low ambitions. To lift this self up into a higher range of being when it had done with the uses of this, — that was his work. Self-salvation, self-elevation, — the ideas that give birth to, and destroy half of our Christianity, half of our philanthropy! Sometimes, sleeping instincts in the man strug-

gled up to assert a divinity more terrible than
this growing self-existent soul that he purified
and analyzed day by day : a depth of tender
pity for outer pain ; a fierce longing for rest,
on something, in something, he cared not what.
He stifled such rebellious promptings, — called
them morbid. He called it morbid, too, the
passion now that chilled his strong blood, and
wrung out these clammy drops on his forehead,
at the mere thought of this girl below.

He shut the door of his room tightly: he
had no time to-day for lounging visitors. For
Holmes, quiet and steady, was sought for, if
not popular, even in the free-and-easy West;
one of those men who are unwillingly masters
among men. Just and mild, always ; with a
peculiar gift that made men talk their best
thoughts to him, knowing they would be understood ; if any core of eternal flint lay under
the simple, truthful manner of the man, nobody
saw it.

He laid the bill of sale on the table; it was
an altogether practical matter on which he sat
in judgment, but he was going to do nothing
rashly. A plain business document: he took
Dr. Knowles's share in the factory; the pay-
ments made with short intervals ; John Herne
was to be his endorser: it needed only the
names to make it valid. Plain enough ; no

hint there of the tacit understanding that the
purchase-money was a wedding dowry; even
between Herne and himself it never was
openly put into words. If he did not marry
Miss Herne, the mill was her father's; that of
course must be spoken of, arranged to-morrow.
If he took it, then? if he married her? Holmes
had been poor, was miserably poor yet, with
the position and habits of a man of refinement.
God knows it was not to gratify those tastes
that he clutched at this money. All the slow
years of work trailed up before him, that were
gone, — of hard, wearing work for daily bread,
when his brain had been starving for knowledge, and his soul dulled, debased with sordid
trading. Was this to be always? Were these
few golden moments of life to be traded for the
bread and meat he ate? To eat and drink, —
was that what he was here for?

As he paced the floor mechanically, some
vague recollection crossed his brain of a childish story of the man standing where the two
great roads of life parted. They were open
before him now. Money, money, — he took
the word into his heart as a miser might do.
With it, he was free from these carking cares
that were making his mind foul and muddy.
If he had money! Slow, cool visions of triumphs rose before him outlined on the years

to come, practical, if Utopian. Slow and sure
successes of science and art, where his brain
could work, helpful and growing. Far off, yet
surely to come, — surely for him, — a day
when a pure social system should be universal, should have thrust out its fibres of light,
knitting into one the nations of the earth, when
the lowest slave should find its true place and
rightful work, and stand up, knowing itself
divine. " To insure to every man the freest
development of his faculties : " he said over
the hackneyed dogma again and again, while
the heavy, hateful years of poverty rose before
him that had trampled him down. " To insure to him the freest development," he did
not need to wait for St. Simon, or the golden
year, he thought with a dreary gibe ; money
was enough, and — Miss Herne.

It was curious, that, when this woman, whom
he saw every day, came up in his mind, it was
always in one posture, one costume. You have
noticed that peculiarity in your remembrance of
some persons ? Perhaps you would find, if you
looked closely, that in that look or indelible ges-
ture which your memory has caught there lies
some subtile hint of the tie between your soul
and theirs. Now, when Holmes had resolved
coolly to weigh this woman, brain, heart, and
flesh; to know how much of a hindrance she

would be, he could only see her, with his artist's
sense, as delicate a bloom of colouring as eye
could crave, in one immovable posture, — as he
had seen her once in some masquerade or *tableau
vivant*. June, I think it was, she chose to represent that evening, — and with her usual success; for no woman ever knew more thoroughly
her material of shape or colour, or how to work
it up. Not an ill-chosen fancy, either, that of
the moist, warm month. Some tranced summer's day might have drowsed down into such
a human form by a dank pool, or on the thick
grass-crusted meadows. There was the full con-
tour of the limbs hid under warm green folds,
the white flesh that glowed when you touched
it as if some smothered heat lay beneath, the
snaring eyes, the sleeping face, the amber hair
uncoiled in a languid quiet, while yellow jas-
mines deepened its hue into molten sunshine,
and a great tiger-lily laid its sultry head on her
breast. June? Could June become incarnate
with higher poetic meaning than that which this
woman gave it? Mr. Kitts, the artist I told
you of, thought not, and fell in love with June
and her on the spot, which passion became quite
unbearable after she had graciously permitted
him to sketch her, — for the benefit of Art.
Three medical students and one attorney, Miss
Herne numbered as having been driven into a

state of dogged despair on that triumphal occasion. Mr. Holmes may have quarrelled with
the rendering, doubting to himself if her lip were
not too thick, her eye too brassy and pale a blue
for the queen of months; though I do not believe he thought at all about it. Yet the picture
clung to his memory.

As he slowly paced the room to-day, thinking
of this woman as his wife, light blue eyes and
yellow hair and the unclean sweetness of jas-
mine-flowers mixed with the hot sunshine and
smells of the mill. He could think of her in no
other light. He might have done so; for the
poor girl had her other sides for view. She had
one of those sharp, tawdry intellects whose pos-
sessors are always reckoned " brilliant women,
fine talkers." She was (aside from the necessary sarcasm to keep up this reputation) a good-
humoured soul enough, — when no one stood in
her way. But if her shallow virtues or vices
were palpable at all to him, they became one
with the torpid beauty of the oppressive summer day, and weighed on him alike with a
vague disgust. The woman luxuriated in perfume; some heavy odour always hung about
her. Holmes, thinking of her now, fancied he
felt it stifling the air, and opened the window
for breath. Patchouli or copperas, — what was
the difference ? The mill and his future wife

came to him together; it was scarcely his fault,
if he thought of them as one, or muttered,
" Damnable clog!" as he sat down to write,
his cold eye growing colder. But he did not
argue the question any longer; decision had
come keenly in one moment, fixed, unalterable.

If, through the long day, the starved heart of
the man called feebly for its natural food, he
called it a paltry weakness; or if the old thought
of the quiet, pure little girl in the office below
came back to him, he — he wished her well, he
hoped she might succeed in her work, he would
always be ready to lend her a helping hand. So
many years (he was ashamed to think how many)
he had built the thought of this girl as his wife
into the future, put his soul's strength into the
hope, as if love and the homely duties of husband and father were what life was given for!
A boyish fancy, he thought. He had not learned
then that all dreams must yield to self-reverence
and self-growth. As for taking up this life of
poverty and soul-starvation for the sake of a
little love, it would be an ignoble martyrdom,
the sacrifice of a grand unmeasured life to a
shallow pleasure. He was no longer a young
man now; he had no time to waste. Poor
Margret! he wondered if it hurt her?

He signed the deed, and left it in the slow,
quiet way natural to him, and after a while

6 *

stooped to pat the dog softly, who was trying
to lick his hand, — with the hard fingers shaking
a little, and a smothered fierceness in the half-
closed eye, like a man who is tortured and alone.

There is a miserable drama acted in other
homes than the Tuileries, when men have found
a woman's heart in their way to success, and
trampled it down under an iron heel. Men like
Napoleon must live out the law of their natures, I suppose, — on a throne, or in a mill.

So many trifles that day roused the under-
current of old thoughts and old hopes that
taunted him, — trifles, too, that he would not
have heeded at another time. Pike came in on
business, a bunch of bills in his hand. A wily,
keen eye he had, looking over them, — a lean
face, emphasized only by cunning. No wonder
Dr. Knowles cursed him for a "slippery cus-
tomer," and was cheated by him the next hour.
While he and Holmes were counting out the
bills, a little white-headed girl crept shyly in at
the door, and came up to the table, — oddly
dressed, in a frock fastened with great horn
buttons, and with an old-fashioned anxious pair
of eyes, the color of blue Delft. Holmes
smoothed her hair, as she stood beside them;
for he never could help caressing children or
dogs. Pike looked up sharply, — then half
smiled, as he went on counting.

" Ninety, ninety-five, *and* one hundred, all right," — tying a bit of tape about the papers. " My Sophy, Mr. Holmes. Good girl, Sophy is. Bring her up to the mill sometimes," he said, apologetically, " on 'count of not leaving her alone. She gets lonesome at th' house."

Holmes glanced at Pike's felt hat lying on the table : there was a rusty strip of crape on it.

" Yes," said Pike, in a lower tone, " I 'm father and mother, both, to Sophy now."

" I had not heard," said Holmes, kindly. " How about the boys, now ? "

" Pete and John 's both gone West," the man said, his eyes kindling eagerly. " 'S fine boys as ever turned out of Indiana. Good eddica- tions I give 'em both. I 've felt the want of that all my life. Good eddications. Says I, ' Now, boys, you 've got your fortunes, nothing to hinder your bein' President. Let 's see what stuff 's in ye,' says I. So they 're doin' well. Wrote fur me to come out in the fall. But I 'd rather scratch on, and gather up a little for Sophy here, before I stop work."

He patted Sophy's tanned little hand on the table, as if beating some soft tune. Holmes folded up the bills. Even this man.could spare time out of his hard, stingy life to love, and be loved, and to be generous ! But then he had no higher aim, knew nothing better.

"Well," said Pike, rising, "in case you take th' mill, Mr. Holmes, I hope we'll be agreeable. I'll strive to do my best," — in the old fawning manner, to which Holmes nodded a curt reply.

The man stopped for Sophy to gather up her bits of broken "chayney" with which she was making a tea-party on the table, and went down-stairs.

Towards evening Holmes went out, — not going through the narrow passage that led to the offices, but avoiding it by a circuitous route. If it cost him any pain to think why he did it, he showed none in his calm, observant face. Buttoning up his coat as he went: the October sunset looked as if it ought to be warm, but he was deathly cold. On the street the young doctor beset him again with bows and news: Cox was his name, I believe; the one, you remember, who had such a Talleyrand nose for ferreting out successful men. He had to bear with him but for a few moments, however. They met a crowd of workmen at the corner, one of whom, an old man freshly washed, with honest eyes looking out of horn spectacles, waited for them by a fire-plug. It was Polston, the coal-digger, — an acquaintance, a far-off kinsman of Holmes, in fact.

"Curious person making signs to you, yonder," said Cox; "hand, I presume."

" My cousin Polston.   If you do not know
him, you 'll excuse me ? "

Cox sniffed the air down the street, and
twirled his rattan, as he went.   The coal-digger was abrupt and distant in his greeting,
going straight to business.

" I will keep yoh only a minute, Mr.
Holmes " ——

" Stephen," corrected Holmes.

The old man's face warmed.

" Stephen, then," holding out his hand, " sence
old times dawn't shame yoh, Stephen.   That 's
hearty, now.   It 's only a wured I want, but
it 's immediate.   Concernin' Joe Yare, — Lois's
father, yoh know ?   He 's back."

" Back ?   I saw him to-day, following me in
the mill.   His hair is gray ?   I think it was he."

" No doubt.   Yes, he 's aged fast, down in the
lock-up ; goin' fast to the end.   Feeble, pore-
like.   It 's a bad life, Joe Yare's ; I wish 'n' 't
would be better to the end " ——

He stopped with a wistful look at Holmes,
who stood outwardly attentive, but with little
thought to waste on Joe Yare.   The old coal-
digger drummed on the fire-plug uneasily.

" Myself, 't was for Lois's sake I thowt on
it.   To speak plain, — yoh 'll mind that Stokes
affair, th' note Yare forged ?   Yes ?   Ther' 's
none knows o' that but yoh an' me.   He 's safe,

Yare is, only fur yoh an' me. Yoh speak the wured an' back he goes to the lock-up. Fur life. D' yoh see ? "

" I see."

" He 's tryin' to do right, Yare is."

The old man went on, trying not to be eager, and watching Holmes's face.

" He 's tryin'. Sendin' him back — yoh know how *that* 'll end. Seems like as we 'd his soul in our hands. S'pose, — what d' yoh think, if we give him a chance ? It 's yoh he fears. I see him a-watchin' yoh ; what d' yoh think, if we give him a chance ? " catching Holmes's sleeve. " He 's old, an' he 's tryin'. Heh ? "

Holmes smiled.

" We did n't make the law he broke. Justice before mercy. Have n't I heard you talk to Sam in that way, long ago ? "

The old man loosened his hold of Holmes's arm, looked up and down the street, uncertain, disappointed.

" The law. Yes. That 's right ! Yoh 're a just man, Stephen Holmes."

" And yet ? " ——

" Yes. I dun'no'. Law 's right, but Yare 's had a bad chance, an' he 's tryin'. An' we 're sendin' him to hell. Somethin' 's wrong. But I think yoh 're a just man," looking keenly in Holmes's face.

" A hard one, people say," said Holmes, after a pause, as they walked on.

He had spoken half to himself, and received no answer. Some blacker shadow troubled him than old Yare's fate.

" My mother was a hard woman, — you knew her ? " he said, abruptly.

" She was just, like yoh. She was one o' th' elect, she said. Mercy 's fur them, — an' outside, justice. It 's a narrer showin', I 'm thinkin'."

" My father was outside," said Holmes, some old bitterness rising up in his tone, his gray eye lighting with some unrevenged wrong.

Polston did not speak for a moment.

" Dunnot bear malice agin her. They 're dead, now. It was n't left fur her to judge him out yonder. Yoh 've yer father's eyes, Stephen, 'times. Hungry, pitiful, like women's. His got desper't' 't th' last. Drunk hard, — died of 't, yoh know. But *she* killed him, — th' sin was writ down fur her. Never was a boy I loved like him, when we was boys."

There was a short silence.

" Yoh 're like yer mother," said Polston, striving for a lighter tone. " Here," — motioning to the heavy iron jaws. " She never — let go. Somehow, too, she 'd the law on her side in outward showin', an' th' right. But I hated

religion, knowin' her.   Well, ther' 's a day of
makin' things clear, comin'."

They had reached the corner now, and Polston turned down the lane.

"Yoh 'll think o' Yare's case?" he said.

"Yes.   But how can I help it," Holmes said,
lightly, "if I am like my mother, here?" —
putting his hand to his mouth.

God help us, how can yoh?   It 's harrd to
think father and mother leave their souls fight-
in' in their childern, cos th' love was wantin' to
make them one here."

Something glittered along the street as he
spoke : the silver mountings of a low-hung
phaëton drawn by a pair of Mexican ponies.
One or two gentlemen on horseback were
alongside, attendant on a lady within, Miss
Herne.   She turned her fair face, and pale,
greedy eyes, as she passed, and lifted her hand
languidly in recognition of Holmes.   Polston's
face coloured.

"I 've heered," he said, holding out his grimy
hand.   "I wish yoh well, Stephen, boy.   So 'll
the old 'oman.   Yoh 'll come an' see us, soon?
Ye 'r' lookin' fagged, an' yer eyes is gettin' more
like yer father's.   I 'm glad things is takin' a
good turn with yoh ; an' yoh 'll never be like
him, starvin' fur th' kind wured, an' havin' to
die without it.   I 'm glad yoh 've got true love.

She 'd a fair face, I think. I wish yoh well, Stephen."

Holmes shook the grimy hand, and then stood a moment looking back to the mill, from which the hands were just coming, and then down at the phaëton moving idly down the road. How cold it was growing! People passing by had a sickly look, as if they were struck by the plague. He pushed the damp hair back, wiping his forehead, with another glance at the mill-women coming out of the gate, and then followed the phaëton down the hill.

CHAPTER VI.

AN hour after, the evening came on sultry, the air murky, opaque, with yellow trails of colour dragging in the west : a sullen stillness in the woods and farms ; only, in fact, that dark, inexplicable hush that precedes a storm. But Lois, coming down the hill-road, singing to herself, and keeping time with her whip-end on the wooden measure, stopped when she grew conscious of it. It seemed to her blurred fancy more than a deadening sky : a something solemn and unknown, hinting of evil to come. The dwarf-pines on the road-side scowled weakly at her through the gray ; the very silver minnows in the pools she passed, flashed frightened away, and darkened into the muddy niches. There was a vague dread in the sudden silence. She called to the old donkey, and went faster down the hill, as if escaping from some overhanging peril, unseen. She saw Margret coming up the road. There was a phaëton behind Lois, and some horsemen : she jolted the cart off into the stones to let them pass, seeing Mr. Holmes's face in the carriage as she did so. He did not look at her ; had his head turned towards the

gray distance. Lois's vivid eye caught the full
meaning of the woman beside him. The face
hurt her : not fair, as Polston called it : vapid
and cruel. She was dressed in yellow : the
colour seemed jeering and mocking to the girl's
sensitive instinct, keenly alive to every trifle.
She did not know that it is the colour of shams,
and that women like this are the most deadly
of shams. As the phaëton went slowly down,
Margret came nearer, meeting it on the road-
side, the dust from the wheels stifling the air.
Lois saw her look up, and then suddenly stand
still, holding to the fence, as they met her.
Holmes's cold, wandering eye turned on the
little dusty figure standing there, poor and
despised. Polston called his eyes hungry : it
was a savage hunger that sprang into them
now ; a gray shadow creeping over his set face,
as he looked at her, in that flashing moment.
The phaëton was gone in an instant, leaving
her alone in the road. One of the men looked
back, and then whispered something to the lady
with a laugh. She turned to Holmes, when he
had finished, fixing her light, confusing eyes on
his face, and softening her voice.

" Fred swears that woman we passed was
your first love. Were you, then, so chivalric ?
Was it to have been a second romaunt of ' King
Cophetua and the Beggar Maid ? ' "

He met her look, and saw the fierce demand
through the softness and persiflage. He gave
it no answer, but, turning to her, kindled into
the man whom she was so proud to show as her
capture, — a man far off from Stephen Holmes.
Brilliant she called him, — frank, winning, generous. She thought she knew him well; held
him a slave to her fluttering hand. Being proud
of her slave, she let the hand flutter down now
somehow with some flowers it held until it
touched his hard fingers, her cheek flushing
into rose. The nerveless, spongy hand, — what
a death-grip it had on his life! He did not
look back once at the motionless, dusty figure
on the road. What was that Polston had said
about starving to death for a kind word? *Love?*
He was sick of the sickly talk, — crushed it out
of his heart with a savage scorn. He remembered his father, the night he died, had said in
his weak ravings that God was love. Was He?
No wonder, then, He was the God of women,
and children, and unsuccessful men. For him,
he was done with it. He was here with stronger
purpose than to yield to weaknesses of the flesh.
He had made his choice, — a straight, hard path
upwards; he was deaf now and forever to any
word of kindness or pity. As for this woman
beside him, he would be just to her, in justice
to himself: she never should know the loathing

in his heart: just to her as to all living creatures.
Some little, mean doubt kept up a sullen whisper of bought and sold, — sold, — but he laughed
it down. He sat there with his head steadily
turned towards her : a kingly face, she called it,
and she was right, — it was a kingly face : with
the same shallow, fixed smile on his mouth, —
no weary cry went up to God that day so terrible in its pathos, I think : with the same dull
consciousness that this was the trial night of his
life, — that with the homely figure on the road-
side he had turned his back on love and kindly
happiness and warmth, on all that was weak
and useless in the world. He had made his
choice ; he would abide by it, — he would abide
by it. He said that over and over again, dulling
down the death-gnawing of his outraged heart.

Miss Herne was quite contented, sitting by
him, with herself, and the admiring world. She
had no notion of trial nights in life. Not many
temptations pierced through her callous, flabby
temperament to sting her to defeat or triumph.
There was for her no under-current of conflict,
in these people whom she passed, between self
and the unseen power that Holmes sneered at,
whose name was love ; they were nothing but
movables, pleasant or ugly to look at, well- or
ill-dressed. There were no dark iron bars across
her life for her soul to clutch and shake madly,

— nothing " in the world amiss, to be unriddled
by and by." Little Margret, sitting by the
muddy road, digging her fingers dully into the
clover-roots, while she looked at the spot where
the wheels had passed, looked at life differently,
it may be ; — or old Joe Yare by the furnace-
fire, his black face and gray hair bent over a
torn old spelling-book Lois had given him. The
night, perhaps, was going to be more to them
than so many rainy hours for sleeping, — the
time to be looked back on through coming lives
as the hour when good and ill came to them,
and they made their choice, and, as Holmes
said, did abide by it.

It grew cool and darker. Holmes left the
phaëton before they entered town, and turned
back. He was going to see this Margret Howth,
tell her what he meant to do. Because he was
going to leave a clean record. No one should
accuse him of want of honour. This girl alone
of all living beings had a right to see him as he
stood, justified to himself. Why she had this
right, I do not think he answered to himself.
Besides, he must see her, if only on business.
She must keep her place at the mill : he would
not begin his new life by an act of injustice,
taking the bread out of Margret's mouth. *Little
Margret!* He stopped suddenly, looking down
into a deep pool of water by the road-side.

What madness of weariness crossed his brain just then I do not know. He shook it off. Was he mad. Life was worth more to him than to other men, he thought; and perhaps he was right. He went slowly through the cool dusk, looking across the fields, up at the pale, frightened face of the moon hooded in clouds: he did not dare to look, with all his iron nerve, at the dark figure beyond him on the road. She was sitting there just where he had left her : he knew she would be. When he came closer, she got up, not looking towards him; but he saw her clasp her hands behind her, the fingers plucking weakly at each other. It was an old, childish fashion of hers, when she was frightened or hurt. It would only need a word, and he could be quiet and firm, — she was such a child compared to him : he always had thought of her so. He went on up to her slowly, and stopped; when she looked at him, he untied the linen bonnet that hid her face, and threw it back. How thin and tired the little face had grown! Poor child! He put his strong arm kindly about her, and stooped to kiss her hand, but she drew it away. God! what did she do that for ? Did not she know that he could put his head beneath her foot then, he was so mad with pity for the woman he had wronged ? Not love, he thought, controlling himself, — it was only justice to be kind to her.

"You have been ill, Margret, these two years,
while I was gone?"

He could not hear her answer; only saw that
she looked up with a white, pitiful smile. Only
a word it needed, he thought, — very kind and
firm: and he must be quick, — he could not
bear this long. But he held the little worn
fingers, stroking them with an unutterable tenderness.

"You must let these fingers work for me,
Margret," he said, at last, "when I am master
in the mill."

"It is true, then, Stephen?"

"It is true, — yes."

She lifted her hand to her head, uncertainly:
he held it tightly, and then let it go. What
right had he to touch the dust upon her shoes,
— he, bought and sold? She did not speak for
a time; when she did, it was a weak and sick
voice.

"I am glad. I saw her, you know. She is
very beautiful."

The fingers were plucking at each other
again; and a strange, vacant smile on her
face, trying to look glad.

"You love her, Stephen?"

He was quiet and firm enough now.

"I do not. Her money will help me to become what I ought to be. She does not care

for love. You want me to succeed, Margret?
No one ever understood me as you did, child
though you were."

Her whole face glowed.

" I know! I know! I did understand you!"

She said, lower, after a little while, —

" I knew you did not love her."

" There is no such thing as love in real life,"
he said, in his steeled voice. " You will know
that, when you grow older. I used to believe
in it once, myself."

She did not speak, only watched the slow
motion of his lips, not looking into his eyes,
— as she used to do in the old time. Whatever secret account lay between the souls of this
man and woman came out now, and stood bare
on their faces.

" I used to think that I, too, loved," he went
on, in his low, hard tone. " But it kept me back,
Margret, and " ——

He was silent.

" I know, Stephen. It kept you back " ——

" And I put it away. I put it away to-night,
forever."

She did not speak; stood quite quiet, her
head bent on her breast. His conscience was
clear now. But he almost wished he had not
said it, she was such a weak, sickly thing. She
sat down at last, burying her face in her hands,

7

with a shivering sob.   He dared not trust himself to speak again.

" I am not proud, — as a woman ought to be,"
she said, wearily, when he wiped her clammy
forehead.

" You loved me, then ? " he whispered.

Her face flashed at the unmanly triumph; her
puny frame started up, away from him.

" I did love you, Stephen.   I did love you, —
as you might be, not as you are, — not with
those inhuman eyes.   I do understand you, —
I do.   I know you for a better man than you
know yourself this night."

She turned to go.   He put his hand on her
arm ; something we have never seen on his face
struggled up, — the better soul that she knew.

" Come back," he said, hoarsely ; " don't leave
me with myself.   Come back, Margret."

She did not come ; stood leaning, her sudden
strength gone, against the broken wall.   There
was a heavy silence.   The night throbbed slow
about them.   Some late bird rose from the
sedges of the pool, and with a frightened cry
flapped its tired wings, and drifted into the
dark.   His eyes, through the gathering shadow,
devoured the weak, trembling body, met the
soul that looked at him, strong as his own.
Was it because it knew and trusted him that
all that was pure and strongest in his crushed

nature struggled madly to be free? He thrust it down; the self-learned lesson of years was not to be conquered in a moment.

"There have been times," he said, in a smothered, restless voice, "when I thought you belonged to me. Not here, but before this life. My soul and body thirst and hunger for you, then, Margret."

She did not answer; her hands worked feebly together, the dull blood fainting in her veins.

Knowing only that the night yawned intolerable about her, that she was alone, — going mad with being alone. No thought of heaven or God in her soul: her craving eyes seeing him only. The strong, living man that she loved: her tired-out heart goading, aching to lie down on his brawny breast for one minute, and die there, — that was all.

She did not move: underneath the pain there was power, as Knowles thought.

He came nearer, and held up his arms to where she stood, — the heavy, masterful face pale and wet.

"I need you, Margret. I shall be nothing without you, now. Come, Margret, little Margret!"

She came to him, then, and put her hands in his.

"No, Stephen," she said.

If there were any pain in her tone, she kept it down, for his sake.

"Never, I could never help you, — as you are. It might have been, once. Good-by, Stephen."

Her childish way put him in mind of the old days when this girl was dearer to him than his own soul. She was so yet. He held her close to his breast, looking down into her eyes. She moved uneasily; she dared not trust herself.

"You will come?" he said. "It might have been, — it shall be again."

"It may be," she said, humbly. "God is good. And I believe in you, Stephen. I will be yours some time: we cannot help it, if we would: but not as you are."

"You do not love me?" he said, flinging her off, his face whitening.

She said nothing, gathered her damp shawl around her, and turned to go. Just a moment they stood, looking at each other. If the dark square figure standing there had been an iron fate trampling her young life down into hopeless wretchedness, she forgot it now. Women like Margret are apt to forget. His eye never abated in its fierce question.

"I will wait for you yonder, if I die first," she whispered.

He came closer, waiting for an answer.

"And — I love you, Stephen."

He gathered her in his arms, and put his cold lips to hers, without a word; then turned, and left her slowly.

She made no sign, shed no tear, as she stood, watching him go. It was all over: she had willed it, herself, and yet — he could not go! God would not suffer it! Oh, he could not leave her, — he could not! — He went down the hill, slowly. If it were a trial of life and death for her, did he know or care? — He did not look back. What if he did not? his heart was true; he suffered in going; even now he walked wearily. God forgive her, if she had wronged him! — What did it matter, if he were hard in this life, and it hurt her a little? It would come right, — beyond, some time. But life was long. — She would not sit down, sick as she was: he might turn, and it would vex him to see her suffer. — He walked slowly; once he stopped to pick up something. She saw the deep-cut face and half-shut eyes. How often those eyes had looked into her soul, and it had answered! They never would look so any more. — There was a tree by the place where the road turned into town. If he came back, he would be sure to turn there. — How tired he walked, and slow! — If he was sick, that beautiful woman could be near him, — help him. — *She* never would touch his hand again, — never

again, never, — unless he came back now. —
He was near the tree : she closed her eyes, turning away. When she looked again, only the
bare road lay there, yellow and wet. It was
over, now.

How long she sat there she did not know.
She tried once or twice to go to the house, but
the lights seemed so far off that she gave it up
and sat quiet, unconscious, except of the damp
stone-wall her head leaned on, and the stretch
of muddy road.   Some time, she knew not
when, there was a heavy step beside her, and
a rough hand shook hers where she stooped,
feebly tracing out the lines of mortar between
the stones. It was Knowles. She looked up,
bewildered.

" Hunting catarrhs, eh ? " he growled, eying
her keenly. " Got your father on the Bourbons,
so took the chance to come and find you. He 'll
not miss *me* for an hour. That man has a natural hankering after treason against the people.
Lord, Margret! what a stiff old head he 'd have
carried to the guillotine! How he 'd have looked
at the *canaille !* "

He helped her up gently enough.

" Your bonnet 's like a wet rag," — with a
furtive glance at the worn-out face. A hungry
face always, with her life unfed by its stingy
few crumbs of good ; but to-night it was vacant
with utter loss.

She got up, trying to laugh cheerfully, and went beside him down the road.

" You saw that painted Jezebel to-night, and " —— stopping abruptly.

She had not heard him, and he followed her doggedly, with an occasional snort or grunt or other inarticulate damn at the obstinate mud. She stopped at last, with a quick gasp. Looking at her, he chafed her limp hands, — his huge, uncouth face growing pale. When she was better, he said, gravely, —

" I want you, Margret. Not at home, child. I want to show you something."

He turned with her suddenly off the main road into a by-path, helping her along, watching her stealthily, but going on with his disjointed, bearish growls. If it stung her from her pain, vexing her, he did not care.

" I want to show you a bit of hell : outskirt. You 're in a fit state : it 'll do you good. I 'm minister there.   The clergy can't attend to it just now : they 're too busy measuring God's truth by the States'-Rights doctrine, or the Chicago Platform.   Consequence, religion yields to majorities.   Are you able ?   It 's only a step."

She went on indifferently.   The night was breathless and dark.   Black, wet gusts dragged now and then through the skyless fog, striking her face with a chill.   The Doctor quit talking, hurrying her, watching her anxiously. They came at last to the railway-track, with long trains of empty freight-cars.

"We are nearly there," he whispered. "It's time you knew your work, and forgot your weakness. The curse of pampered generations. 'High Norman blood,' — pah!"

There was a broken gap in the fence. He led her through it into a muddy yard. Inside was one of those taverns you will find in the suburbs of large cities, haunts of the lowest vice. This one was a smoky frame, standing on piles over an open space where hogs were rooting. Half a dozen drunken Irishmen were playing poker with a pack of greasy cards in an out-house. He led her up the rickety ladder to the one room, where a flaring tallow-dip threw a saffron glare into the darkness. A putrid odour met them at the door. She drew back, trembling.

"Come here!" he said, fiercely, clutching her hand. "Women as fair and pure as you have come into dens like this, — and never gone away. Does it make your delicate breath faint? And you a follower of the meek and lowly Jesus! Look here! and here!"

The room was swarming with human life. Women, idle trampers, whiskey-bloated, filthy, lay half-asleep, or smoking, on the floor, and set up a chorus of whining begging when they entered. Half-naked children crawled about in rags. On the damp, mildewed walls there was hung a picture of the Benicia Boy, and close by, Pio Nono, crook in hand, with the usual inscription, "Feed my sheep." The Doctor looked at it.

"'*Tu es Petrus, et super hanc*'——— Good God! what *is* truth?" he muttered, bitterly.

He dragged her closer to the women, through the darkness and foul smell.

"Look in their faces," he whispered. "There is not one of them that is not a living lie. Can they help it? Think of the centuries of serf-dom and superstition through which their blood has crawled. Come closer, — here."

In the corner slept a heap of half-clothed blacks. Going on the underground railroad to Canada. Stolid, sensual wretches, with here and there a broad, melancholy brow, and des-perate jaws. One little pickaninny rubbed its sleepy eyes, and laughed at them.

"So much flesh and blood out of the market, unweighed!"

Margret took up the child, kissing its brown face. Knowles looked at her.

"Would you touch her? I forgot you were born down South. Put it down, and come on."

They went out of the door. Margret stopped, looking back.

7 *

"Did I call it a bit of hell? It's only a glimpse of the under-life of America, — God help us! — where all men are born free and equal."

The air in the passage grew fouler. She leaned back faint and shuddering. He did not heed her. The passion of the man, the terrible pity for these people, came out of his soul now, writhing his face, and dulling his eyes.

"And you," he said, savagely, "you sit by the road-side, with help in your hands, and Christ in your heart, and call your life lost, quarrel with your God, because that mass of selfishness has left you, — because you are balked in your puny hope! Look at these women. What is their loss, do you think? Go back, will you, and drone out your life whimpering over your lost dream, and go to Shakspeare for tragedy when you want it? Tragedy! Come here, — let me hear what you call this."

He led her through the passage, up a narrow flight of stairs. An old woman in a flaring cap sat at the top, nodding, — wakening now and then, to rock herself to and fro, and give the shrill Irish keen.

"You know that stoker who was killed in the mill a month ago? Of course not, — what

are such people to you? There was a girl who
loved him, — you know what *that* is? She's
dead now, here. She drank herself to death,
— a most unpicturesque suicide. I want you
to look at her. You need not blush for her
life of shame, now; she's dead. — Is Hetty
here?"

The woman got up.

"She is, Zur. She is, Mem. She's lookin'
foine in her Sunday suit. Shrouds is gone
out, Mem, they say."

She went tipping over the floor to something
white that lay on a board, a candle at the head,
and drew off the sheet. A girl of fifteen, almost a child, lay underneath, dead, — her lithe,
delicate figure decked out in a dirty plaid skirt,
and stained velvet bodice, — her neck and arms
bare. The small face was purely cut, haggard,
patient in its sleep, — the soft, fair hair gathered
off the tired forehead. Margret leaned over her,
shuddering, pinning her handkerchief about the
child's dead neck.

"How young she is!" muttered Knowles.
"Merciful God, how young she is! — What
is that you say?" sharply, seeing Margret's
lips move.

"'He that is without sin among you, let
him first cast a stone at her.'"

"Ah, child, that is old-time philosophy. Put

your hand here, on her dead face. Is your loss like hers?" he said lower, looking into the dull pain in her eyes. Selfish pain he called it.

"Let me go," she said. "I am tired."

He took her out into the cool, open road, leading her tenderly enough, — for the girl suffered, he saw.

"What will you do?" he asked her then. "It is not too late, — will you help me save these people?"

She wrung her hands helplessly.

"What do you want with me?" she cried. "I have enough to bear."

The burly black figure before her seemed to tower and strengthen; the man's face in the wan light showed a terrible life-purpose coming out bare.

"I want you to do your work. It is hard; it will wear out your strength and brain and heart. Give yourself to these people. God calls you to it. There is none to help them. Give up love, and the petty hopes of women. Help me. God calls you to the work."

She went on blindly: he followed her. For years he had set apart this girl to help him in his scheme: he would not be balked now. He had great hopes from his plan: he meant to give all he had: it was the noblest of aims. He thought some day it would work like leaven through the festering mass under the country he loved so well, and raise it to a new life. If it failed, — if it failed, and saved one life, his work was not lost. But it could not fail.

"Home!" he said, stopping her as she reached the stile, — "oh, Margret, what is home? There is a cry going up night and day from homes like that den yonder, for help, — and no man listens."

She was weak; her brain faltered.

"Does God call me to this work?· Does He call me?" she moaned.

He watched her eagerly.

"He calls you. He waits for your answer. Swear to me that you will help His people. Give up father and mother and love, and go down as Christ did. Help me to give liberty and truth and Jesus' love to these wretches on the brink of hell. Live with them, raise them with you."

She looked up, white; she was a weak, weak woman, sick for her natural food of love.

"Is it my work?"

"It is your work. Listen to me, Margret," softly. "Who cares for you? You stand alone to-night. There is not a single human heart that calls you nearest and best. Shiver, if you will, — it is true. The man you wasted

your soul on left you in the night and cold to
go to his bride, — is sitting by her now, holding her hand in his."

He waited a moment, looking down at her,
until she should understand.

"Do you think you deserved this of God?
I know that yonder on the muddy road you
looked up to Him, and knew it was not just;
that you had done right, and this was your reward. I know that for these two years you
have trusted in the Christ you worship to make
it right, to give you your heart's desire. Did
He do it? Did He hear your prayer? Does
He care for your weak love, when the nations
of the earth are going down? What is your
poor hope to Him, when the very land you live
in is a wine-press that will be trodden some
day by the fierceness and wrath of Almighty
God? O Christ! — if there be a Christ, —
help me to save it!"

He looked up, — his face white with pain.
After a time he said to her, —

"Help me, Margret! Your prayer was selfish; it was not heard. Give up your idle hope
that Christ will aid you. Swear to me, this
night when you have lost all, to give yourself
to this work."

The storm had been dark and windy: it
cleared now slowly, the warm summer rain

falling softly, the fresh blue stealing broadly
from behind the gray.   It seemed to Margret
like a blessing; for her brain rose up stronger,
more healthful.

"I will not swear," she said, weakly.   "I
think He heard my prayer. I think He will
answer it. He was a man, and loved as we
do. My love is not selfish; it is the best gift
God has given me."

Knowles went slowly with her to the house.
He was not baffled.   He knew that the struggle
was yet to come ; that, when she was alone, her
faith in the far-off Christ would falter ; that she
would grasp at this work, to fill her empty hands
and starved heart, if for no other reason, — to
stifle by a sense of duty her unutterable feeling of loss.   He was keenly read in woman's
heart, this Knowles.   He left her silently, and
she passed through the dark passage to her own
room.

Putting her damp shawl off, she sat down on
the floor, leaning her head on a low chair, — one
her father had given her for a Christmas gift
when she was little.   How fond Holmes and
her father used to be of each other!   Every
Christmas he spent with them.   She remembered them all now.   "He was sitting by her
now, holding her hand in his."   She said that
over to herself, though it was not hard to understand.

After a long time, her mother came with a candle to the door.

"Good-night, Margret. Why, your hair is wet, child!"

For Margret, kissing her good-night, had laid her head down a minute on her breast. She stroked the hair a moment, and then turned away.

"Mother, could you stay with me to-night?"

"Why, no, Maggie, — your father wants me to read to him."

"Oh, I know. Did he miss me to-night, — father?"

"Not much; we were talking old times over, — in Virginia, you know."

"I know; good-night."

She went back to the chair. Tige was there, — for he used to spend half of his time on the farm. She put her arm about his head. God knows how lonely the poor child was when she drew the dog so warmly to her heart: not for his master's sake alone; but it was all she had. He grew tired at last, and whined, trying to get out.

"Will you go, Tige?" she said, and opened the window.

He jumped out, and she watched him going towards town. Such a little thing, it was! But not even a dog "called her nearest and best."

Let us be silent; the story of the night is not for us to read. Do you think that He, who in the far, dim Life holds the worlds in His hand, knew or cared how alone the child was? What if she wrung her thin hands, grew sick with the slow, mad, solitary tears? — was not the world to save, as Knowles said?

He, too, had been alone; He had come unto His own, and His own received him not: so, while the struggling world rested, unconscious, in infinite calm of right, He came close to her with human eyes that had loved, and not been loved, and had suffered with that pain. And, trusting Him, she only said, "Show me my work! Thou that takest away the pain of the world, have mercy upon me!"

CHAPTER VII.

FOR that night, at least, Holmes swept his soul clean of doubt and indecision; one of his natures was conquered, — finally, he thought. Polston, if he had seen his face as he paced the street slowly home to the mill, would have remembered his mother's the day she died. How the stern old woman met death half-way! why should she fear? she was as strong as he. Wherein had she failed of duty? her hands were clean: she was going to meet her just reward.

It was different with Holmes, of course, with his self-existent soul. It was life he accepted to-night, he thought, — a life of growth, labour, achievement, — eternal.

" *Ohne Hast, aber ohne Rast,*" — favourite words with him. He liked to study the nature of the man who spoke them; because, I think, it was like his own, — a Titan strength of endurance, an infinite capability of love, and hate, and suffering, and over all, (the peculiar identity of the man,) a cold, speculative eye of reason, that looked down into the passion and depths of his growing self, and calmly noted them, a lesson for all time.

"*Ohne Hast.*" Going slowly through the
night, he strengthened himself by marking how
all things in Nature accomplish a perfected life
through slow, narrow fixedness of purpose, —
each life complete in itself : why not his own,
then ? The windless gray, the stars, the stone
under his feet, stood alone in the universe, each
working out its own soul into deed. If there
were any all-embracing harmony, one soul
through all, he did not see it. Knowles — that
old sceptic — believed in it, and called it Love.
Even Göthe himself, what was it he said?
" *Der Allumfasser, der Allerhalter, fasst und er-
hält er nicht, dich, mich, sich selbst ?* "

There was a curious power in the words, as
he lingered over them, like half-comprehended
music, — as simple and tender as if they had
come from the depths of a woman's heart : it
touched him deeper than his power of control.
Pah ! it was a dream of Faust's ; he, too, had
his Margaret ; he fell, through that love.

He went on slowly to the mill. If the name
or the words woke a subtile remorse or longing,
he buried them under restful composure. Whether they should ever rise like angry ghosts of what
might have been, to taunt the man, only the
future could tell.

Going through the gas-lit streets, Holmes met
some cordial greeting at every turn. What a

just, clever fellow he was! people said: one of
those men improved by success: just to the
defrauding of himself: saw the true worth of
everybody, the very lowest: had n't one spark
of self-esteem: despised all humbug and show,
one could see, though he never said it: when he
was a boy, he was moody, with passionate likes
and dislikes; but success had improved him,
vastly. So Holmes was popular, though the
beggars shunned him, and the lazy Italian organ-
grinders never held their tambourines up to him.

The mill street was dark; the building threw
its great shadow over the square. It was empty,
he supposed; only one hand generally remained
to keep in the furnace-fires. Going through one
of the lower passages, he heard voices, and
turned aside to examine. The management
was not strict, and in case of a fire the mill was
not insured: like Knowles's carelessness.

It was Lois and her father, — Joe Yare being
feeder that night. They were in one of the
great furnace-rooms in the cellar, — a very comfortable place that stormy night. Two or three
doors of the wide brick ovens were open, and
the fire threw a ruddy glow over the stone floor,
and shimmered into the dark recesses of the
shadows, very home-like after the rain and mud
without. Lois seemed to think so, at any rate,
for she had made a table of a store-box, put a

white cloth on it, and was busy getting up a
regular supper for her father, — down on her
knees before the red coals, turning something
on an iron plate, while some slices of ham sent
up a cloud of juicy, hungry smell.

The old stoker had just finished slaking the
out-fires, and was putting some blue plates on
the table, gravely straightening them. He had
grown old, as Polston said, — Holmes saw,
stooped much, with a low, hacking cough; his
coarse clothes were curiously clean: that was
to please Lois, of course. She put the ham on
the table, and some bubbling coffee, and then,
from a hickory board in front of the fire, took
off, with a jerk, brown, flaky slices of Virginia
johnny-cake.

" Ther' yoh are, father, hot 'n' hot," with her
face on fire, — " ther' — yoh — are, — coaxin' to
be eatin'. — Why, Mr. Holmes! Father! Now,
ef yoh jes' hed n't hed yer supper? "

She came up, coaxingly. What brooding
brown eyes the poor cripple had! Not many
years ago he would have sat down with the
two poor souls, and made a hearty meal of it:
he had no heart for such follies now.

Old Yare stood in the background, his hat
in his hand, stooping in his submissive negro
fashion, with a frightened watch on Holmes.

" Do you stay here, Lois? " he asked, kindly,
turning his back on the old man.

" On'y to bring his supper.   I could n't bide
all night 'n th' mill," — the old shadow coming
on her face, — " I could n't, yoh know.   *He*
does n't mind it."

She glanced quickly from one to the other in
silence, seeing the fear on her father's face.

" Yoh know father, Mr. Holmes ?   He 's
back now.   This is him."

The old man came forward, humbly.

" It 's me, Marster Stephen."

The sullen, stealthy face disgusted Holmes.
He nodded, shortly.

" Yoh 've been kind to my little girl while I
was gone," he said, catching his breath.   " I
thank yoh, Marster."

" You need not.   It was for Lois."

" 'T was fur her I comed back hyur.   'T was
a resk," — with a dumb look of entreaty at
Holmes, — " but fur her I thort I 'd try it.   I
know 't was a resk ; but I thort them as cared
fur Lo wud be merciful.   She 's a good girl,
Lo.   She 's all I hev."

Lois brought a box over, lugging it heavily.

" We hev n't chairs ; but yoh 'll sit down,
Mr. Holmes ? " laughing as she covered it with
a cloth.   " It 's a warm place, here.   Father
studies 'n his watch, 'n' I 'm teacher," — showing the torn old spelling-book.

The old man came eagerly forward, seeing
the smile flicker on Holmes's face.

" It 's slow work, Marster, — slow. But Lo
's a good teacher, 'n' I 'm tryin', — I 'm tryin'
hard."

" It 's not slow, Sir, seein' father hed n't
'dvantages, like me. He was a "——

She stopped, lowering her voice, a hot flush
of shame on her face.

" I know."

" Be n't that 'n 'xcuse, Marster, seein' I
knowed noght at the beginnin'? Thenk o'
that, Marster. I 'm tryin' to be a different
man. Fur Lo. I *am* tryin'."

Holmes did not notice him.

" Good-night, Lois," he said, kindly, as she
lighted his lamp.

He put some money on the table.

" You must take it," as she looked uneasy.
" For Tiger's board, say. I never see him now.
A bright new frock, remember."

She thanked him, her eyes brightening, looking at her father's patched coat.

The old man followed Holmes out.

" Marster Holmes "——

" Have done with this," said Holmes, sternly.
" Whoever breaks law abides by it. It is no
affair of mine."

The old man clutched his hands together
fiercely, struggling to be quiet.

" Ther' 's none knows it but yoh," he said,

in a smothered voice. "Fur God's sake be
merciful! It 'll kill my girl, — it 'll kill her.
Gev me a chance, Marster."

"You trouble me. I must do what is just."

"It 's not just," he said, savagely. "What
good 'll it do me to go back ther'? I was goin'
down, down, an' bringin' th' others with me.
What good 'll it do you or the rest to hev me
ther'? To make me afraid? It 's poor learn-
in' frum fear. Who taught me what was
right? Who cared? No man cared fur my
soul, till I thieved 'n' robbed; 'n' then judge
'n' jury 'n' jailers was glad to pounce on me.
Will yoh gev me a chance? will yoh?"

It was a desperate face before him; but
Holmes never knew fear.

"Stand aside," he said, quietly. "To-morrow I will see you. You need not try to escape."

He passed him, and went slowly up through
the vacant mill to his chamber.

The man sat down on the lower step a few
moments, quite quiet, crushing his hat up in
a slow, steady way, looking up at the mouldy
cobwebs on the wall. He got up at last, and
went in to Lois. Had she heard? The old
scarred face of the girl looked years older, he
thought, — but it might be fancy. She did not
say anything for a while, moving slowly, with

a new gentleness, about him; her very voice
was changed, older. He tried to be cheerful,
eating his supper: she need not know until
to-morrow. He would get out of the town to-
night, or —— There were different ways to
escape. When he had done, he told her to
go; but she would not.

"Let me stay th' night," she said. "I be
n't afraid o' th' mill."

"Why, Lo," he said, laughing, "yoh used
to say yer death was hid here, somewheres."

"I know. But ther' 's worse nor death.
But it 'll come right," she said, persistently,
muttering to herself, as she leaned her face on
her knees, watching, — "it 'll come right."

The glimmering shadows changed and faded
for an hour. The man sat quiet. There was
not much in the years gone to soften his
thought, as it grew desperate and cruel: there
was oppression and vice heaped on him, and
flung back out of his bitter heart. Nor much
in the future: a blank stretch of punishment
to the end. He was an old man: was it easy
to bear? What if he were black? what if he
were born a thief? what if all the sullen revenge of his nature had made him an outcast
from the poorest poor? Was there no latent
good in this soul for which Christ died, that a
kind hand might not have brought to life?

8

None? Something, I think, struggled up in the touch of his hand, catching the skirt of his child's dress, when it came near him, with the timid tenderness of a mother touching her dead baby's hair, — as something holy, far off, yet very near: something in his old crime-marked face, — a look like this dog's, putting his head on my knee, — a dumb, unhelpful love in his eyes, and the slow memory of a wrong done to his soul in a day long past. A wrong to both, you say, perhaps; but if so, irreparable, and never to be recompensed. Never?

" Yoh must go, my little girl," he said at last.

Whatever he did must be done quickly. She came up, combing the thin gray hairs through her fingers.

" Father, I dunnot understan' what it is, rightly. But stay with me, — stay, father!"

" Yoh 've a many frien's, Lo," he said, with a keen flash of jealousy. " Ther' 's none like yoh, — none."

" Father, look here."

She put her misshapen head and scarred face down on his hand, where he could see them. If it had ever hurt her to be as she was, if she had ever compared herself bitterly with fair, beloved women, she was glad now, and thankful, for every fault and deformity that brought her nearer to him, and made her dearer.

" They 're kind, but ther' 's not many loves me with true love, like yoh. Stay, father! Bear it out, whatever it be. Th' good time 'll come, father."

He kissed her, saying nothing, and went with her down the street. When he left her, she waited, and, creeping back, hid near the mill. God knows what vague dread was in her brain; but she came back to watch and help.

Old Yare wandered through the great loom-rooms of the mill with but one fact clear in his cloudy, faltering perception, — that above him the man lay quietly sleeping who would bring worse than death on him to-morrow. Up and down, aimlessly, with his stoker's torch in his hand, going over the years gone and the years to come, with the dead hatred through all of the pitiless man above him, — with now and then, perhaps, a pleasanter thought of things that had been warm and cheerful in his life, — of the corn-huskings long ago, when he was a boy, down in " th' Alabam'," — of the scow his young master gave him once, the first thing he really owned : he was almost as proud of it as he was of Lois when she was born. Most of all remembering the good times in his life, he went back to Lois. It was all good, there,

to go back to. What a little chub she used to
be! Remembering, with bitter remorse, how
all his life he had meant to try and do better,
on her account, but had kept putting off and
putting off until now. And now —— Did
nothing lie before him but to go back and rot
yonder? Was that the end, because he never
had learned better, and was a " dam' nigger " ?

" I 'll *not* leave my girl!" he muttered, going
up and down, — " I 'll *not* leave my girl! "

If Holmes did sleep above him, the trial of
the day, of which we have seen nothing, came
back sharper in sleep. While the strong self
in the man lay torpid, whatever holier power
was in him came out, undaunted by defeat,
and unwearied, and took the form of dreams,
those slighted messengers of God, to soothe
and charm and win him out into fuller, kindlier life. Let us hope that they did so win
him; let us hope that even in that unreal
world the better nature of the man triumphed
at last, and claimed its reward before the terrible reality broke upon him.

Lois, over in the damp, fresh-smelling lum-
ber-yard, sat coiled up in one of the creviced
houses made by the jutting boards. She remembered how she used to play in them, before she went into the mill. The mill, — even
now, with the vague dread of some uncertain

evil to come, the mill absorbed all fear in its old hated shadow. Whatever danger was coming to them lay in it, came from it, she knew, in her confused, blurred way of thinking. It loomed up now, with the square patch of ashen sky above, black, heavy with years of remembered agony and loss. In Lois's hopeful, warm life this was the one uncomprehended monster. Her crushed brain, her unwakened powers, resented their wrong dimly to the mass of iron and work and impure smells, unconscious of any remorseless power that wielded it. It was a monster, she thought, through the sleepy, dreading night, — a monster that kept her wakeful with a dull, mysterious terror.

When the night grew sultry and deepest, she started from her half-doze to see her father come stealthily out and go down the street. She must have slept, she thought, rubbing her eyes, and watching him out of sight, — and then, creeping out, turned to glance at the mill. She cried out, shrill with horror. It was a live monster now, — in one swift instant, alive with fire, — quick, greedy fire, leaping like serpents' tongues out of its hundred jaws, hungry sheets of flame maddening and writhing towards her, and under all a dull and hollow roar that shook the night. Did it call her to her death? She turned to fly, and then —— He was alone, dying! He had been so kind to her! She wrung her hands, standing there a moment. It was a brave hope that was in her heart, and a prayer on her lips never left unanswered, as she hobbled, in her lame, slow way, up to the open black door, and, with one backward look, went in.

CHAPTER VIII.

THERE was a dull smell of camphor; a farther sense of coolness and prickling wet on Holmes's hot, cracking face and hands; then silence and sleep again. Sometime — when, he never knew — a gray light stinging his eyes like pain, and again a slow sinking into warm, unsounded darkness and unconsciousness. It might be years, it might be ages. Even in after-life, looking back, he never broke that time into weeks or days: people might so divide it for him, but he was uncertain, always: it was a vague vacuum in his memory: he had drifted out of coarse, measured life into some out-coast of eternity, and slept in its calm. When, by long degrees, the shock of outer life jarred and woke him, it was feebly done: he came back reluctant, weak: the quiet clinging to him, as if he had been drowned in Lethe, and had brought its calming mist with him out of the shades.

The low chatter of voices, the occasional lifting of his head on the pillow, the very sooth-

ing draught, came to him unreal at first : parts
only of the dull, lifeless pleasure. There was
a sharper memory pierced it sometimes, making him moan and try to sleep, — a remembrance of great, cleaving pain, of falling giddily, of owing life to some one, and being
angry that he owed it, in the pain. Was it
he that had borne it? He did not know, —
nor care : it made him tired to think. Even
when he heard the name, Stephen Holmes, it
had but a far-off meaning : he never woke
enough to know if it were his or not. He
learned, long after, to watch the red light curling among the shavings in the grate when they
made a fire in the evenings, to listen to the
voices of the women by the bed, to know that
the pleasantest belonged to the one with the
low, shapeless figure, and to call her Lois,
when he wanted a drink, long before he knew
himself.

They were very long, pleasant days in early
December. The sunshine was pale, but it
suited his hurt eyes better : it crept slowly in
the mornings over the snuff-coloured carpet on
the floor, up the brown foot-board of the bed,
and, when the wind shook the window-cur-
tains, made little crimson pools of mottled
light over the ceiling, — curdling pools, that
he liked to watch : going off, from the clean

gray walls, and rustling curtain, and transparent crimson, into sleeps that lasted all day.

He was not conscious how he knew he was in a hospital : but he did know it, vaguely; thought sometimes of the long halls outside of the door, with ranges of rooms opening into them, like this, and of very barns of rooms on the other side of the building with rows of white cots where the poorer patients lay : a stretch of travel from which his brain came back to his snug fireplace, quite tired, and to Lois sitting knitting by it. He called the little Welsh-woman, " Sister," too, who used to come in a stuff dress, and white bands about her face, to give his medicine, and gossip with Lois in the evening : she had a comical voice, like a cricket chirping. There was another with a real Scotch brogue, who came and listened sometimes, bringing a basket of undarned stockings : the doctor told him one day how fearless and skilful she was, every summer going to New Orleans when the yellow fever came. She died there the next June : but Holmes never, somehow, could realize a martyr in the cheery, freckled-faced woman whom he always remembered darning stockings in the quiet firelight. It was very quiet ; the voices about him were pleasant and low. If he had drifted from any shock of pain into a sleep like death,

some of the stillness hung about him yet;
but the outer life was homely and fresh and
natural.

The doctor used to talk to him a little; and
sometimes one or two of the patients from the
eye-ward would grow tired of sitting about in
the garden-alleys, and would loiter in, if Lois
would give them leave; but their talk wearied
him, jarred him as strangely as if one had begun on politics and price-currents to the silent
souls in Hades. It was enough thought for
him to listen to the whispered stories of the
sisters in the long evenings, and, half-heard,
try and make an end to them; to look drowsily
down into the garden, where the afternoon sunshine was still so summer-like that a few holly-
hocks persisted in showing their honest red faces
along the walls, and the very leaves that filled
the paths would not wither, but kept up a
wholesome ruddy brown. One of the sisters
had a poultry-yard in it, which he could see:
the wall around it was of stone covered with
a brown feathery lichen, which every rooster
in that yard was determined to stand on, or
perish in the attempt; and Holmes would
watch, through the quiet, bright mornings, the
frantic ambition of the successful aspirant with
an amused smile.

" One 'd thenk," said Lois, sagely, " a chicken

never stood on a wall before, to hear 'em, or a hen laid an egg."

Nor did Holmes smile once because the chicken burlesqued man : his thought was too single for that yet.   It was long, too, before he thought of the people who came in quietly to see him as anything but shadows, or wished for them to come again.   Lois, perhaps, was the most real thing in life then to him : growing conscious, day by day, as he watched her, of his old life over the gulf.   Very slowly conscious : with a weak groping to comprehend the sudden, awful change that had come on him, and then forgetting his old life, and the change, and the pity he felt for himself, in the vague content of the fire-lit room, and his nurse with her interminable knitting through the long afternoons, while the sky without would thicken and gray, and a few still flakes of snow would come drifting down to whiten the brown fields, — with no chilly thought of winter, but only to make the quiet autumn more quiet.   Whatever honest, commonplace affection was in the man came out in a simple way to this Lois, who ruled his sick whims and crotchets in such a quiet, sturdy fashion.   Not because she had risked her life to save his ; even when he understood that, he recalled it with an uneasy, heavy gratitude ; but the drinks she made him, and the plot they

laid to smuggle in some oysters in defiance of
all rules, and the cheerful, pock-marked face, he
never forgot.

Doctor Knowles came sometimes, but seldom : never talked, when he did come : late
in the evening generally : and then would punch
his skin, and look at his tongue, and shake the
bottles on the mantel-shelf with a grunt that
terrified Lois into the belief that the other doctor was a quack, and her patient was totally
undone. He would sit, grum enough, with his
feet higher than his head, chewing an unlighted
cigar, and leave them both thankful when he
saw proper to go.

The truth is, Knowles was thoroughly out
of place in these little mending-shops called
sick-chambers, where bodies are taken to
pieces, and souls set right. He had no faith
in your slow, impalpable cures : all reforms
were to be accomplished by a wrench, from
the abolition of slavery to the pulling of a
tooth.

He had no especial sympathy with Holmes,
either : the men were started in life from oppo-
site poles : and with all the real tenderness under his surly, rugged habit, it would have been
hard to touch him with the sudden doom fallen
on this man, thrown crippled and penniless
upon the world, helpless, it might be, for life.

He would have been apt to tell you, savagely, that " he wrought for it."

Besides, it made him out of temper to meet the sisters. Knowles could have sketched for you with a fine decision of touch the *rôle* played by the Papal power in the progress of humanity, — how far it served as a stepping-stone, and the exact period when it became a wearisome clog. The world was done with it now, utterly. Its breath was only poisoned, with coming death. So the homely live charity of these women, their work, which no other hands were ready to take, jarred against his abstract theory, and irritated him, as an obstinate fact always does run into the hand of a man who is determined to clutch the very heart of a matter. Truth will not underlie all facts, in this muddle of a world, in spite of the Positive Philosophy, you know.

Don't sneer at Knowles. Your own clear, tolerant brain, that reflects all men and creeds alike, like colourless water, drawing the truth from all, is very different, doubtless, from this narrow, solitary soul, who thought the world waited for him to fight down his one evil before it went on its slow way. An intolerant fanatic, of course. But the truth he did know was so terribly real to him, there was such sick, throbbing pity in his heart for men who suffered as he had done! And then, fanatics must make history for conservative men to learn from, I suppose.

If Knowles shunned the hospital, there was another place he shunned more, — the place where his Communist buildings were to have stood. He went out there once, as one might go alone to bury his dead out of his sight, the day after the mill was burnt, — looking first at the smoking mass of hot bricks and charred shingles, so as clearly to understand how utterly dead his life-long scheme was. He stalked gravely around it, his hands in his pockets; the hodmen who were raking out their winter's fire-wood from the ashes remarking, that " old Knowles did n't seem a bit cut up about it." Then he went out to the farm he had meant to buy, as I told you, and looked at it in the same stolid way. It was a dull day in October. The Wabash crawled moodily past his feet, the dingy prairie stretched drearily away on the other side, while the heavy-browed Indiana hills stood solemnly looking down the plateau where the buildings were to have risen.

Well, most men have some plan of life, into which all the strength and the keen, fine feeling of their nature enter; but generally they try to make it real in early youth, and, balked then, laugh ever afterwards at their own folly. This poor old Knowles had begun to block out his dream when he was a gaunt, gray-haired man of sixty. I have known men so build their heart's blood, and brains into their work, that, when it tumbled down, their lives went with it. His fell that dull day in October; but if it hurt him, no man knew it. He sat there, looking at the broad plateau, whistling softly to himself, a long time. He had meant that a great many hearts should be made better and happier there; he had dreamed —— God knows what he had dreamed, of which this reality was the foundation, — of how much world-freedom, or beauty, or kindly life this was the heart or seed. It was all over now. All the afternoon the muddy sky hung low over the hills and dull prairie, while he sat there looking at the dingy gloom : just as you and I have done, perhaps, some time, thwarted in some true hope, — sore and bitter against God, because He did not see how much His universe needed our pet reform.

He got up at last, and without a sigh went slowly away, leaving the courage and self-reliance of his life behind him, buried with that one beautiful, fair dream of life. He never came back again. People said Knowles was quieter since his loss; but I think only God saw the depth of the difference. When he was leaving the plateau, that day, he looked back at

it, as if to say good-bye,— not to the dingy
fields and river, but to the Something he had
nursed so long in his rugged heart, and given
up now forever. As he looked, the warm, red
sun came out, lighting up with a heartsome
warmth the whole gray day. Some blessing
power seemed to look at him from this grave-
yard of his hopes, from the gloomy hills, the
prairie, and the river, which he never was to see
again. His hope accomplished could not have
looked at him with surer content and fulfilment.
He turned away, ungrateful and moody. Long
afterwards he remembered the calm and bright-
ness which his hand had not been raised to
make, and understood the meaning of its
promise.

He went to work now in earnest : he had to
work for his bread-and-butter, you understand ?
Restless, impatient at first ; but we will forgive
him that : you yourself were not altogether submissive, perhaps, when the slow-built expecta-
tion of life was destroyed by some chance, as
you called it, no more controllable than this
paltry burning of a mill. Yet, now that the
great hope was gone on which his brain had
worked with rigid, fierce intentness, now that
his hands were powerless to redeem a perishing
class, he had time to fall into careless, kindly
habit : he thought it wasted time, remorsefully,

of course. He was seized with a curiosity to
know what plan in living these people had who
crossed his way on the streets; if they were
disappointed, like him. Humbled, he hardly
knew why: vague, uncertain in action. Quit
dogging old Huff with his advice; trotted about
the streets with a cowed look, that, if one could
have seen into the jaded old heart under his
snuffy waistcoat, would have seemed pitiful
enough. He went sometimes to read the papers to old Tim Poole, who was bed-ridden, and
did not pish or pshaw once at his maundering
about secession, or the misery in his back. Went
to church sometimes: the sermons were bigotry,
always, to his notion, sitting on a back seat,
squirting tobacco-juice about him; but the simple, old-fashioned hymns brought the tears to
his eyes: — " They sounded to him like his
mother's voice, singing in Paradise:" he hoped
she could not see how things had gone on here,
— how all that was honest and strong in his life
had fallen in that infernal mill. Once or twice
he went down Crane Alley, and lumbered up
three pair of stairs to the garret where Kitts
had his studio, — got him orders, in fact, for
two portraits; and when that pale-eyed young
man, in a fit of confidence, one night, with a
very red face drew back the curtain from his
grand " Fall of Chapultepec," and watched him

with a lean and hungry look, Knowles, who knew no more about painting than a gorilla, walked about, looking through his fist at it, saying, " how fine the *chiaroscuro* was, and that it was a devilish good thing altogether." " Well, well," he soothed his conscience, going down-stairs, " maybe that bit of canvas is as much to that poor chap as the Phalanstery was once to another fool." And so went on through the gas-lit streets into his parishes in cellars and alleys, with a sorer heart, but cheerfuller words, now that he had nothing but words to give.

The only place where he hardened his heart was in the hospital with Holmes. After he had wakened to full consciousness, Knowles thought the man a beast to sit there uncomplaining day after day, cold and grave, as if the lifeful warmth of the late autumn were enough for him. Did he understand the iron fate laid on him? Where was the strength of the self-existent soul now? Did he know that it was a balked, defeated life, that waited for him, vacant of the triumphs he had planned? " The self-existent soul! stopped in its growth by chance, this omnipotent deity, — the chance burning of a mill!" Knowles muttered to himself, looking at Holmes. With a dim flash of doubt, as he said it, whether there might not, after all, be a Something, — some deep of calm, of eternal order, where he and

Holmes, these coarse chances, these wrestling
souls, these creeds, Catholic or Humanitarian,
even that namby-pamby Kitts and his picture,
might be unconsciously working out their part.
Looking out of the hospital-window, he saw
the deep of the stainless blue, impenetrable,
with the stars unconscious in their silence of
the maddest raging of the petty world. There
was such calm! such infinite love and justice!
it was around, above him; it held him, it held
the world, — all Wrong, all Right! For an instant the turbid heart of the man cowered, awe-
struck, as yours or mine has done when some
swift touch of music or human love gave us a
cleaving glimpse of the great I AM. The next,
he opened the newspaper in his hand. What
part in the eternal order could *that* hold? or
slavery, or secession, or civil war? No harmony could be infinite enough to hold such
discords, he thought, pushing the whole matter
from him in despair. Why, the experiment of
self-government, the problem of the ages, was
crumbling in ruin! So he despaired, just as
Tige did the night the mill fell about his ears,
in full confidence that the world had come to an
end now, without hope of salvation, — crawling
out of his cellar in dumb amazement, when the
sun rose as usual the next morning.

Knowles sat, peering at Holmes over his pa-

per, watching the languid breath that showed
how deep the hurt had been, the maimed body,
the face outwardly cool, watchful, reticent as
before. He fancied the slough of disappointment into which God had crushed the soul of
this man : would he struggle out? Would he
take Miss Herne as the first step in his stair-way,
or be content to be flung down in vigorous
manhood to the depth of impotent poverty?
He could not tell if the quiet on Holmes's face
were stolid defiance or submission : the dumb
kings might have looked thus beneath the feet
of Pharaoh. When he walked over the floor,
too, weak as he was it was with the old iron
tread. He asked Knowles presently what business he had gone into.

"My old hobby in an humble way, — the
House of Refuge."

They both laughed.

"Yes, it is true. The janitor points me out
to visitors as 'under-superintendent, a philanthropist in decayed circumstances.' Perhaps
it is my life-work," — growing sad and earnest.

"If you can inoculate these infant beggars
and thieves with your theory, it will be practice
when you are dead."

"I think that," said Knowles, gravely, his eye
kindling, — "I think that."

" As thankless a task as that of Moses," said the other, watching him curiously. " For *you* will not see the pleasant land, — *you* will not go over."

The old man's flabby face darkened.

" I know," he said.

He glanced involuntarily out at the blue, and the clear-shining, eternal stars.

" I suppose," he said, after a while, cheerfully, " I must content myself with Lois's creed, here, — ' It 'll come right some time.' "

Lois looked up from the saucepan she was stirring, her face growing quite red, nodding emphatically some half-dozen times.

"After all," said Holmes, kindly, " this chance may have forced you on the true road to success for your new system of Sociology. Only untainted natures could be fitted for self-government. Do you find the fallow field easily worked ? "

Knowles fidgeted uneasily.

" No. Fact is, I 'm beginning to think there 's a good deal of an obstacle in blood. I find difficulty, much difficulty, Sir, in giving to the youngest child true ideas of absolute freedom, and unselfish heroism."

" You teach them these by reason alone ? " said Holmes, gravely.

" Well, — of course, — that is the true theory ;

reason is the only yoke that should be laid upon
a free-born soul; but I — I find it necessary to
have them whipped, Mr. Holmes."

Holmes stooped suddenly to pat Tiger, hiding
a furtive smile.   The old man went on, anxiously, —

" Old Mr. Howth says that is the end of all
self-governments : from anarchy to despotism, he
says.   Brute force must come in.   Old people
are apt to be set in their ways, you know.   Honestly, we do not find unlimited freedom answer
in the House.   I hope much from a woman's
assistance : I have destined her for this work
always : she has great latent power of sympathy and endurance, such as can bring the Christian teaching home to these wretches."

" The Christian ? " said Holmes.

" Well, yes.   I am not a believer myself, you
know; but I find that it takes hold of these
people more vitally than more abstract faiths : I
suppose because of the humanity of Jesus.   In
Utopia, of course, we shall live from scientific
principles ; but they do not   answer in   the
House."

" Who is the woman ? " asked Holmes, carelessly.

The other watched him keenly.

" She is coming for five years.   Margret
Howth."

He patted the dog with the same hard, unmoved touch.

"It is a religious duty with her. Besides, she must do something. They have been almost starving since the mill was burnt."

Holmes's face was bent; he could not see it. When he looked up, Knowles thought it more rigid, immovable than before.

When Knowles was going away, Holmes said to him, —

"When does Margret Howth go into that devils' den?"

"The House? On New-Year's." The scorn in him was too savage to be silent. "It is the best time to begin a new life. Yourself, now, you will have fulfilled your design by that time, — of marriage?"

Holmes was leaning on the mantel-shelf; his very lips were pale.

"Yes, I shall, I shall," — in his low, hard tone.

Some sudden dream of warmth and beauty flashed before his gray eyes, lighting them as Knowles never had seen before.

"Miss Herne is beautiful, — let me congratulate you, in Western fashion."

The old man did not hide his sneer.

Holmes bowed.

"I thank you, for her."

Lois held the candle to light the Doctor out of the long passages.

"Yoh hev n't seen Barney out 't Mr. Howth's, Doctor? He 's ther' now."

"No. When shall you have done waiting on this — man, Lois? God help you, child!"

Lois's quick instinct answered, —

"He 's very kind. He 's like a woman fur kindness to such as me. When I come to die, I 'd like eyes such as his to look at, tender, pitiful."

"Women are fools alike," grumbled the Doctor. "Never mind. ' When you come to die?' What put that into your head? Look up."

The child sheltered the flaring candle with her hand.

"I 've no tho't o' dyin'," she said, laughing.

There was a gray shadow about her eyes, a peaked look to the face, he never saw before, looking at her now with a physician's eyes.

"Does anything hurt you here?" touching her chest.

"It 's better now. It was that night o' th' fire. Th' breath o' th' mill, I thenk, — but it 's nothin'."

"Burning copperas? Of course it 's better Oh, that 's nothing!" he said, cheerfully.

When they reached the door, he held out his hand, the first time he ever had done it to her, and then waited, patting her on the head.

"I think it 'll come right, Lois," he said, dreamily, looking out into the night. "You 're a good girl. I think it 'll all come right. For you and me. Some time. Good-night, child."

After he was a long way down the street, he turned to nod good-night again to the comical little figure in the door-way.

CHAPTER IX.

IF Knowles hated anybody that night, he hated the man he had left standing there with pale, heavy jaws, and heart of iron; he could have cursed him, standing there. He did not see how, after he was left alone, the man lay with his face to the wall, holding his bony hand to his forehead, with a look in his eyes that if you had seen, you would have thought his soul had entered on that path whose steps take hold on hell.

There was no struggle in his face; whatever was the resolve he had reached in the solitary hours when he had stood so close upon the borders of death, it was unshaken now; but the heart, crushed and stifled before, was taking its dire revenge. If ever it had hungered, through the cold, selfish days, for God's help, or a woman's love, it hungered now, with a craving like death. If ever he had thought how bare and vacant the years would be, going down to the grave with lips that never had known a true wife's kiss, he remembered it now, when it was too late, with bitterness such as wrings a man's heart but once in a lifetime. If ever he had denied to his own soul this Margret, called her alien or foreign, it called her now, when it was too late, to her rightful place; there was not a thought nor a hope in the darkest depths of his nature that did not cry out for her help that night, — for her, a part of himself, — now, when it was too late. He went over all the years gone, and pictured the years to come; he remembered the money that was to help his divine soul upward; he thought of it with a curse, getting up and pacing the floor of the narrow room, slowly and quietly. Looking out into the still starlight and the quaint garden, he tried to fancy this woman as he knew her, after the restless power of her soul should have been chilled and starved into a narrow, lifeless duty. He fancied her old, and stern, and sick of life, she that might have been —— what might they not have been, together? And he had driven her to this for money, — money!

It was of no use to repent of it now. He had frozen the love out of her heart, long ago. He remembered (all that he did remember of the blank night after he was hurt) that he had seen her white, worn-out face looking down at him; that she did not touch him; and that,

when one of the sisters told her she might take
her place, and sponge his forehead, she said,
bitterly, she had no right to do it, that he was
no friend of hers. He saw and heard that, unconscious to all else ; he would have known it,
if he had been dead, lying there. It was too
late now : why need he think of what might
have been ?   Yet he did think of it through the
long winter's night, — each moment his thought
of the life to come, or of her, growing more tender and more bitter. Do you wonder at the
remorse of this man ? Wait, then, until you
lie alone, as he had done, through days as slow,
revealing as ages, face to face with God and
death. Wait until you go down so close to
eternity that the life you have lived stands out
before you in the dreadful bareness in which
God sees it, — as you shall see it some day
from heaven or hell : money, and hate, and
love will stand in their true light then. Yet,
coming back to life again, he held whatever
resolve he had reached down there with his old
iron will : all the pain he bore in looking back
to the false life before, or the ceaseless remembrance that it was too late now to atone for
that false life, made him the stronger to abide
by that resolve, to go on the path self-chosen,
let the end be what it might. Whatever the
resolve was, it did not still the gnawing hun-

ger in his heart that night, which every trifle
made more fresh and strong.

There was a wicker-basket that Lois had left
by the fire, piled up with bits of cloth and
leather out of which she was manufacturing
Christmas gifts; a pair of great woollen socks,
which one of the sisters had told him privately
Lois meant for him, lying on top. As with all
of her people, Christmas was the great day of
the year to her. Holmes could not but smile,
looking at them. Poor Lois! — Christmas
would be here soon, then? And sitting by
the covered fire, he went back to Christmases
gone, the thought of all others that brought
Margret nearest and warmest to him : since
he was a boy they had been together on that
day. With his hand over his eyes, he sat quiet
by the fire until morning. He heard some boy
going by in the gray dawn call to another that
they would have holiday on Christmas week.
It was coming, he thought, rousing himself, —
but never as it had been : that could never be
again. Yet it was strange how this thought
of Christmas took hold of him, after this, —
famished his heart. As it approached in the
slow-coming winter, the days growing shorter,
and the nights longer and more solitary, so
Margret became more real to him, — not rejected and lost, but as the wife she might have

been, with the simple, passionate love she gave
him once. The thought grew intolerable to
him ; yet there was not a homely pleasure of
those years gone, when the old school-master
kept high holiday on Christmas, that he did
not recall and linger over with a boyish yearning, now that these things were over forever.
He chafed under his weakness. If the day
would but come when he could go out and
conquer his fate, as a man ought to do! On
Christmas eve he would put an end to these
torturing taunts, be done with them, let the sacrifice be what it might. For I fear that even
now Stephen Holmes thought of his own need
and his own hunger.

He watched Lois knitting and patching her
poor little gifts, with a vague feeling that every
stitch made the time a moment shorter until
he should be free, with his life in his hand
again. She left the hospital at last, sorrowfully enough, but he made her go : he fancied
the close air was hurting her, seeing at night
the strange shadow growing on her face. I
do not think he ever said to her that he knew
all she had done for him, or thanked her ; but
no dog or woman that Stephen Holmes loved
could look into his eyes, and doubt that love.
Sad, masterful eyes, such as are seen but once
or twice in a lifetime : no woman but would

wish, like Lois, for such eyes to be near her when she came to die, for her to remember the world's love in. She came hobbling back every day to see him after she had gone, and would stay to make his soup, telling him, child-like, how many days it was until Christmas. He knew that, as well as she, waiting through the cold, slow hours, in his solitary room. He thought sometimes she had some eager petition to offer him, when she stood watching him wistfully, twisting her hands together; but she always smothered it with a sigh, and, tying her little woollen cap, went away, walking more slowly, he thought, every day.

Do you remember how Christmas came that year? how there was a waiting pause, when the States stood still, and from the peoples came the first awful murmurs of the storm that was to shake the earth? how men's hearts failed them for fear, how women turned pale, and held their children closer to their breasts, while they heard a far cry of lamentation for their country that had fallen? Do you remember how, amidst the fury of men's anger, the storehouses of God were opened for that land? how the very sunshine gathered new splendours, the rains more fruitful moisture, until the earth poured forth an unknown fulness of life and beauty? Was there no promise there, no proph-

ecy ?   Do you remember, while the very life of
the people hung in doubt before them, while the
angel of death came again to pass over the
land, and there was no blood on any door-post
to keep him from that house, how serenely the
old earth folded in her harvest, dead, till it
should waken to a stronger life ? how quietly,
as the time came near for the birth of Christ,
this old earth made ready for his coming, heed-
less of the clamour of men ? how the air grew
fresher above, day by day, and the gray deep
silently opened for the snow to go down and
screen and whiten and make holy that fouled
earth ?   I think the slow-falling snow did not
fail in its quiet warning ; for I remember that
men, too, in a feeble way tried to make ready
for the birth of Christ.   There was a healthier
glow than terror stirred in their hearts ; because
of the vague, great dread without, it may be,
they drew closer together round household fires,
were kindlier in the good old-fashioned way ;
old friendships were wakened, old times talked
over, fathers and mothers and children planned
homely ways to show the love in their hearts
and to welcome in Christmas.   Who knew but
it might be the last ?   Let us be thankful for
that happy Christmas-day.   What if it were
the last ?   What if, when another comes, and
another, one voice, the kindest and cheerfullest

then, shall never say " Happy Christmas " to us
again ?   Let us be thankful for that day the
more, — accept it the more as a sign of that
which will surely come.

Holmes, even, in his dreary room and drearier
thought, felt the warmth and expectant stir
creeping through the land as the day drew near.
Even in the hospital, the sisters were in a busy
flutter, decking their little chapel with flowers,
and preparing a *fête* for their patients.   The
doctor, as he bandaged his broken arm, hinted
at faint rumours in the city of masquerades and
concerts.   Even Knowles, who had not visited
the hospital for weeks, relented and came back,
moody and grum.   He brought Kitts with him,
and started him on talking of how they kept
Christmas in Ohio on his mother's farm ; and
the poor soul, encouraged by the silence of two
of his auditors, and the intense interest of Lois
in the background, mazed on about Santa-
Claus trees and Virginia reels until the clock
struck twelve, and Knowles began to snore.

Christmas was coming.   As he stood, day
after day, looking out of the gray window, he
could see the signs of its coming even in the
shop-windows glittering with miraculous toys,
in the market-carts with their red-faced drivers
and heaps of ducks and turkeys, in every stage-
coach or omnibus that went by crowded with

9 *

boys home for the holidays, hallooing for Bell
or Lincoln, forgetful that the election was over,
and Carolina out.

Pike came to see him one day, his arms full
of a bundle, which turned out to be an accor-
dion for Sophy.

" Christmas, you know," he said, taking off
the brown paper, while he was cursing the Cot-
ton States the hardest, and gravely kneading at
the keys, and stretching it until he made as
much discord as five Congressmen. " I think
Sophy will like that," he said, looking at it side-
ways, and tying it up carefully.

" I am sure she will," said Holmes, — and
did not think the man a fool for one moment.

Always going back, this Holmes, when he
was alone, to the certainty that home-comings
or children's kisses or Christmas feasts were
not for such as he, — never could be, though he
sought for the old time in bitterness of heart;
and so, dully remembering his resolve, and waiting for Christmas eve, when he might end it all.
Not one of the myriads of happy children listened more intently to the clock clanging off
hour after hour than the silent, stern man who
had no hope in that day that was coming.

He learned to watch even for poor Lois coming up the corridor every day, — being the only
tie that bound the solitary man to the inner

world of love and warmth. The deformed little
body was quite alive with Christmas now, and
brought its glow with her, in her weak way.
Different from the others, he saw with a curious
interest. The day was more real to her than to
them. Not because, only, the care she had of
everybody, and everybody had of her seemed to
reach its culmination of kindly thought for the
Christmas time ; not because, as she sat talking slowly, stopping for breath, her great fear
seemed to be that she would not have gifts
enough to go round ; but deeper than that, —
the day was real to her. As if it were actually
true that the Master in whom she believed was
freshly born into the world once a year, to
waken all that was genial and noble and pure
in the turbid, worn-out hearts ; as if new honour and pride and love did flash into the realms
below heaven with the breaking of Christmas
morn. It was a beautiful faith ; he almost
wished it were his. A beautiful faith ! it gave
a meaning to the old custom of gifts and kind
words. *Love* coming into the world ! — the
idea pleased his artistic taste, being simple and
sublime. Lois used to tell him, while she feebly
tried to set his room in order, of all her plans, —
of how Sam Polston was to be married on
New-Year's, — but most of all of the Christmas
coming out at the old school-master's : how the

old house had been scrubbed from top to bot-
tom, was fairly glowing with shining paint and
hot fires, — how Margret and her mother
worked, in terror lest the old man should find
out how poor and bare it was, — how he and
Joel had some secret enterprise on foot at the
far end of the plantation out in the swamp,
and were gone nearly all day.

She ceased coming at last. One of the sisters went out to see her, and told him she was
too weak to walk, but meant to be better soon,
— quite well by the holidays. He wished the
poor thing had told him what she wanted of
him, — wished it anxiously, with a dull presen-
timent of evil.

The days went by, cold and slow. He
watched grimly the preparations the hospital
physician was silently making in his case, for
fever, inflammation.

"I must be strong enough to go out cured
on Christmas eve," he said to him one day,
coolly.

The old doctor glanced up shrewdly. He
was an old Alsatian, very plain-spoken.

"You say so?" he mumbled. "Chut! Then
you will go. There are some — bull-dog men.
They do what they please, — they never die unless they choose, begar! We know them in our
practice, Herr Holmes!"

Holmes laughed. Some acumen there, he thought, in medicine or mind: as for himself, it was true enough; whatever success he had gained in life had been by no flush of enthusiasm or hope; a dogged persistence of "holding on," rather.

A long time; but Christmas eve came at last: bright, still, frosty. "Whatever he had to do, let it be done quickly;" but not till the set hour came. So he laid his watch on the table beside him, waiting until it should mark the time he had chosen: the ruling passion of self-control as strong in this turn of life's tide as it would be in its ebb, at the last. The old doctor found him alone in the dreary room, coming in with the frosty breath of the eager street about him. A grim, chilling sight enough, as solitary and impenetrable as the Sphinx. He did not like such faces in this genial and gracious time, so hurried over his examination. The eye was cool, the pulse steady, the man's body, battered though it was, strong in its steely composure. "*Ja wohl! — ja wohl!*" he went on chuffily, summing up: latent fever, — the very lips were blue, dry as husks; "he would go, — *oui?* — then go!" — with a chuckle. "All right, *glück zu!*" And so shuffled out. Latent fever? Doubtless, yet hardly from broken bones, the doctor thought, — with no sus-

picion of the subtile, intolerable passion smouldering in every drop of this man's phlegmatic
blood.

Evening came at last. He stopped until the
cracked bell of the chapel had done striking
the Angelus, and then put on his overcoat, and
went out. Passing down the garden walk a
miserable chicken staggered up to him, chirping a drunken recognition. For a moment, he
breathed again the hot smoke of the mill, remembering how Lois had found him in Margret's office, not forgetting the cage : chary of
this low life, even in the peril of his own. So,
going out on the street, he tested his own nature by this trifle in his old fashion. " The ruling passion strong in death," eh ? It had not
been self-love ; something deeper : an instinct
rather than reason. Was he glad to think this
of himself? He looked out more watchful of the
face which the coming Christmas bore. · The
air was cold and pungent. The crowded city
seemed wakening to some keen enjoyment ;
even his own weak, deliberate step rang on the
icy pavement as if it wished to rejoice with the
rest. I said it was a trading city : so it was,
but the very trade to-day had a jolly Christmas
face on ; the surly old banks and pawnbrokers'
shops had grown ashamed of their doings, and
shut their doors, and covered their windows

with frosty trees, and cathedrals, and castles; the shops opened their inmost hearts; some child's angel had touched them, and they flushed out into a magic splendour of Christmas trees, and lights, and toys; Santa Claus might have made his head-quarters in any one of them. As for children, you stumbled over them at every step, quite weighed down with the heaviness of their joy, and the money burning their pockets; the acrid old brokers and pettifoggers, that you met with a chill on other days, had turned into jolly fathers of families, and lounged laughing along with half a dozen little hands pulling them into candy-stores or toy-shops; all of the churches whose rules permitted them to show their deep rejoicing in a simple way, had covered their cold stone walls with evergreens, and wreaths of glowing fire-berries : the child's angel had touched them too, perhaps, — not unwisely.

He passed crowds of thin-clad women looking in through open doors, with red cheeks and hungry eyes, at red-hot stoves within, and a placard, " Christmas dinners for the poor, gratis ; " out of every window on the streets came a ruddy light, and a spicy smell; the very sunset sky had caught the reflection of the countless Christmas fires, and flamed up to the zenith, blood-red as cinnabar.

Holmes turned down one of the back streets: he was going to see Lois, first of all. I hardly know why: the child's angel may have touched him, too ; or his heart, full of a yearning pity for the poor cripple, who, he believed now, had given her own life for his, may have plead for indulgence, as men remember their childish prayers, before going into battle. He came at last, in the quiet lane where she lived, to her little brown frame-shanty, to which you mounted by a flight of wooden steps : there were two narrow windows at the top, hung with red curtains ; he could hear her feeble voice singing within. As he turned to go up the steps, he caught sight of something crouched underneath them in the dark, hiding from him : whether a man or a dog he could not see. He touched it.

" What d' ye want, Mas'r ? " said a stifled voice.

He touched it again with his stick. The man stood upright, back in the shadow : it was old Yare.

" Had ye any word wi' me, Mas'r ? "

He saw the negro's face grow gray with fear.

" Come out, Yare," he said, quietly. " Any word ? What word is arson, eh ? "

The man did not move. Holmes touched him with the stick.

" Come out," he said.

He came out, looking gaunt, as with famine.

" I 'll not flurr myself," he said, crunching his ragged hat in his hands, — " I 'll not."

He drove the hat down upon his head, and looked up with a sullen fierceness.

" Yoh 've got me, an' I 'm glad of 't. I 'm tired, fearin'. I was born for hangin', they say," with a laugh. " But I 'll see my girl. I 've waited hyur, runnin' the resk, — not darin' to see her, on 'count o' yoh. I thort I was safe on Christmas-day, — but what 's Christmas to yoh or me ? "

Holmes's quiet motion drove him up the steps before him. He stopped at the top, his cowardly nature getting the better of him, and sat down whining on the upper step.

" Be marciful, Mas'r ! I wanted to see my girl, — that 's all. She 's all I hev."

Holmes passed him and went in. Was Christmas nothing to him ? How did this foul wretch know that they stood alone, apart from the world ?

It was a low, cheerful little room that he came into, stooping his tall head : a tea-kettle humming and singing on the wood-fire, that lighted up the coarse carpet and the gray walls, but spent its warmest heat on the low settee where Lois lay sewing, and singing to herself. She was wrapped up in a shawl, but

the hands, he saw, were worn to skin and
bone; the gray shadow was heavier on her
face, and the brooding brown eyes were like
a tired child's. She tried to jump up when
she saw him, and not being able, leaned on
one elbow, half-crying as she laughed.

"It 's the best Christmas gift of all! I can
hardly b'lieve it!" — touching the strong hand
humbly that was held out to her.

Holmes had a gentle touch, I told you, for
dogs and children and women : so, sitting quietly by her, he listened for a long time with
untiring patience to her long story ; looked at
the heap of worthless trifles she had patched
up for gifts, wondering secretly at the delicate
sense of colour and grace betrayed in the bits
of flannel and leather ; and took, with a grave
look of wonder, his own package, out of which
a bit of woollen thread peeped forth.

"Don't look till to-morrow mornin'," she said,
anxiously, as she lay back trembling and exhausted.

The breath of the mill! The fires of the
world's want and crime had finished their work
on her life, — so! She caught the meaning of
his face quickly.

"It 's nothin'," she said, eagerly. "I 'll be
strong by New-Year's ; it 's only a day or two
rest I need. I 've no tho't o' givin' up."

And to show how strong she was, she got up
and hobbled about to make the tea. He had
not the heart to stop her; she did not want to
die, — why should she? the world was a great,
warm, beautiful nest for the little cripple, —
why need he show her the cold without? He
saw her at last go near the door where old
Yare sat outside, then heard her breathless cry,
and a sob. A moment after the old man came
into the room, carrying her, and, laying her
down on the settee, chafed her hands, and misshapen head.

"What ails her?" he said, looking up, bewildered, to Holmes. "We 've killed her
among us."

She laughed, though the great eyes were
growing dim, and drew his coarse gray hair
into her hand.

"Yoh wur long comin'," she said, weakly.
"I hunted fur yoh every day, — every day."

The old man had pushed her hair back, and
was reading the sunken face with a wild fear.

"What ails her?" he cried. "Ther' 's somethin' gone wi' my girl. Was it my fault? Lo,
was it my fault?"

"Be quiet!" said Holmes, sternly.

"Is it *that?*" he gasped, shrilly. "My God!
not that! I can't bear it!"

Lois soothed him, patting his face childishly.

"Am I dyin' now?" she asked, with a frightened look at Holmes.

He told her no, cheerfully.

"I've no tho't o' dyin'. I dunnot thenk o'
dyin'. Don't mind, dear! Yoh 'll stay with me,
fur good?"

The man's paroxysm of fear for her over, his
spite and cowardice came uppermost.

"It's him," he yelped, looking fiercely at
Holmes. "He's got my life in his hands. He
kin take it. What does he keer fur me or my
girl? I 'll not stay wi' yoh no longer, Lo.
Mornin' he 'll send me t' th' lock-up, an' after " ——

"I care for *you*, child," said Holmes, stooping
suddenly close to the girl's livid face.

"To-morrow?" she muttered. "My Christmas-day?"

He wet her face while he looked over at the
wretch whose life he held in his hands. It was
the iron rule of Holmes's nature to be just; but
to-night dim perceptions of a deeper justice
than law opened before him, — problems he had
no time to solve : the sternest fortress is liable
to be taken by assault, — and the dew of the
coming morn was on his heart.

"So as I 've hunted fur him!" she whispered,
weakly. "I did n't thenk it wud come to this.
So as I loved him! Oh, Mr. Holmes, he 's hed

a pore chance in livin',—forgive him this! Him
that 'll come to-morrow 'd say to forgive him
this."

She caught the old man's head in her arms
with an agony of tears, and held it tight.

" I hev hed a pore chance," he said, looking
up, — " that's God's truth, Lo! I dunnot keer
fur that: it's too late goin' back. But Lo —
Mas'r," he mumbled, servilely, " it's on'y a little
time t' th' end: let me stay with Lo. She loves
me, — Lo does."

A look of disgust crept over Holmes's face.

" Stay, then," he muttered, — " I wash my
hands of you, you old scoundrel!"

He bent over Lois with his rare, pitiful smile.

" Have I his life in my hands? I put it into
yours, — so, child! Now put it all out of your
head, and look up here to wish me good-bye."

She looked up cheerfully, hardly conscious
how deep the danger had been; but the flush
had gone from her face, leaving it sad and
still.

" I must go to keep Christmas, Lois," he said,
playfully.

" Yoh're keepin' it here, Sir." She held her
weak gripe on his hand still, with the vague
outlook in her eyes that came there sometimes.
" Was it fur me yoh done it?"

" Yes, for you."

"And fur Him that 's comin', Sir ? " smiling.

Holmes's face grew graver.

" No, Lois." She looked into his eyes bewildered. " For the poor child that loved me "
he said, half to himself, smoothing her hair.

Perhaps in that day when the under-currents
of the soul's life will be bared, this man will know
the subtile instincts that drew him out of his
self-reliance by the hand of the child that loved
him to the Love beyond, that was man and
died for him, as well as she. He did not see
it now.

The clear evening light fell on Holmes, as he
stood there looking down at the dying little
lamiter: a powerful figure, with a face supreme,
masterful, but tender: you will find no higher
type of manhood. Did God make him of the
same blood as the vicious, cringing wretch
crouching to hide his black face at the other
side of the bed ? Some such thought came
into Lois's brain, and vexed her, bringing the
tears to her eyes : he was her father, you know.
She drew their hands together, as if she would
have joined them, then stopped, closing her eyes
wearily.

" It 's all wrong," she muttered, — " oh, it 's
far wrong ! Ther' 's One could make them 'like.
Not me."

She stroked her father's hand once, and

then let it go. There was a long silence. Holmes glanced out, and saw the sun was down.

"Lois," he said, "I want you to wish me a happy Christmas, as people do."

Holmes had a curious vein of superstition : he knew no lips so pure as this girl's, and he wanted them to wish him good-luck that night. She did it, looking up laughing and growing red : riddles of life did not trouble her childish fancy long. And so he left her, with a dull feeling, as I said before, that it was good to say a prayer before the battle came on. For men who believed in prayers : for him, it was the same thing to make one day for Lois happier.

CHAPTER X.

It was later than Holmes thought: a gray, cold evening. The streets in that suburb were lonely: he went down them, the new-fallen snow dulling his step. It had covered the peaked roofs of the houses too, and they stood in listening rows, white and still. Here and there a pale flicker from the gas-lamps struggled with the ashy twilight. He met no one: people had gone home early on Christmas eve. He had no home to go to: pah! there were plenty of hotels, he remembered, smiling grimly. It was bitter cold: he buttoned up his coat tightly, as he walked slowly along as if waiting for some one, — wondering dully if the gray air were any colder or stiller than the heart hardly beating under the coat. Well, men had conquered Fate, conquered life and love, before now. It grew darker: he was pacing now slowly in the shadow of a long low wall surrounding the grounds of some building. When he came near the gate, he would stop and listen: he could have heard a sparrow on the snow, it was so still. After a while he did hear footsteps, crunching the snow heavily; the gate clicked as they came out : it was Knowles, and the clergyman whom Dr. Cox did not like; Vandyke was his name.

"Don't bolt the gate," said Knowles; "Miss Howth will be out presently."

They sat down on a pile of lumber near by, waiting, apparently. Holmes went up and joined them, standing in the shadow of the lumber, talking to Vandyke. He did not meet him, perhaps, once in six months; but he believed in the man, thoroughly.

"I've just helped Knowles build a Christmas-tree in yonder, — the House of Refuge, you know. He could not tell an oak from an arbor-vitæ, I believe."

Knowles was in no mood for quizzing.

"There are other things I don't know," he said, gloomily, recurring to some subject Holmes had interrupted. "The House is going to the Devil, Charley, headlong."

"There's no use in saying no," said the other; "you'll call me a lying diviner."

Knowles did not listen.

"Seems as if I were to go groping and stumbling through the world like some forsaken Cyclops with his eye out, dragging down whatever I touched. If there were anything to hold by, anything certain!"

10

Vandyke looked at him gravely, but did not answer; rose and walked indolently up and down to keep himself warm. A lithe, slow figure, a clear face with delicate lips, and careless eyes that saw everything: the face of a man quick to learn, and slow to teach.

" There she comes!" said Knowles, as the lock of the gate rasped.

Holmes had heard the slow step in the snow long before. A small woman came out, and went down the silent street into the road beyond. Holmes kept his back turned to her, lighting his cigar; the other men watched her eagerly.

" What do you think, Vandyke?" demanded Knowles. " How will she do?"

" Do for what?" — resuming his lazy walk. " You talk as if she were a machine. It is the way with modern reformers. Men are so many ploughs and harrows to work on ' the classes.' Do for what?"

Knowles flushed hotly.

" The work the Lord has left for her. Do you mean to say there is none to do, — you, pledged to Missionary labour?"

The young man's face coloured.

" I know this street needs paving terribly, Knowles; but I don't see a boulder in your hands. Yet the great Task-master does not

despise the pavers. He did not give you the
spirit and understanding for paving, eh, is that
it? How do you know He gave this Margret
Howth the spirit and understanding of a reformer? There may be higher work for her to
do."

"Higher!" The old man stood aghast. "I
know your creed, then, — that the true work for
a man or a woman is that which develops their
highest nature?"

Vandyke laughed.

"You have a creed-mania, Knowles. You
have a confession of faith ready-made for everybody, but yourself. I only meant for you to
take care what you do. That woman looks
as the Prodigal Son might have done when
he began to be in want, and would fain have
fed himself with the husks that the swine did
eat."

Knowles got up moodily.

"Whose work is it, then?" he muttered, following the men down the street; for they walked
on. "The world has waited six thousand years
for help. It comes slowly, — slowly, Vandyke;
even through your religion."

The young man did not answer: looked up,
with quiet, rapt eyes, through the silent city,
and the clear gray beyond. They passed a little church lighted up for evening service: as if

to give a meaning to the old man's words, they were chanting the one anthem of the world, the *Gloria in Excelsis.* Hearing the deep organ-roll, the men stopped outside to listen : it heaved and sobbed through the night, as if bearing up to God the wrong of countless aching hearts, then was silent, and a single voice swept over the moors in a long, lamentable cry : — " Thou that takest away the sins of the world, have mercy upon us ! "

The men stood silent, until the hush was broken by a low murmur : — " For Thou only art holy." Holmes had taken off his hat, unconscious that he did it; he put it on slowly, and walked on. What was it that Knowles had said to him once about mean and selfish taints on his divine soul ? " For Thou only art holy :" if there were truth in that!

" How quiet it is ! " he said, as they stopped to leave him. It was, — a breathless quiet; the great streets of the town behind them were shrouded in snow; the hills, the moors, the prairie swept off into the skyless dark, a gray and motionless sea lit by a low watery moon. " The very earth listens," he said.

" Listens for what ? " said the literal old Doctor.

" I think it listens always," said Vandyke, his eye on fire. " For its King — that shall be.

Not as He came before. It has not long to wait now: the New Year is not far off."

" I 've no faith in holding your hands, waiting for it; nor have you either, Charley," growled Knowles. " There 's an infernal lot of work to be done before it comes, I fancy. Here, let me light my cigar."

Holmes bade them good-night, laughing, and struck into the by-road through the hills. He shook hands with Vandyke before he went, — a thing he scarce ever did with anybody. Knowles noticed it, and, after he was out of hearing, mumbled out some sarcasm at " a minister of the gospel consorting with a cold, silent scoundrel like that!" Vandyke listened to his scolding in his usual lazy way, and they went back into town.

The road Holmes took was rutted deep with wagon-wheels, not easily travelled; he walked slowly therefore, being weak, stopping now and then to gather strength. He had not counted the hours until this day, to be balked now by a little loss of blood. The moon was nearly down before he reached the Cloughton hills : he turned there into a narrow path which he remembered well. Now and then he saw the mark of a little shoe in the snow, — looking down at it with a hot panting in his veins, and a strange flash in his eye, as he walked on steadily.

There was a turn in the path at the top of
the hill, a sunken wall, with a broad stone from
which the wind had blown the snow. This
was the place. He sat down on the stone, rest-
ing. Just there she had stood, clutching her
little fingers behind her, when he came up and
threw back her hood to look in her face : how
pale and worn it was, even then ! He had not
looked at her to-night : he would not, if he had
been dying, with those men standing there.
He stood alone in the world with this little
Margret. How those men had carped, and
criticised her, chattered of the duties of her
soul ! Why, it was his, it was his own, softer
and fresher. There was not a glance with
which they followed the weak little body in its
poor dress that he had not seen, and savagely
resented. They measured her strength ? counted
how long the bones and blood would last in
their House of Refuge ? There was not a mor-
sel of her flesh that was not pure and holy in
his eyes. His Margret ? He chafed with an
intolerable fever to make her his, but for one
instant, as she had been once. Now, when it
was too late. For he went back over every
word he had spoken that night, forcing himself
to go through with it, — every cold, poisoned
word. It was a fitting penance. " There is
no such thing as love in real life : " he had told

her that! How he had stood, with all the power of his " divine soul " in his will, and told her, — he, — a man, — that he put away her love from him then, forever! He spared himself nothing, — slurred over nothing; spurned himself, as it were, for the meanness, in which he had wallowed that night. How firm he had been! how kind! how masterful! — pluming himself on his man's strength, while he held her in his power as one might hold an insect, played with her shrinking woman's nature, and trampled it under his feet, coldly and quietly. She was in his way, and he had put her aside. How the fine subtile spirit had risen up out of its agony of shame, and scorned him! How it had flashed from the puny flame standing there in the muddy road despised and jeered at, and calmly judged him! He might go from her as he would, toss her off like a worn-out plaything, but he could not blind her : let him put on what face he would to the world, whether they called him a master among men, or a miser, or, as Knowles did to-night after he turned away, a scoundrel, this girl laid her little hand on his soul with an utter recognition : she alone. " She knew him for a better man than he knew himself that night : " he remembered the words.

The night was growing murky and bitingly cold : there was no prospect on the snow-cov-

ered hills, or the rough road at his feet with
its pools of ice-water, to bring content into his
face, or the dewy light into his eyes; but they
came there, slowly, while he sat thinking. Some
old thought was stealing into his brain, perhaps,
fresh and warm, like a soft spring air, — some
hope of the future, in which this child-woman
came close to him, and near. It was an idle
dream, only would taunt him when it was over,
but he opened his arms to it: it was an old
friend; it had made him once a purer and better man than he could ever be again. A warm,
happy dream, whatever it may have been: the
rugged, sinister face grew calm and sad, as the
faces of the dead change when loving tears fall
on them.

He sighed wearily: the homely little hope
was fanning into life stagnant depths of desire and purpose, stirring his resolute ambition.
Too late? Was it too late? Living or dead
she was his, though he should never see her
face, by some subtile power that had made
them one, he knew not when nor how. He
did not reason now, — abandoned himself, as
morbid men only do, to this delirious hope of
a home, and cheerful warmth, and this woman's love fresh and eternal: a pleasant dream
at first, to be put away at pleasure. But it
grew bolder, touched under-deeps in his nature

of longing and intense passion; all that he knew or felt of power or will, of craving effort, of success in the world, drifted into this dream, and became one with it. He stood up, his vigorous frame starting into a nobler manhood, with the consciousness of right, — with a willed assurance, that, the first victory gained, the others should follow.

It was late; he must go on; he had not meant to sit idling by the road-side. He went through the fields, his heavy step crushing the snow, a dry heat in his blood, his eye intent, still, until he came within sight of the farm-house; then he went on, cool and grave, in his ordinary port.

The house was quite dark; only a light in one of the lower windows, — the library, he thought. The broad field he was crossing sloped down to the house, so that, as he came nearer, he saw the little room quite plainly in the red glow of the fire within, the curtains being undrawn. He had a keen eye; did not fail to see the marks of poverty about the place, the gateless fences, even the bare room with its worn and patched carpet: noted it all with a triumphant gleam of satisfaction. There was a black shadow passing and repassing the windows: he waited a moment looking at it, then came more slowly towards them, intenser heats

10 *

smouldering in his face.   He would not sur-
prise her; she should be as ready as he was
for the meeting.   If she ever put her pure
hand in his again, it should be freely done,
and of her own good-will.

She saw him as he came up on the porch,
and stopped, looking out, as if bewildered, —
then resumed her walk, mechanically.   What
it cost her to see him again he could not tell:
her face did not alter.   It was lifeless and
schooled, the eyes looking straight forward always, indifferently.   Was this his work?   If
he had killed her outright, it would have been
better than this.

The windows were low: it had been his old
habit to go in through them, and he now went
up to one unconsciously.   As he opened it, he
saw her turn away for an instant; then she
waited for him, entirely tranquil, the clear fire
shedding a still glow over the room, no cry or
shiver of pain to show how his coming broke
open the old wound.   She smiled even, when
he leaned against the window, with a careless
welcome.

Holmes stopped, confounded.   It did not suit
him, — this.   If you know a man's nature, you
comprehend why.   The bitterest reproach, or a
proud contempt would have been less galling
than this gentle indifference.   His hold had

slipped from off the woman, he believed. A
moment before he had remembered how he had
held her in his arms, touched her cold lips, and
then flung her off, — he had remembered it,
every nerve shrinking with remorse and unutterable tenderness : now ——! The utter quiet
of her face told more than words could do.
She did not love him ; he was nothing to her.
Then love was a lie. A moment before he
could have humbled himself in her eyes as
low as he lay in his own, and accepted her
pardon as a necessity of her enduring, faithful nature : now, the whole strength of the
man sprang into rage, and mad desire of con-
quest.

He came gravely across the room, holding
out his hand with his old quiet control. She
might be cold and grave as he, but underneath
he knew there was a thwarted, hungry spirit,
— a strong, fine spirit as dainty Ariel. He
would sting it to life, and tame it : it was
his.

"I thought you would come, Stephen," she
said, simply, motioning him to a chair.

Could this automaton be Margret ? He
leaned on the mantel-shelf, looking down with
a cynical sneer.

"Is that the welcome ? Why, there are a
thousand greetings for this time of love and

good words you might have chosen. Besides,
I have come back ill and poor, — a beggar
perhaps. How do women receive such, —
generous women ? Is there no etiquette ?
no hand-shaking ? nothing more ? remembering that I was once — not indifferent to
you."

He laughed. She stood still and grave as
before.

" Why, Margret, I have been down near
death since that night."

He thought her lips grew gray, but she looked
up clear and steady.

" I am glad you did not die. Yes, I can say
that. As for hand-shaking, my ideas may be
peculiar as your own."

" She measures her words," he said, as to
himself; " her very eye-light is ruled by deco-
rum; she is a machine, for work. She has
swept her child's heart clean of anger and revenge, even scorn for the wretch that sold himself for money. There was nothing else to
sweep out, was there ? " — bitterly, — " no
friendships, such as weak women nurse and
coddle into being, — or love, that they live in,
and die for sometimes, in a silly way ? "

" Unmanly ! "

" No, not unmanly. Margret, let us be serious and calm. It is no time to trifle or wear

masks. That has passed between us which leaves no room for sham courtesies."

"There needs none," — meeting his eye unflinchingly. "I am ready to meet you and hear your good-bye. Dr. Knowles told me your marriage was near at hand. I knew you would come, Stephen. You did before."

He winced, — the more that her voice was so clear of pain.

"Why should I come? To show you what sort of a heart I have sold for money? Why, you think you know, little Margret. You can reckon up its deformity, its worthlessness, on your cool fingers. You could tell the serene and gracious lady who is chaffering for it what a bargain she has made, — that there is not in it one spark of manly honour or true love. Don't venture too near it in your coldness and prudence. It has tiger passions I will not answer for. Give me your hand, and feel how it pants like a hungry fiend. It will have food, Margret."

She drew away the hand he grasped, and stood back in the shadow.

"What is it to me?" — in the same measured voice.

Holmes wiped the cold drops from his forehead, a sort of shudder in his powerful frame. He stood a moment looking into the fire, his head dropped on his arm.

"Let it be so," he said at last, quietly. "The worn old heart can gnaw on itself a little longer. I have no mind to whimper over pain."

Something that she saw on the dark sardonic face, as the red gleams lighted it, made her start convulsively, as if she would go to him; then controlling herself, she stood silent. He had not seen the movement, — or, if he saw, did not heed it. He did not care to tame her now. The firelight flashed and darkened, the crackling wood breaking the dead silence of the room.

"It does not matter," he said, raising his head, laying his arm over his strong chest unconsciously, as if to shut in all complaint. "I had an idle fancy that it would be good on this Christmas night to bare the secrets hidden in here to you, — to suffer your pure eyes to probe the sorest depths: I thought perhaps they would have a blessing power. It was an idle fancy. What is my want or crime to you?"

The answer came slowly, but it did come.

"Nothing to me."

She tried to meet the gaunt face looking down on her with its proud sadness, — did meet it at last with her meek eyes.

"No, nothing to you. There is no need that I should stay longer, is there? You made

ready to meet me, and have gone through your
part well."

" It is no part. I speak God's truth to you as
I can."

" I know. There is nothing more for us to
say to each other in this world, then, except
good-night. Words — polite words — are bit-
terer than death, sometimes. If ever we happen to meet, that courteous smile on your face
will be enough to speak — God's truth for you.
Shall we say good-night now ? "

" If you will."

She drew farther into the shadow, leaning on
a chair.

He stopped, some sudden thought striking
him.

" I have a whim," he said, dreamily, " that I
would like to satisfy. It would be a trifle to
you : will you grant it ? — for the sake of some
old happy day, long ago ? "

She put her hand up to her throat; then it
fell again.

" Anything you wish, Stephen," she said,
gravely.

" Yes. Come nearer, then, and let me see
what I have lost. A heart so cold and strong
as yours need not fear inspection. I have a
fancy to look into it, for the last time."

She stood motionless and silent.

" Come," — softly, — "there is no hurt in
your heart that fears detection ? "

She came out into the full light, and stood
before him, pushing back the hair from her
forehead, that he might see every wrinkle, and
the faded, lifeless eyes.   It was a true woman's
motion, remembering even then to scorn decep-
tion.   The light glowed brightly in her face, as
the slow minutes ebbed without a sound : she
only saw his face in shadow, with the fitful
gleam of intolerable meaning in his eyes.   Her
own quailed and fell.

" Does it hurt you that I should even look at
you ? " he said, drawing back.   " Why, even
the sainted dead suffer us to come near them
after they have died to us, — to touch their
hands, to kiss their lips, to find what look
they left in their faces for us.   Be patient, for
the sake of the old time.   My whim is not
satisfied yet."

" I am patient."

" Tell me something of yourself, to take
with me when I go, for the last time.   Shall
I think of you as happy in these days ? "

" I am contented," — the words oozing from
her white lips in the bitterness of truth.   " I
asked God, that night, to show me my work ;
and I think He has shown it to me.   I do not
complain.   It is a great work."

" Is that all ? " he demanded, fiercely.

" No, not all. It pleases me to feel I have a warm home, and to help keep it cheerful. When my father kisses me at night, or my mother says, ' God bless you, child,' I know that is enough, that I ought to be happy."

The old clock in the corner hummed and ticked through the deep silence, like the humble voice of the home she toiled to keep warm, thanking her, comforting her.

" Once more," as the light grew stronger on her face, — " will you look down into your heart that you have given to this great work, and tell me what you see there ? Dare you do it, Margret ? "

" I dare do it," — but her whisper was husky.

" Go on."

He watched her more as a judge would a criminal, as she sat before him : she struggled weakly under the power of his eye, not meeting it. He waited relentless, seeing her face slowly whiten, her limbs shiver, her bosom heave.

" Let me speak for you," he said at last. " I know who once filled your heart to the exclusion of all others : it is no time for mock shame. I know it was my hand that held the very secret of your being. Whatever I may have been, you loved me, Margret. Will you say that now ? "

" I loved you, — once."

Whether it were truth that nerved her, or self-delusion, she was strong now to utter it all.

" You love me no longer, then ? "

" I love you no longer."

She did not look at him ; she was conscious only of the hot fire wearing her eyes, and the vexing click of the clock. After a while he bent over her silently, — a manly, tender presence.

" When love goes once," he said, " it never returns. Did you say it was gone, Margret ? "

One effort more, and Duty would be satisfied.

" It is gone."

In the slow darkness that came to her she covered her face, knowing and hearing nothing. When she looked up, Holmes was standing by the window, with his face toward the gray fields. It was a long time before he turned and came to her.

" You have spoken honestly : it is an old fashion of yours. You believed what you said. Let me also tell you what you call God's truth, for a moment, Margret. It will not do you harm."
— He spoke gravely, solemnly. — " When you loved me long ago, selfish, erring as I was, you fulfilled the law of your nature ; when you put

that love out of your heart, you make your duty
a tawdry sham, and your life a lie. Listen to
me. I am calm."

It was calmness that made her tremble as she
had not done before, with a strange suspicion of
the truth flashing on her. That she, casing herself in her pride, her conscious righteousness,
hugging her new-found philanthropy close, had
sunk to a depth of niggardly selfishness, of
which this man knew nothing. Nobler than
she ; half angry as she felt that, sitting at his
feet, looking up. He knew it, too ; the grave
judging voice told it ; he had taken his rightful
place. Just, as only a man can be, in his judgment of himself and her : her love that she
had prided herself with, seemed weak and
drifting, brought into contact with this cool
integrity of meaning. I think she was glad to
be humbled before him. Women have strange
fancies, sometimes.

" You have deceived yourself," he said: " when
you try to fill your heart with this work, you
serve neither your God nor your fellow-man.
You tell me," stooping close to her, " that I
am nothing to you : you believe it, poor child !
There is not a line on your face that does
not prove it false. I have keen eyes, Margret!"— He laughed. — " You have wrung this
love out of your heart ? If it were easy to do,

did it need to wring with it every sparkle of
pleasure and grace out of your life! Your
very hair is gathered out of your sight: you
feared to remember how my hand had touched
it? Your dress is stingy and hard; your step,
your eyes, your mouth under rule. So hard
it was to force yourself into an old worn-out
woman! Oh, Margret! Margret!"

She moaned under her breath.

" I notice trifles, child! Yonder, in that corner, used to stand the desk where I helped you
with your Latin. How you hated it! Do you
remember?"

" I remember."

" It always stood there: it is gone now.
Outside of the gate there was that elm I planted, and you promised to water while I was
gone. It is cut down now by the roots."

" I had it done, Stephen."

" I know. Do you know why? Because
you love me: because you do not dare to think
of me, you dare not trust yourself to look at the
tree that I had planted."

She started up with a cry, and stood there in
the old way, her fingers catching at each other.

" It is cruel, — let me go!"

" It is not cruel." — He came up closer to her.
— " You think you do not love me, and see
what I have made you! Look at the torpor

of this face, — the dead, frozen eyes! It is a
' nightmare death in life.' Good God, to think
that I have done this! To think of the countless days of agony, the nights, the years of solitude that have brought her to this, — little
Margret!"

He paced the floor, slowly. She sat down
on a low stool, leaning her head on her hands.
The little figure, the bent head, the quivering
chin brought up her childhood to him. She
used to sit so when he had tormented her, waiting to be coaxed back to love and smiles again.
The hard man's eyes filled with tears, as he
thought of it. He watched the deep, tearless
sobs that shook her breast: he had wounded
her to death, — his bonny Margret! She was
like a dead thing now : what need to torture
her longer? Let him be manly and go out to
his solitary life, taking the remembrance of
what he had done with him for company. He
rose uncertainly, — then came to her : was that
the way to leave her?

" I am going, Margret," he whispered, " but
let me tell you a story before I go, — a Christmas story, say. It will not touch you, — it is
too late to hope for that, — but it is right that
you should hear it."

She looked up wearily.

" As you will, Stephen."

Whatever impulse drove the man to speak words that he knew were useless, made him stand back from her, as though she were something he was unfit to touch : the words dragged from him slowly.

"I had a curious dream to-night, Margret, — a waking dream : only a clear vision of what had been once. Do you remember — the old time ?"

What disconnected rambling was this ? Yet the girl understood it, looked into the low fire with sad, listening eyes.

"Long ago. That was a free, strong life that opened before us then, little one, — before you and me ? Do you remember the Christmas before I went away ? I had a strong arm and a hungry brain to go out into the world with, then. Something better, too, I had. A purer self than was born with me came late in life, and nestled in my heart. Margret, there was no fresh loving thought in my brain for God or man that did not grow from my love of you ; there was nothing noble or kindly in my nature that did not flow into that love, and deepen there. I was your master, too. I held my own soul by no diviner right than I held your love and owed you mine. I understand it, now, when it is too late." — He wiped the cold drops from his face. — "Now do you

know whether it is remorse I feel, when I think
how I put this purer self away, — how I went
out triumphant in my inhuman, greedy brain,
— how I resolved to know, to be, to trample
under foot all weak love or homely pleasures?
I have been punished. Let those years go. I
think, sometimes, I came near to the nature of
the damned who dare not love: I would not.
It was then I hurt you, Margret, — to the death:
your true life lay in me, as mine in you."

He had gone on drearily, as though holding
colloquy with himself, as though great years of
meaning surged up and filled the broken words.
It may have been thus with the girl, for her face
deepened as she listened. For the first time for
many long days tears welled up into her eyes,
and rolled between her fingers unheeded.

" I came through the streets to-night baffled
in life, — a mean man that might have been
noble, — all the years wasted that had gone before, — disappointed, — with nothing to hope
for but time to work humbly and atone for the
wrongs I had done. When I lay yonder, my
soul on the coast of eternity, I resolved to atone
for every selfish deed. I had no thought of
happiness ; God knows I had no hope of it. I
had wronged you most: I could not die with
that wrong unforgiven."

" Unforgiven, Stephen ? " she sobbed ; " I for-
gave it long ago."

He looked at her a moment, then by some master effort choked down the word he would have spoken, and went on with his bitter confession.

" I came through the crowded town, a homeless, solitary man, on the Christmas eve when love comes to every man. If ever I had grown sick for a word or touch from the one soul to whom alone mine was open, I thirsted for it then. The better part of my nature was crushed out, and flung away with you, Margret. I cried for it, — I wanted help to be a better, purer man. I need it now. And so," he said, with a smile that hurt her more than tears, " I came to my good angel, to tell her I had sinned and repented, that I had made humble plans for the future, and ask her —— God knows what I would have asked her then! She had forgotten me, — she had another work to do!"

She wrung her hands with a helpless cry. Holmes went to the window : the dull waste of snow looked to him as hopeless and vague as his own life.

" I have deserved it," he muttered to himself. " It is too late to amend."

Some light touch thrilled his arm.

" Is it too late, Stephen ? " whispered a childish voice.

The strong man trembled, looking at the little dark figure standing near him.

" We were both wrong : I have been untrue, selfish. More than you. Stephen, help me to be a better girl; let us be friends again."

She went back unconsciously to the old words of their quarrels long ago. He drew back.

" Do not mock me," he gasped. " I suffer, Margret. Do not mock me with more courtesy."

" I do not ; let us be friends again."

She was crying like a penitent child ; her face was turned away; love, pure and deep, was in her eyes.

The red fire-light grew stronger ; the clock hushed its noisy ticking to hear the story. Holmes's pale lip worked : what was this coming to him ? His breast heaved, a dry heat panted in his veins, his deep eyes flashed fire.

" If my little friend comes to me," he said, in a smothered voice, " there is but one place for her, — her soul with my soul, her heart on my heart." — He opened his arms. — " She must rest her head here. My little friend must be — my wife."

She looked into the strong, haggard face, — a smile crept out on her own, arch and debonair like that of old time.

" I am tired, Stephen," she whispered, and softly laid her head down on his breast.

The red fire-light flashed into a glory of

11

crimson through the room, about the two figures standing motionless there, — shimmered
down into awe-struck shadow : who heeded it ?
The old clock ticked away furiously, as if rejoicing that weary days were over for the pet
and darling of the house : nothing else broke
the silence.   Without, the deep night paused,
gray, impenetrable.   Did it hope that far angel-
voices would break its breathless hush, as once
on the fields of Judea, to usher in Christmas
morn ?   A hush, in air, and earth, and sky, of
waiting hope, of a promised joy.   Down there
in the farm-window two human hearts had
given the joy a name ; the hope throbbed into
being ; the hearts touching each other beat in a
slow, full chord of love as pure in God's eyes
as the song the angels sang, and as sure a promise of the Christ that is to come.   Forever and
ever, — not even death would part them ; he
knew that, holding her closer, looking down
into her face.

What a pale little face it was ?   Through the
intensest heat of his passion the sting touched
him.   Some instinct made her glance up at him,
with a keen insight, seeing the morbid gloom
that was the man's sin, in his face.   She lifted
her head from his breast, and when he stooped
to touch her lips, shook herself free, laughing
carelessly.   Alas, Stephen Holmes ! you will

have little time for morbid questionings in those years to come : her cheerful work has begun : no more self-devouring reveries : your very pauses of silent content and love will be rare and well-earned. No more tranced raptures for to-night, — let to-morrow bring what it would.

" You do not seem to find your purer self altogether perfect ? " she demanded. " I think the pale skin hurts your artistic eye, or the frozen eyes, — which is it ? "

" They have thawed into brilliant fire, — something looks at me half-yielding and half-defiant, — you know that, you vain child ! But, Margret, nothing can atone " ———

He stopped.

" Yes, stop. That is right, Stephen. Remorse grows maudlin when it goes into words," laughing again at his astounded look.

He took her hand, — a dewy, healthy hand, — the very touch of it meant action and life.

" What if I say, then," he said, earnestly, " that I do not find my angel perfect, be the fault mine or hers ? The child Margret, with her sudden tears, and laughter, and angry heats, is gone, — I killed her, I think, — gone long ago. I will not take in place of her this worn, pale ghost, who wears clothes as chilly as if she came from the dead, and stands alone, as ghosts do."

She stood a little way off, her great brown eyes flashing with tears. It was so strange a joy to find herself cared for, when she had believed she was old and hard : the very idle jesting made her youth and happiness real to her. Holmes saw that with his quick tact. He flung playfully a crimson shawl that lay there about her white neck.

" My wife must suffer her life to flush out in gleams of colour and light: her cheeks must hint at a glow within, as yours do now. I will have no hard angles, no pallor, no uncertain memory of pain in her life : it shall be perpetual summer."

He loosened her hair, and it rolled down about the bright, tearful face, shining in the red fire-light like a mist of tawny gold.

" I need warmth and freshness and light : my wife shall bring them to me. She shall be no strong-willed reformer, standing alone : a sovereign lady with kind words for the world, who gives her hand only to that man whom she trusts, and keeps her heart and its secrets for me alone."

She paid no heed to him other than by a deepening colour ; the clock, however, grew tired of the long soliloquy, and broke in with an asthmatic warning as to the time of night.

" There is midnight," she said. " You shall

go, now, Stephen Holmes, — quick ! before
your sovereign lady fades, like Cinderella, into grayness and frozen eyes!"

When he was gone, she knelt down by her
window, remembering that night long ago, —
free to sob and weep out her joy, — very sure
that her Master had not forgotten to hear even
a woman's prayer, and to give her her true work,
— very sure, — never to doubt again.   There
was a dark, sturdy figure pacing up and down the
road, that she did not see.   It was there when
the night was over, and morning began to dawn.
Christmas morning! he remembered, — it was
something to him now!   Never again a homeless, solitary man!   You would think the man
weak, if I were to tell you how this word
" home " had taken possession of him, — how
he had planned out work through the long
night : success to come, but with his wife
nearest his heart, and the homely farm-house,
and the old school-master in the centre of the
picture.   Such an humble castle in the air!
Christmas morning was surely something to
him.   Yet, as the night passed, he went back
to the years that had been wasted, with an
unavailing bitterness.   He would not turn from
the truth, that, with his strength of body and
brain to command happiness and growth, his
life had been a failure.   I think it was first on

that night that the story of the despised Nazarene came to him with a new meaning, — One
who came to gather up these broken fragments
of lives and save them with His own. But
vaguely, though: Christmas-day as yet was to
him the day when love came into the world.
He knew the meaning of that. So he watched
with an eagerness new to him the day-breaking.
He could see Margret's window, and a dim light
in it: she would be awake, praying for him,
no doubt. He pondered on that. Would you
think Holmes weak, if he forsook the faith of
Fichte, sometime, led by a woman's hand?
Think of the apostle of the positive philoso-
phers, and say no more. He could see a flickering light at dawn crossing the hall: he remembered the old school-master's habit well, — calling
" Happy Christmas " at every door: he meant
to go down there for breakfast, as he used to
do, imagining how the old man would wring his
hands, with a " Holloa! you 're welcome home,
Stephen, boy! " and Mrs. Howth would bring
out the jars of pine-apple preserve which her
sister sent her every year from the West Indies.
And then —— Never mind what then. Stephen
Holmes was very much in love, and this Christmas-day had much to bring him. Yet it was
with a solemn shadow on his face that he
watched the dawn, showing that he grasped

the awful meaning of this day that "brought love into the world." Through the clear, frosty night he could hear a low chime of distant bells shiver the air, hurrying faint and far to tell the glad tidings. He fancied that the dawn flushed warm to hear the story, — that the very earth should rejoice in its frozen depths, if it were true. If it were true! — if this passion in his heart were but a part of an all-embracing power, in whose clear depths the world struggled vainly! — if it were true that this Christ did come to make that love clear to us! There would be some meaning then in the old school-master's joy, in the bells wakening the city yonder, in even poor Lois's thorough content in this day, — for it would be, he knew, a thrice happy day to her. A strange story that of the Child coming into the world, — simple! He thought of it, watching, through his cold, gray eyes, how all the fresh morning told it, — it was in the very air; thinking how its echo stole through the whole world, — how innumerable children's voices told it in eager laughter, — how even the lowest slave half-smiled, on waking, to think it was Christmas-day, the day that Christ was born. He could hear from the church on the hill that they were singing again the old song of the angels. Did this matter to him? Did not he care, with the new throb in his heart, who was born this day? There is no smile on his face as he listens to the words, " Glory to God in the highest, and on earth peace, good-will toward men;" it bends lower, — lower only. But in his soul-lit eyes there are warm tears, and on his worn face a sad and solemn joy.

CHAPTER XI.

I AM going to end my story now. There are phases more vivid in the commonplace lives of these men and women, I do not doubt: love, as poignant as pain in its joy; crime, weak and foul and foolish, like all crime; silent self-sacrifices: but I leave them for you to paint; you will find colours enough in your own house and heart.

As for Christmas-day, neither you nor I need try to do justice to that theme: how the old school-master went about, bustling, his thin face quite hot with enthusiasm, and muttering, " God bless my soul!" — hardly recovered from the sudden delight of finding his old pupil waiting for him when he went down in the morning; how he insisted on being led by him, and nobody else, all day, and before half an hour had confided, under solemn pledges of secrecy, the great project of the book about Bertrand de Born ; how even easy Mrs. Howth found her hospitable Virginian blood in a glow at the unexpected breakfast-guest, — settling into more confident pleasure as dinner came on, for which success

11 *

was surer; how cold it was, outside; how Joel
piled on great fires, and went off on some mysterious errand, having " other chores to do than
idling and duddering; " how the day rose into
a climax of perfection at dinner-time, to Mrs.
Howth's mind, — the turkey being done to a
delicious brown, the plum-pudding quivering
like luscious jelly (a Christian dinner to-day, if
we starve the rest of the year!). Even Dr.
Knowles, who brought a great bouquet out for
the school-master, was in an unwonted good-
humour; and Mr. Holmes, of whom she stood a
little in dread, enjoyed it all with such zest,
and was so attentive to them all, but Margret.
They hardly spoke to each other all day; it
quite fretted the old lady; indeed, she gave the
girl a good scolding about it out in the pantry,
until she was ready to cry. She had looked
that way all day, however.

Knowles was hurt deep enough when he saw
Holmes, and suspected the worst, under all his
good-humour. It was a bitter disappointment to
give up the girl; for, beside the great work, he
loved her in an uncouth fashion, and hated
Holmes. He met her alone in the morning;
but when he saw how pale she grew, expecting
his outbreak, and how she glanced timidly in
at the room where Stephen was, he relented.
Something in the wet brown eye perhaps re-

called a forgotten dream of his boyhood; for
he sighed sharply, and did not swear as he
meant to. All he said was, that " women will
be women, and that she had a worse job on her
hands than the House of Refuge," — which she
put down to the account of his ill-temper, and
only laughed, and made him shake hands.

Lois and her father came out in the old cart
in high state across the bleak, snowy hills, quite
aglow with all they had seen at the farm-houses
on the road. Margret had arranged a settle for
the sick girl by the kitchen-fire, but they all
came out to speak to her.

As for the dinner, it was the essence of all
Christmas dinners: Dickens himself, the priest
of the genial day, would have been contented.
The old school-master and his wife had hearts
big and warm enough to do the perpetual hon-
ours of a baronial castle; so you may know how
the little room and the faces about the homely
table glowed and brightened. Even Knowles
began to think that Holmes might not be so
bad, after all, recalling the chicken in the mill,
and, — " Well, it was better to think well of all
men, poor devils!"

I am sorry to say there was a short thunder-
storm in the very midst of the dinner. Knowles
and Mr. Howth, in their anxiety to keep off
from ancient subjects of dispute, came, for

a wonder, on modern politics, and of course
there was a terrible collision, which made Mrs.
Howth quite breathless: it was over in a minute, however, and it was hard to tell which was
the most repentant. Knowles, as you know,
was a disciple of Garrison, and the old school-
master was a States'-rights man, as you might
suppose from his antecedents, — suspected, indeed, of being a contributor to " DeBow's Review." I may as well come out with the whole
truth, and acknowledge that at the present writing the old gentleman is the very hottest Se-
cessionist I know. If it hurts the type, write it
down a vice of blood, O printers of New England!

The dinner, perhaps, was fresher and heartier
after that. Then Knowles went back to town ;
and in the middle of the afternoon, as it grew
dusk, Lois started, knowing how many would
come into her little shanty in the evening to wish
her Happy Christmas, although it was over. They
piled up comforts and blankets in the cart, and
she lay on them quite snugly, her scarred child's-
face looking out from a great woollen hood Mrs.
Howth gave her. Old Yare held Barney, with
his hat in his hand, looking as if he deserved
hanging, but very proud of the kindness they all
showed his girl. Holmes gave him some money
for a Christmas gift, and he took it, eagerly

enough. For some unexpressed reason, they stood a long time in the snow bidding Lois good-bye; and for the same reason, it may be, she was loath to go, looking at each one earnestly as she laughed and grew red and pale answering them, kissing Mrs. Howth's hand when she gave it to her. When the cart did drive away, she watched them standing there until she was out of sight, and waved her scrap of a handkerchief; and when the road turned down the hill, lay down and softly cried to herself.

Now that they were alone they gathered close about the fire, while the day without grew gray and colder, — Margret in her old place by her father's knee. Some dim instinct had troubled the old man all day; it did now : whenever Margret spoke, he listened eagerly, and forgot to answer sometimes, he was so lost in thought. At last he put his hand on her head, and whispered, " What ails my little girl ? " And then his little girl sobbed and cried, as she had been ready to do all day, and kissed his trembling hand, and went and hid on her mother's neck, and left Stephen to say everything for her. And I think you and I had better come away.

It was quite dark before they had done talking, — quite dark ; the wood-fire had charred down into a great bed of crimson ; the tea stood till it grew cold, and no one drank it.

The old man got up at last, and Holmes led
him to the library, where he smoked every
evening. He held Maggie, as he called her, in
his arms a long time, and wrung Holmes's
hand. "God bless you, Stephen!" he said, —
"this is a very happy Christmas-day to me."
And yet, sitting alone, the tears ran over his
wrinkled face as he smoked; and when his
pipe went out, he did not know it, but sat
motionless. Mrs. Howth, fairly confounded by
the shock, went up-stairs, and stayed there a
long time. When she came down, the old
lady's blue eyes were tenderer, if that were possible, and her face very pale. She went into
the library and asked her husband if she did
n't prophesy this two years ago, and he said
she did, and after a while asked her if she remembered the barbecue-night at Judge Clapp's
thirty years ago. She blushed at that, and then
went up and kissed him. She had heard Joel's
horse clattering up to the kitchen-door, so con-
cluded she would go out and scold him. Under
the circumstances it would be a relief.

If Mrs. Howth's nerves had been weak, she
might have supposed that free-born serving-
man seized with sudden insanity, from the
sight that met her, going into the kitchen.
His dinner, set on the dresser, was flung contemptuously on the ashes; a horrible cloud of

burning grease rushed from a dirty pint-pot on
the table, and before this Joel was capering and
snorting like some red-headed Hottentot before
his fetich, occasionally sticking his fingers into
the nauseous stuff, and snuffing it up as if it
were roses.   He was a church-member : he
could *not* be drunk ?   At the sight of her, he
tried to regain the austere dignity usual to him
when women were concerned, but lapsed into
an occasional giggle, which spoiled the effect.

" Where have you been," she inquired, se-
verely, " scouring the country like a heathen
on this blessed day ?   And what is that you
have burning ?   You 're disgracing the house,
and strangers in it."

Joel's good-humour was proof against even
this.

" I 've scoured to some purpose, then.   Dun't
tell the mester : it 'll muddle his brains t'-night.
Wait till mornin'.   Squire More 'll be down his-
self t' 'xplain."

He rubbed the greasy fingers into his hair,
while Mrs. Howth's eyes were fixed in dumb
perplexity.

" Ye see," — slowly, determined to make it
clear to her now and forever, — "it 's water : no,
t' a'n't water : it 's troubled me an' Mester
Howth some time in Poke Run, atop o' 't.   I
hed my suspicions, — so 'd he ; lay low, though,

frum all women-folks. So 's I tuk a bottle
down, unbeknown, to Squire More, an' it 's oil!"
— jumping like a wild Indian, — " thank the
Lord fur his marcies, it 's oil!"

" Well, Joel," she said, calmly, " very disa-
greeable smelling oil it is, I must say."

" Good save the woman!" he broke out, *sotto
voce*, " she 's a born natural! Did ye never
hear of a shaft? or millions o' gallons a day?
It 's better nor a California ranch, I tell ye.
Mebbe," charitably, " ye did n't know Poke
Run 's the mester's?"

" I certainly do. But I do not see what this
green ditch-water is to me. And I think,
Joel," ——

" It 's more to ye nor all yer States'-rights as
I 'm sick o' hearin' of. It 's carpets, an' bun-
nets, an' slithers of railroad-stock, an' some
colour on Margot's cheeks, — ye 'ed best think
o' that! That 's what it is to ye! I 'm goin'
to take stock myself. I 'm glad that gell 'll git
rest frum her mills an' her Houses o' Deviltry,
— she 's got gumption fur a dozen women."

He went on muttering, as he gathered up his
pint-pot and bottle, —

" I 'm goin' to send my Tim to college soon 's
the thing 's in runnin' order. Lord! what a
lawyer that boy 'll make!"

Mrs. Howth's brain was still muddled.

" You are better pleased than you were at Lincoln's election," she observed, placidly.

" Politics be darned!" he broke out, forgetting the teachings of Mr. Clinche. " Now, Mem, dun't ye muddle the mester's brain t'-night wi' 't, I say. I 'm goin' t' 'xperiment myself a bit."

Which he did, accordingly, — shutting himself up in the smoke-house and burning the compound in divers sconces and Wide-Awake torches, giving up the entire night to his diabolical orgies.

Mrs. Howth did not tell the master ; for one reason : it took a long time for so stupendous an idea to penetrate the good lady's brain ; and for another : her motherly heart was touched by another story than this Aladdin's lamp of Joel's wherein burned petroleum. She watched from her window until she saw Holmes crossing the icy road : there was a little bitterness, I confess, in the thought that he had taken her child from her ; but the prayer that rose for them both took her whole woman's heart with it.

The road was rough over the hills ; the wind that struck Holmes's face bitingly keen : perhaps the life coming for him would be as cold a struggle, having not only poverty to conquer, but himself. But he is a strong man, — no stronger

puts his foot down with cool, resolute tread; and
to-night there is a thrill on his lips that never
rested there before, — a kiss, dewy and warm.
Something, some new belief, too, stirs in his
heart, like a subtile atom of pure fire, that he
hugs closely, — his for all time. No poverty or
death shall ever drive it away. Perhaps he en-
tertains an angel unaware.

After that night Lois never left her little
shanty. The days that followed were like one
long Christmas; for her poor neighbors, black
and white, had some plot among themselves,
and worked zealously to make them seem so to
her. It was easy to make these last days happy for the simple little soul who had always
gathered up every fragment of pleasure in her
featureless life, and made much of it, and re-
joiced over it. She grew bewildered, sometimes, lying on her wooden settle by the fire;
people had always been friendly, taken care of
her, but now they were eager in their kindness,
as though the time were short. She did not
understand the reason, at first; she did not
want to die: yet if it hurt her, when it grew
clear at last, no one knew it; it was not her
way to speak of pain. Only, as she grew
weaker, day by day, she began to set her house
in order, as one might say, in a quaint, almost
comical fashion, giving away everything she

owned, down to her treasures of colored bottles and needle-books, mending her father's
clothes, and laying them out in her drawers;
lastly, she had Barney brought in from the
country, and every day would creep to the
window to see him fed and chirrup to him,
whereat the poor old beast would look up with
his dim eye, and try to neigh a feeble answer.
Kitts used to come every day to see her, though
he never said much when he was there : he lug-
ged his great copy of the Venus del Pardo along
with him one day, and left it, thinking she would
like to look at it; Knowles called it trash, when
he came. The Doctor came always in the morning ; he told her he would read to her one day,
and did it always afterwards, putting on his
horn spectacles, and holding her old Bible close
up to his rugged, anxious face. He used to
read most from the Gospel of St. John. She
liked better to hear him than any of the others,
even than Margret, whose voice was so low and
tender: something in the man's half-savage nature was akin to the child's.

As the day drew near when she was to go,
every pleasant trifle seemed to gather a deeper,
solemn meaning. Jenny Balls came in one
night, and old Mrs. Polston.

" We thought you 'd like to see her weddin'-
dress, Lois," said the old woman, taking off

Jenny's cloak, " seein' as the weddin' was to
hev been to-morrow, and was put off on 'count
of you."

Lois did like to see it ; sat up, her face quite
flushed to see how nicely it fitted, and stroked
back Jenny's soft hair under the veil. And
Jenny, being a warm-hearted little thing, broke
into a sobbing fit, saying that it spoiled it all
to have Lois gone.

" Don't muss your veil, child," said Mrs. Polston.

But Jenny cried on, hiding her face in Lois's
skinny hand, until Sam Polston came in, when
she grew quiet and shy. The poor deformed
girl lay watching them, as they talked. Very
pretty Jenny looked, with her blue eyes and
damp pink cheeks ; and it was a manly, grave
love in Sam's face, when it turned to her. A
different love from any she had known : better,
she thought. It could not be helped ; but it
was better.

After they were gone, she lay a long time
quiet, with her hand over her eyes. Forgive
her ! she, too, was a woman. Ah, it may be
there are more wrongs that shall be righted
yonder in the To-Morrow than are set down in
your theology !

And so it was, that, as she drew nearer to
this To-Morrow, the brain of the girl grew

clearer, — struggling, one would think, to shake
off whatever weight had been put on it by blood
or vice or poverty, and become itself again.
Perhaps, even in her cheerful, patient life, there
had been hours when she had known the wrongs
that had been done her, known how cruelly the
world had thwarted her ; her very keen insight
into whatever was beautiful or helpful may
have made her see her own mischance, the
blank she had drawn in life, more bitterly.
She did not see it bitterly now. Death is honest ; all things grew clear to her, going down
into the valley of the shadow ; so, wakening to
the consciousness of stifled powers and ungiven
happiness, she saw that the fault was not hers,
nor His who had appointed her lot; He had
helped her to bear it, — bearing worse himself.
She did not say once, " I might have been,"
but day by day, more surely, " I shall be."
There was not a tear on the homely faces turning from her bed, not a tint of colour in the
flowers they brought her, not a shiver of light
in the ashy sky, that did not make her more
sure of that which was to come. More loving
she grew, as she went away from them, the
touch of her hand more pitiful, her voice more
tender, if such a thing could be, — with a look
in her eyes never seen there before. Old Yare
pointed it out to Mrs. Polston one day.

" My girl 's far off frum us," he said, sobbing
in the kitchen, — " my girl 's far off now."

It was the last night of the year that she
died.   She was so much better that they all
were quite cheerful.   Kitts went away as it
grew dark, and she bade him wrap up his
throat with such a motherly dogmatism that
they all laughed at her ; she, too, with the rest.

" I 'll make you a New-Year's call," he said,
going out; and she called out that she should
be sure to expect him.

She seemed so strong that Holmes and Mrs.
Polston and Margret, who were there, were
going home; besides, old Yare said, " I 'd like
to take care o' my girl alone to-night, ef yoh 'd
let me," — for they had not trusted him before.
But Lois asked them not to go until the Old
Year was over; so they waited down-stairs.

The old man fell asleep, and it was near midnight when he wakened with a cold touch on
his hand.

" It 's come, father ! "

He started up with a cry, looking at the new
smile in her eyes, grown strangely still.

" Call them all, quick, father ! "

Whatever was the mystery of death that met
her now, her heart clung to the old love that had
been true to her so long.

He did not move.

"Let me hev yoh to myself, Lo, 't th' last; yoh're all I hev; let me hev yoh 't th' last."

It was a bitter disappointment, but she roused herself even then to smile, and tell him yes, cheerfully. You call it a trifle, nothing? It may be; yet I think the angels looking down had tears in their eyes, when they saw the last trial of the unselfish, solitary heart, and kept for her a different crown from his who conquers a city.

The fire-light grew warmer and redder; her eyes followed it, as if all that had been bright and kindly in her life were coming back in it. She put her hand on her father, trying vainly to smooth his gray hair. The old man's heart smote him for something, for his sobs grew louder, and he left her a moment; then she saw them all, faces very dear to her even then. She laughed and nodded to them all in the old childish way; then her lips moved. "It's come right!" she tried to say; but the weak voice would never speak again on earth.

"It's the turn o' the night," said Mrs. Polston, solemnly; "lift her head; the Old Year's goin' out."

Margret lifted her head, and held it on her breast. She could hear cries and sobs; the faces, white now, and wet, pressed nearer, yet fading slowly: it was the Old Year going out,

the worn-out year of her life. Holmes opened
the window : the cold night-wind rushed in,
bearing with it snatches of broken harmony :
some idle musician down in the city, playing
fragments of some old, sweet air, heavy with
love and regret. It may have been chance : yet,
let us think it was not chance; let us believe
that He, who had made the world warm and
happy for her, chose that this best voice of all
should bid her good-bye at the last.

So the Old Year went out in that music.
The dull eyes, loving to the end, wandered
vaguely as the sounds died away, as if losing
something, — losing all, suddenly. She sighed
as the clock struck, and then a strange calm,
unknown before, stole over her face ; her eyes
flashed open with a living joy. Margret stooped
to close them, kissing the cold lids ; and Tiger,
who had climbed upon the bed, whined and
crept down.

" It is the New Year," said Holmes, bending
his head.

The cripple was dead ; but *Lois*, free, loving,
and beloved, trembled from her prison to her
Master's side in the To-Morrow.

I can show you her grave out there in the
hills, — a short, stunted grave, like a child's.
No one goes there, although there are many
firesides where they speak of " Lois " softly,

as of something holy and dear: but they think of her always as not there; as gone home; even old Yare looks up, when he talks of " my girl." Yet, knowing that nothing in God's just universe is lost, or fails to meet the late fulfilment of its hope, I like to think of her poor body lying there: I like to believe that the great mother was glad to receive the form that want and crime of men had thwarted, — took her uncouth child home again, that had been so cruelly wronged, — folded it in her warm bosom with tender, palpitating love.

It pleased me in the winter months to think that the worn-out limbs, the old scarred face of Lois rested, slept: crumbled into fresh atoms, woke at last with a strange sentience, and, when God smiled permission through the summer sun, flashed forth in a wild ecstasy of the true beauty that she loved so well. In no questioning, sad pallor of sombre leaves or gray lichens: throbbed out rather in answering crimsons, in lilies, white, exultant in a chordant life!

Yet, more than this: I strive to grope, with dull, earthy sense, at her freed life in that earnest land where souls forget to hunger or to hope, and learn to be. And so thinking, the certainty of her aim and work and love yonder comes with a new, vital reality, beside which the story

12

of the yet living men and women of whom I
have told you grows vague and incomplete,
like unguessed riddles. I have no key to solve
them with, — no right to solve them.

My story is but a mere groping hint? It
lacks determined truth, a certain yea and nay?
It has no conduit of God's justice running
through it, awarding apparent good and ill?
I know : it is a story of To-Day. The Old
Year is on us yet. Poor old Knowles will
tell you it is a dark day ; bewildered at the inexplicable failure of the cause for which his old
blood ran like water that dull morning at Ball's
Bluff. He doubts everything in the bitterness
of wasted effort ; doubts sometimes, even, if
the very flag he fights for, be not the symbol of
a gigantic selfishness : if the Wrong he calls
his enemy, have not caught a certain truth to
give it strength. A dark day, he tells you :
that the air is filled with the cry of the slave,
and of nations going down into darkness, their
message untold, their work undone : that now,
as eighteen centuries ago, the Helper stands
unwelcome in the world ; that your own heart,
as well as the great humanity, asks an unren-
dered justice. Does he utter all the problem
of To-Day. Vandyke, standing higher, perhaps,
or, at any rate, born with hopefuller brain,

would show you how, by the very instant peril
of the hour, is lifted clearer into view the
eternal prophecy of coming content : could tell
you that the unquiet earth, and the unanswer-
ing heaven are instinct with it : that the un-
granted prayer of your own life should teach it
to you : that in that Book wherein God has
not scorned to write the history of America, he
finds the quiet surety that the rescue of the
world is near at hand.

Holmes, like most men who make destiny,
does not pause in his cool, slow work for'their
prophecy or lamentation. " Such men will
mould the age," old Knowles says, drearily,
for he does not like Holmes: follows him unwillingly, even knowing him nearer the truth
than he. " Born for mastership, as I told you
long ago: they strike the blow, while ———.
I 'm tired of theorists, exponents of the abstract
right : your Hamlets, and your Sewards, that
let occasion slip until circumstance or — mobs
drift them as they will."

But Knowles's growls are unheeded, as usual.

What is this To-Day to Margret ? She has
no prophetic insight, cares for none, I am afraid:
the common things of every-day wear their old
faces to her, dear and real. Her haste is too
eager to allay the pain about her, her husband's
touch too strong and tender, the Master beside

her too actual a presence, for her to waste her life in visions. Something of Lois's live, universal sympathy has come into her narrow, intenser nature; through its one love, it may be. What is To-Morrow until it comes? This moment the evening air thrills with a purple of which no painter as yet has caught the tint, no poet the meaning; no silent face passes her on the street on which a human voice might not have charm to call out love and power: the Helper yet waits near her. Here is work, life: the Old Year you despise holds beauty, pain, content yet unmastered: let us leave Margret to master them.

It does not satisfy you? Child-souls, you tell me, like that of Lois, may find it enough to hold no past and no future, to accept the work of each moment, and think it no wrong to drink every drop of its beauty and joy: we, who are wiser, laugh at them. It may be: yet I say unto you, their angels only do always behold the face of our Father in the New Year.

THE END.

NOTES TO THE TEXT OF *MARGRET HOWTH* BY JEAN FAGAN YELLIN

P. 17, line 28: Arians, Calvinists: the Arian doctrine holds that the Son is not the same substance as the Father, but was made as an agent for creating the world; Calvinist thought emphasizes the sovereignty of God and the doctrine of predestination. That they worshipped together signifies that the chapel in the country tolerated diverse beliefs.

P. 23, line 12: Bysshe Shelley: Percy Bysshe Shelley (1792–1822) was an English romantic poet.

P. 24, lines 14–15: Phalanstery or Community: A Fourierist cooperative community was called a Phalanstery. Brook Farm, the best known cooperative community, was for a time organized on Fourierist principles.

P. 25, line 4: Cornwallis: British Gen. Charles Cornwallis (1738–1805) surrendered to Washington and Lafayette at Yorktown, ending the Revolutionary War.

P. 27, line 10: Comte: Auguste Comte (1798–1857) was a French mathematician and philosopher.

P. 28, lines 6–7: Jeffersonian Democracy, Federalism: During the post-Revolutionary period, Jeffersonian Democracy advocated states' rights and a strict interpretation of the Constitution, individual liberties, and the primacy of agrarian life; Federalists advocated a strong federal government and a liberal interpretation of Constitutional powers.

P. 28, lines 22–23: Abraham, Dives: See Luke 16: 19–31.

P. 29, line 14: Abolitionist, Fourierite: An Abolitionist supported the abolition of slavery; a Fourierite was a

follower of French sociologist and reformer Francois Marie
Charles Fourier (1772–1827).

P. 30, line 20: Spinoza, Fichte, Saint Simon: The Dutch
Jewish philosopher Baruch Spinoza (1632–1677) anticipated
the school of historical criticism and argued that through
knowledge, man can free himself of bondage to his emotions; Spinoza's thought influenced the German poet and
dramatist Johann Wolfgang von Goethe (1749–1832). The
German philosopher Johann Gottlieb Fichte (1762–1814)
was an important influence on the development of German
romanticism. Comte de Claude Henri Saint-Simon
(1760–1825) was a French socialistic reformer.

P. 35, lines 13–14: *"io non averei creduto, che [vita] tanta
n' avesse disfatta"*: "I should never have believed that death
had undone so many" is taken from Dante's *Inferno*
3.56–57.

P. 35, line 30: *"Onorate l'altissimo poeta!"*: "Honor the
great poet" is quoted from Dante's *Inferno* 4.80.

P. 39, line 6: Tintoret, Copley: Italian Jacopo Robusti Tin-
toretto (1518–1594) and American John Singleton Copley
(1738–1815) were master painters.

P. 71, lines 20–21: Could it be that the blood of these her
brothers called against *her* from the ground?: The reference
is to Genesis 4:10.

P. 72, line 2: Was she her brother's keeper?: See Genesis
4:9.

P. 86, line 20: Carlyle: Thomas Carlyle (1795–1881) was a
Scottish essayist and historian.

P. 137, lines 29–30: "King Cophetua and the Beggar
Maid": The legend of King Cophetua who married the beg-
gar maid Phenelophon is the subject of Tennyson's poem
"The Beggar Maid."

P. 149, lines 24–25: States'-Rights doctrine, Chicago Platform: The doctrine of states' rights was invoked by the
secessionists; the Chicago Platform was adopted by the

Republican Convention, held at Chicago, that nominated Abraham Lincoln for president in 1860.

P. 151, lines 8–9: *"Tu es Petrus, et super hanc"*: "You are Peter and upon this": See Matthew 16:18.

P. 153, lines 28–29: "He that is without sin among you, let him first cast a stone at her": See John 8:7.

P. 160, line 15: *"Ohne Hast, aber ohne Rast"*: "Without haste, but without rest."

P. 161, lines 13–14: *"Der Allumfasser, der Allerhalter, fasst und erhalt er nicht, dich, mich, sich selbst?"*: "The All-embracing, the All-sustaining, does he not embrace and sustain you, me, and Himself?"

P. 161, lines 20–21: Faust's ... Margret: The protagonist of *Faust* of the German poet Goethe (1749–1832) destroys innocent Gretchen, who loves him.

P. 179, line 18: Positive Philosophy: Positivists argue that positive knowledge is based on natural phenomena and their properties and relations, as verified empirically.

P. 186, lines 4–5: slough of disappointment: The reference is to John Bunyan's (1628–1688) *Pilgrim's Progress.*

P. 198, lines 2–5: the angel of death came again to pass over the land, and there was no blood on any door-post to keep him from that house: See Exodus 12: 12, 13.

P. 200, lines 1–3: Bell, Lincoln, Carolina out: John Bell (1797–1869) was the 1860 presidential nominee of the Constitutional Union party; Abraham Lincoln (1809–1865) was the successful Republican candidate; South Carolina seized Fort Sumter from the Union on April 12, 1861 and seceded shortly afterward.

P. 247, line 25: Bertrand de Born: Bertrand de Born (1140–c. 1209) was a French troubadour and warrior; Dante mentions him in the *Inferno*, 28.

P. 249, line 15: Dickens: Charles Dickens (1812–1870) was an English novelist.

P. 250, lines 6–10: Garrison, a States'-rights man,

"DeBow's Review": William Lloyd Garrison (1805–1879) was the leading American abolitionist; states' rights was the doctrine of the secessionists; *DeBow's Review* (1846–1880) was a monthly magazine that championed slavery.

AFTERWORD

For her first novel, which we now know as *Margret Howth*, Rebecca Harding chose the title "The Deaf and the Dumb." Although the thirty-year-old author set her story in Indiana, she describes her hometown of Wheeling, Virginia. The time is now, 1861, and the Union is in danger. The problem is not, however, slavery, secession, and civil war. Instead, the book considers whether American democracy can survive the effects of urban industrialization. Raising the extraordinary voice Harding had sounded in "Life in the Iron Mills," *Margret Howth* critiques both emerging industrial capitalism and genteel American literature. But Harding's book also demonstrates the consequences of a young writer trimming her work to conform to the requirements of the literary establishment. The transformation of the despairing "The Deaf and the Dumb" into the affirmative "A Story of To-Day" (later renamed *Margret Howth: A Story of To-Day*) charts the "feminization" of a text by a woman writer and helps explain the gaps in that text, the ubiquity of patriarchy's True Woman in American fiction, and Rebecca Harding's subsequent success as a popular writer.[1]

In the absence of Harding's original text, the only version that we have is "A Story of To-Day," which she rewrote and serialized in the *Atlantic Monthly,* then published as *Margret Howth.* Here, in her first novel, the young writer pursues the innovative literary project she had inaugurated in "Life in the Iron Mills." Then she had written:

> I want you to hide your disgust, take no heed of your clean clothes, and come right down with me,—here, into the thickest of the fog and mud and foul effluvia. I want you to hear this story. There is a secret down here. . . . I will tell you plainly that I have a great hope; and I bring it to you to be tested. It is this: that this terrible dumb question is its own reply . . . the most solemn prophecy which the world has known of the Hope to Come. (*LIIM,* 13–14)

Now, she again challenges her reader:

> I want you to dig into this commonplace, this vulgar American life, and see what is in it. Sometimes I think it has a new and awful significance that we do not see. (P. 6)

Although Harding was writing her "Story of To-Day" as the Civil War began, she demands that her reader consider not politics, but economics, not the struggle for the Union, but the struggle

> for bread and butter. I want you to go down into this common, every-day drudgery, and consider if there might not be in it also a great warfare. Not a serfish war; not altogether ignoble, though even its only end may appear to be your daily food. A great warfare, I think, with a history as old as the world, and not

without its pathos. It has its slain. Men and women, lean-jawed, crippled in the slow, silent battle, are in your alleys, sit beside you at your table; its martyrs sleep under every green hill-side. (Pp. 6–7)

Unlike the later turn-of-the-century realists such as Upton Sinclair, and unlike the still later proletarian writers of the 1930s, Harding does not present her treatment of economic problems in America within the framework of a political program for social change.[2] Instead, she proposes spiritual solutions. Harding's narrator views her untraditional subject from the perspective of post-Calvinist Christianity: Even in these desperate times, she writes, "The voice of the meek Nazarene, which we have deafened down as ill-timed, unfit to teach the watchword of the hour, renews the quiet promise of its coming in simple, humble things" (p. 4).

When Harding wrote these words in 1861, clearly she had decided to create a new kind of fiction. At the beginning of *Margret Howth,* she announces:

My story is very crude and homely, as I said—only a rough sketch of one or two of those people whom you see every day, and call "dregs," sometimes—a dull, plain bit of prose, such as you might pick for yourself out of any of these ware-houses or back-streets. (P. 6)

Later, she explains her literary program:

I live in the commonplace. Once or twice I have rashly tried my hand at dark conspiracies, and women rare and radiant in Italian bowers; but I have a friend who is sure to say, "Try and tell us about the butcher next

door, my dear," . . . I must show men and women as
they are in that especial State of the Union where I
live. (Pp. 102–5)

Readers immediately recognized the importance of
Harding's new discourse and the significance, in
Margret Howth, of the glimpses of waged labor
—Margret's office drudgery, Lois's recollections of
her childhood in "th' shadders o' th' looms" (p. 69),
and Yare's presence among the "red-faced and pale,
whiskey-bloated and heavy-brained, Irish, Dutch,
black" porters (p. 16). A half-century ago, critics
noted that Harding had revealed the "fictional
possibilities in people who had been presumed to be
inarticulate, or whom economic or social oppression
had submerged";[3] that, "Russian-like in their grim
and sordid realism," Harding's early works represent
"distinct landmarks in the evolution of American fiction."[4] More recently, literary historians concurred
that "Mrs. Davis . . . pioneered in . . . the literature of
industrialism, critically concerned with contemporary
social problems, which would ultimately give rise to
American naturalism";[5] that she "presented the sordid side of midcentury America as no one else. . . ."[6]
Within the past decade, spurred by Tillie Olsen's
homage to Rebecca Harding Davis in the Feminist
Press edition of "Life in the Iron Mills," they have
reiterated that she "introduced the industrial revolu-
tion into American literature and helped launch the
literary movement of American realism."[7]

Rebecca Harding wrote her extraordinary new literature in Wheeling, Virginia, her home since childhood.[8] Oldest of the five children of a prosperous family, she later recalled that she had early internalized the precapitalist ethics that characterized money as "Mammon, the chief agent of the flesh and the devil" and assumed that "if you were born into a good family, and were 'converted,' you were considered safe for this world and the next" (*BOG*, p. 2). These doctrines may explain both Harding's shock, in early adulthood, at the disparity between wealth and poverty resulting from the rise of industrial capitalism in America, and her recourse to Christianity as a solution.

She later wrote that in childhood she read "Bunyan and Miss Edgeworth and Sir Walter." But most important for the little girl in her tree house in Virginia had been some sketches by Hawthorne in which "the commonplace folk and things which I saw every day took on a sudden mystery and charm, and for the first time, I found that they, too, belonged to the magic world of knights and pilgrims and fiends" (*BOG*, p. 30).

Like her younger brothers and sisters, the girl was first taught by her mother (to whom she would dedicate her first novel). Rachel Wilson Harding, her daughter later recalled, was "the most accurate historian and grammarian I have ever known, and had enough knowledge to fit out half a dozen modern college bred women."[9] The family had literary taste;

they hired tutors for their children as they grew
older, and when Rebecca was fourteen, sent her to attend the Female Seminary in her mother's hometown
of Washington, Pennsylvania.

Harding later commented that "before the birth of
the New Woman the country was not an intellectual
desert, as she is apt to suppose. There were teachers
of the highest grade, and libraries, and countless
circles in our towns and villages of scholarly, leisurely
folk, who loved books, and music, and Nature, and
lived much apart with them" (*BOG,* p. 101). Certainly
Washington, Pennsylvania, was no intellectual
desert. The lyceum movement was flourishing;
among provocative speakers who came to town, Harding was especially impressed by Oliver Wendell
Holmes and Horace Greeley. Among interesting local
residents was Dr. Francis Julius LeMoyn, chosen in
1839 as candidate for vice president of the United
States by the antislavery Liberty party. (Harding
would later use him as a model for *Margret Howth's*
Dr. Knowles.)[10] In the spring of 1848, Rebecca Harding graduated at the head of her class, wrote and
delivered her valedictory address, and returned to
Wheeling. She was seventeen. Thirteen years later,
she mailed off "Life in the Iron Mills" to the *Atlantic
Monthly.*

We know too little of Harding's life during those
thirteen years. Apparently, upon returning home, she
assumed a daughter's traditional role, helping her
mother with cooking, sewing, and teaching the
younger children. In a house with servants, like the

Hardings', this work was not onerous; biographers note that from her brother Wilson, who was then in college, she learned German—a skill that enabled her to write familiarly of Goethe and Fichte in *Margret Howth*. In her parents' home in Wheeling, Harding had both time and privacy to write, and it is certain that she was writing during these years. Although she later claimed to have produced nothing that she wished to see again, in a letter to James T. Fields she acknowledged that she had published "reviews of new books. A few verses and stories, impelled by the necessity or whim of the moment."[11]

Then in 1861, Harding published two short stories and a serialized novel; and in 1862, when the hard-cover edition of her book appeared, eight more short stories. Both the pace and the quality of this work testify that Harding had become a professional. She continued to publish following her 1863 marriage to Lemuel Clark Davis and throughout the years her three children grew up. Rebecca Harding Davis sustained a successful career as a writer for more than four decades. After *Margret Howth*, she produced eleven more books—eight novels, two collections of short works, and a memoir—as well as more than a dozen serialized novels and scores of short stories in the pages of magazines (serious fiction for the *Atlantic* and potboilers for *Peterson's)*. In addition, she served as contributing editor to the *New York Tribune*, wrote articles for the *Independent, Harper's Bazaar,* the *Outlook,* and the *North American Review,* and composed juveniles for the *Youth's Com-*

panion and *St. Nicholas.* But she never fulfilled her early promise, and by 1909, when her last story appeared, had outlived her popularity. When she died a year later, Rebecca Harding Davis was first identified in a newspaper obituary as "mother of Richard Harding Davis, the novelist and dramatist," then remembered as "herself a novelist and editorial writer of power."[12]

The theme the young Rebecca Harding chose for her first book, a subject that would become major in our national letters, is hunger in America.[13] Like "Life in the Iron Mills," *Margret Howth* dramatizes both the struggle "for bread and butter" and spiritual starvation. This double need—for bread and for spiritual food—constitutes the inarticulate cry of the "dumb," the cry that the "deaf" (readers like ourselves, the narrator asserts) do not hear. The first two-thirds of *Margret Howth* dramatizes this economy of scarcity. Hunger for daily bread has prodded Margret to work in the mill: she has seen her mother's "wild, hopeless" eyes "staring down into years of starvation and misery" (pp. 37–38). Yet the mill itself harbors "the ghosts of Want and Hunger and Crime . . . that do not wait for night to walk our streets" (p. 116). Margret has both "empty hands and a starved heart" (p. 157). Although she desperately tries to transform duty into happiness and "to give it to her silent gnawing heart to feed on," it is obvious that duty is not enough; without her "natural food of love," Margret is spiritually and emotionally starving (pp. 44, 155).

Harding's book begins and ends with Margret Howth, but it is Stephen Holmes's need that propels the novel. Rebelling against "all the slow years of work . . . of hard, wearing work for daily bread, when his brain had been starving for knowledge, and his soul dulled, debased with sordid trading," Holmes asks, "Was this to be always? Were these few golden moments of life to be traded for the bread and meat he ate? To eat and drink,—was that what he was here for?" (p. 123). Rebelling against the "soul-starvation" that poverty brings, he decides to marry for money, not realizing that this decision will leave his heart starved for Margret.[14] Later, finally identifying both Margret's hunger and his own, he proposes marriage. Holmes's "hungry insatiate soul," we are told, demands "air and freedom and knowledge"; and in his hunger, the narrator writes, Holmes is a representative American:

All men around him were doing the same,—thrusting and jostling and struggling, up, up. It was the American motto, Go ahead; mothers taught it to their children; the whole system was a scale of glittering prizes. (P. 121)

Margret Howth is important not because it presents individuals hungry amidst American plenty, but because it presents industrializing America as a society that is starving. Like Thoreau's Concord, Harding's western town is structured, shaped, pinched by money. By day, she writes, the town has

> an anxious, harassed look, like a speculator con-
> cluding a keen bargain; the very dwelling-houses
> smelt of trade, having shops in the lower stories; in
> the outskirts, where there are cottages in other cities,
> there were mills here; the trees, which some deluded
> dreamer had planted on the flat pavements, had all
> grown up into abrupt Lombardy poplars, knowing
> their best policy was to keep out of the way; the boys,
> playing marbles under them, played sharply "for
> keeps . . ." (P. 17)

By night, the town's back alleys are, in Dr. Knowles's
words, "a bit of hell: outskirt." He insists that Margret learn about the slum dwellers, that she look at
"women, idle trampers, whiskey-bloated. . . . half-
naked children . . ." and among them, seeking refuge,
"half-clothed blacks. Going on the underground
railroad to Canada." Then dragging Margret up a
stair, he shows her a girl who, after her lover was
killed in a mill accident, "drank herself to death—a
most unpicturesque suicide." He spells out his lesson:
"Did I call it a bit of hell? It's only a glimpse of the
under-life of America—God help us! where all men are
born free and equal" (pp. 149, 150, 151, 153, 152).

    Margret Howth presents not only a surprising view
of the underside of urban life in midcentury America,
but also an extraordinary range of commentary on
that life. Surveying her yeasty mix of slaves,
fugitives, and free people, of laborers and the
leisured, of poor and rich, Harding's white male

characters debate the possibility of democracy. In
Stephen Holmes, Harding dramatizes the debase-
ment of the Emersonian doctrine of self-reliance.
Holmes attempts to practice the ideas about self-
development voiced by the German philosopher
Fichte. But Holmes lacks not abstract liberty, but
concrete cash; a prosperous marriage, he believes,
will make him "free from these carking cares that
were making his mind foul and muddy" (p. 123).
Although capable of envisioning "a day . . . when the
lowest slave should find its true place and rightful
work, and stand up, knowing itself divine," Holmes is
no reformer: " 'To insure to him the freest development,' he did not need to wait for St. Simon, or the
golden year, he thought with a dreary gibe; money
was enough, and —Miss Herne" (p. 124).

In contrast, the philanthropist Dr. Knowles dreams
of selling his half-ownership in the mill in order to
finance a communist community for people broken
and discarded in capitalist America. Harding's most
interesting character, Knowles perceives America
around him as

> a seething caldron, in which the people I tell you of
> were atoms, where the blood of uncounted races was
> fused, but not mingled,—where creeds, philosophies,
> centuries old, grappled hand to hand in their death-
> struggle,—where innumerable aims and beliefs and
> powers of intellect, smothered rights and triumphant
> wrongs, warred together, struggling for victory.
> Vulgar American life? He thought it a life more po-

tent, more tragic in its history and prophecy, than any
that has gone before. (P. 90)

Margret's father, old Mr. Howth, voices a third
political philosophy. An aristocrat, a devotee of
"honor," a student of the Middle Ages, and a diehard
supporter of states' rights and secession, Howth con-
demns democracy:

> " 'Happy, proud America!' . . . 'Cursed, abased
> America!' better if they had said. Look at her, in the
> warm vigour of her youth, most vigorous in decay!
> Look at the germs and dregs of nations, creeds,
> religions, fermenting together! As for the theory of
> self-government, it will muddle down here, as in the
> three great archetypes of the experiment, into a pul-
> ing, miserable failure!" (P. 26)

While *Margret Howth* includes polemics about the
problems of democracy in an industrial capitalist
society within its dramatization of American hunger,
it offers as a solution spiritual—not economic—
reform. Lois, the crippled mulatto millgirl, exempli-
fies the Christian faith, hope, and charity (as well as
the Christian suffering and transcendence) that are
to save the nation. A child laborer in the mill from age
seven to age sixteen, Lois's health and her wits were
destroyed, she reports, by "th' air 'n th' work" (p.
69). Unemployed, Lois was rescued from the poor-
house by Holmes's charity, and she now earns her living as a peddler. She apparently perceives her func-
tion, however, not in terms of profits, but as a
mediator between rich and poor, black and white,

worker and farmer, bad and good—and "whatever good there was in the vilest face (and there was always something,) she was sure to see it" (pp. 95–96). By the end of the book, Lois's simple creed of Christian love has been embraced by all of the other characters and by the narrator. Public problems have been privatized, economic hunger forgotten, and spiritual hunger eradicated in the endorsement of Lois's religion.

Surveying the American scene, *Margret Howth* concerns itself not only with the problem of class, but also with other social issues. Although the Civil War is not its focus, echoes of that war, close at hand in Harding's Virginia, reverberate throughout. This is not surprising. In April, 1861, a few days after Howth began her novel, Fort Sumter was fired upon and Virginia seceded from the Union.[15] A month later, in a private letter signalling her father's opposition to the proposed enlistment of her brother and reporting on local responses to Lincoln's call for volunteers, she commented on the general confusion among Wheeling's residents:

> Dick has consented to stay. He was all ready to start on Monday, but the Mayor sent him and the other boys word that if they went it would ruin their families—spoke of Pa particularly, so Dick gave it up. . . . About a hundred started for Harper's Ferry this week, and last night sixty more. A good many families are leaving town. . . .[16]

Harding's home town was occupied by Federal troops and put under martial law that summer. By July 30, when she mailed off her revised manuscript, Wheeling had become the center of loyal Virginia.[17] In August, she wrote, "Just now 'New Virginia' and its capital are in a state of panic and preparation not to be described." Rebecca Harding learned that year that war was terrible, and she included antiwar passages in *Margret Howth*.[18] Closer to the center of her novel, however, are issues of gender and race.

Perhaps the misattribution to Harding of the antifeminist *Pro Aris et Focis—A Plea for Our Altars and Hearths* has skewed critics' readings of her female characters.[19] Although she shaped her book around Holmes, Harding made Margret Howth an active figure. The story begins on the girl's twentieth birthday, the day she starts working in the mill to support her destitute parents. In the early chapters, Margret asserts her selfhood by rejecting both Holmes's spontaneous plea that they reconcile (she realizes that she will be a "clog" on his fierce ambition) and Dr. Knowles's demands that she join his utopian commune. After the fire has cost her her mill job, however, she agrees to work with Knowles among the homeless, and she later is convinced by the transformed Holmes that her devotion to familial duty is false. Recognizing that her destiny lies with Holmes, Margret agrees to marry him, and at the book's conclusion, we are told that she is learning to emulate Lois's Christian love. From one perspective, Harding's Margret Howth is an innovative character, a woman who learns that she should assert her own God-given calling instead of sacrificing herself to daughterly duty. But Harding has it both ways: In realizing herself as an independent moral agent, Margret also recognizes that for her, the traditional role of wife and mother is best.[20]

In *Margret Howth,* however, as in other American novels of the period, the quintessential True Woman is a mulatto. Pious, pure, domestic, and obedient, Lois Yare is a Christian victim in a brutal society.[21] But in some respects she, like Margret Howth, is a new character in American letters. A freeborn woman, Lois is not a stock Tragic Mulatto caught in the system of chattel slavery, nor is she a victim of the sexual abuse of a rapacious white master whom she adores. Young and crippled, Lois is seen as asexual, victimized by industrial abuse, destroyed by overwork in the mill she hates and fears (although the imagery of rape is present in the snakes she sees in the shadows of the looms).[22] Despite her physical state, however, her spirit, like that of her sexually-abused and enslaved Tragic Mulatto sisters, is pure. If Harding's novel had been characterized as the *Uncle Tom's Cabin* of wage slavery, instead of *The Jungle,* which earned this title forty years later, Lois would be seen as both its Uncle Tom and its Little Eva. Crippled, confused, a childish female and a mulatto, Lois is a powerless victim on earth who is powerful in heaven. Although like Harriet Beecher Stowe's Uncle Tom she is exploited by an unjust system—wage slavery, child labor, poverty, and urban vice (her

mother died of drink)—Lois does not, like Uncle Tom,
defy her master to assert her belief in Christ. Instead,
like Little Eva, she attempts to live out her Christian
beliefs in the face of disbelief and indifference, then
dies. Lowest of the low, Lois (like Uncle Tom and Little Eva) teaches Christ's truths to all the other
characters.[23]

Harding's narrator has it both ways not only on the
question of gender, but also on the question of race. Is
Lois's problem—or the problem of her black father
Joe Yare—a problem of "blood," of "nature"? Or of
"nurture"? In Yare, Harding presents a Black De-
stroyer, an African-American responding to Old Testament justice with Old Testament vengeance. Unlike
Melville's scheming Babo and Stowe's would-be in-
surrectionist Dred, however, Harding's violent black
man is a free worker in industrial urban America.[24]
But is Yare a criminal because he is black (that is,
because he is somehow racially incapable of civilization)? Or because, when held in slavery, he was denied
access to the Christianity and literacy essential to
civilization? In *Margret Howth,* this question is left
open, and an alternative question is posed: how
should Harding's white middle-class audience respond to this black criminal? Here, as in *Uncle Tom's
Cabin,* African-Americans test their white com-
patriots. Holmes at first responds incorrectly,
demanding justice; later, correctly, he offers mercy.

Given the problems of class, gender, and race cen-
tral to *Margret Howth,* it is hard to accept the book's

conclusion, where social issues become spiritual, public issues become private, and (with the exception of Lois, who dies a "beautiful death") everyone lives happily ever after. Indeed, Harding's letters establish that this was not the way her book originally ended.

The correspondence between Harding, James T. Fields, powerful editor of the *Atlantic Monthly,* and his wife Annie Fields, chronicles the composition, publication, and reception of Rebecca Harding's first novel and helps explain the discrepancies between problems and solutions in *Margret Howth.*[25] When in March, 1861, James Fields accepted "Life in the Iron Mills," he offered Harding an advance on a new story, but she declined, saying she had "nothing written now."[26] A little less than a month later, however, she reported, "I have begun another story entitled 'The Deaf and the Dumb.' If it pleases you, and you accept it, would you wish to insert it in the June issue? If so I will finish it at once. . . ."[27] Fields evidently asked to see the manuscript, then quickly read and rejected her book. His letter has been lost, but Harding's response to Fields's objections suggests clearly what "The Deaf and the Dumb" was:

> Whatever holier meaning life or music has for me, has reached me through the "pathetic minor"—I fear that I only have power to echo the pathos without the meaning. When I began the story, I meant to make it end in full sunshine—to show how even "Lois" was not dumb, how even the meanest things in life, were "voices in the World, and none of them without its signification." Her life and death were to be the only

dark thread. But "Stephen Holmes" was drawn from
life and in my eagerness to show the effects of a creed
like his, I "assembled the gloom" you complain of.

In this letter, Harding proposes to revise her
manuscript to conform to Fields's ideas:

> I tell you this in order to ask you if you think I could
> alter the story so as to make it acceptable by return-
> ing to my original idea. Let her character and death (I
> cannot give up all, you see) remain, and the rest of the
> picture be steeped in warm healthy light. A "perfect
> day in June." Will you tell me if that is your only ob-
> jection—the one you assign? Would the character of
> Holmes be distasteful to your readers? I mean—the
> development in common vulgar life of the Fichtean
> philosophy and its effect upon a self made man, as I
> view it? . . .
> If you do not think I could alter the story, shall I try
> again, or do you care to have me as a contributor? . . .
> If I write for you again, would it be any difference if
> the story was longer than the last? I felt cramped, and
> we of the West like room—you know—[28]

Fields evidently sent a positive reply through his
wife, and ten days later, Harding responded:

> I am glad that Mr. Fields desires me to remain a con-
> tributor to the Atlantic. I will try and meet his wishes
> by being more cheerful. Though humor had need to be
> high and warm as God's sunshine to glow cheerily on
> Virginia soil just now.[29]

Explaining that she has no copy of her manuscript,
in this letter Harding asks that it be returned. Then,
after less than a month, she writes that she has
"sketched a story, which (as Mr. Fields is indifferent

as to length) will extend through three no's." The first part, she reports, is complete; would Fields like to see it before deciding whether to publish?[30]

Fields would not, and six weeks later Harding sent her completely rewritten manuscript. Asking that he "read it in a real July humour,—please—for I *want* you to like it," she expresses mixed feelings about her work:

> If I could have dared write a true history of today! But even in its purest phases I was afraid to touch forbidden subjects so only the husk of the thing was left, of course.[31]

He must have read it at once. Only ten days later, Harding was expressing relief at Field's acceptance and voicing her own dissatisfaction with the revised text:

> I am *very* glad.—The story disappointed me, and I was afraid you would not like it. It was so much like giving people broken bits of apple rind to chew.[32]

In revising "The Deaf and the Dumb," Harding apparently acquiesced to all of Field's suggestions: about dividing it, about changing a name, even about altering the description of the weather to conform to New Englanders' erroneous impressions of the Midwest. Writing that she had again sent him her only copy, she then asked him to return the accepted manuscript: "I think I can improve it, now; although it has not laid away even nine weeks. . . ."[33] A week later, although agreeing that the text should not be risked to wartime mails, Harding tentatively objected to the new title Fields proposed. "I don't like 'Margret Howth' at all, because she is the completest failure in the story, besides *not* being the nucleus of it. However if you do not see this, and really think it a more apt title, alter it, certainly."[34] But after a month, she announced that she was convinced that Fields was right: "I feel ashamed of myself about the name—hereafter you shall direct in everything that I write. . . ."[35]

"Margret Howth—A Story of To-Day" ran in the *Atlantic Monthly* from October, 1861 to March, 1862. Although Harding feared it was "so tedious, every body will be tired," by November Fields was considering publishing it between covers, and Harding was again thinking about revisions:[36]

> If the Story of To-day were in book form it ought to have a more complete ending, don't you think? If you *do* think so, please send me the last four or five pages, and I will alter them now.[37]

Fields didn't think so, and Harding again acquiesced: "If you are contented with the end of the story, so am I. I only intended to kill Dr. Knowles at Manassas, but he may as well see the war out, I suppose."[38] In December, she wrote Fields "you were right, and I was wrong" about the title.[39]

Margret Howth came out in February; it sold about 2000 copies and went through three printings. Although never republished in England, as Harding had hoped, it was evidently well received in America. Charles Leland praised Harding's "noble" book and included a lengthy quotation from the "great-hearted" Harding in the April, 1962 *Knickerbocker*.[40] But the novel also came under attack. One critic, Harding reported to Fields, wrote "denouncing me as a Fourierite and wishing 'he' (I) had an engraving of 'The Light of the World' so that I might know who Christ was!"[41] After the book had been out six months, she expressed unhappiness about its reception:

> Can you not tell now of Margret's probable success? Will a fourth edition be called for? I wish people had liked her better. I *am* disappointed to be honest.[42]

What was the novel Harding originally wrote, what was the first fruit of which, she thought, only "broken bits of apple-rind" remained in *Margret Howth?* What was "The Deaf and the Dumb," the manuscript Fields charged "assembled . . . gloom"? In the absence of a text, any comment must be speculative. But critic William Grayburn has guessed that Harding's book violated the fictional pattern in which a "good woman" saves a flawed hero, instead killing off Stephen Holmes in the fire and leaving Margret Howth to live out her days supporting her parents by working among the slum-dwellers with Dr. Knowles. This conclusion seems reasonable because, as he argues, "the marriage of Margret and Stephen is unthinkable" and because the happy ending "tends to dilute what must have been the major purpose of the book: indictment of social injustice and cruelties."[43] But we can also reach this conclusion on other grounds. Because the first seven chapters of Harding's text so utterly express an economy of scarcity, the affluent ending appears wrong. It is because we know that both the bodies and the souls of the Howths are starved that we choke on the description of their Christmas feast, "the turkey being done to a delicious brown, the plum-pudding quivering like luscious jelly."[44]

Further, this impossible transformation from scarcity to abundance is accompanied by the equally impossible transformation from a narrative that presents itself as a self-conscious critique of conventional fiction to a narrative that presents itself within fictional conventions. Initially, Harding's narrator had accused her audience of wanting

> idyls delicately tinted; passion-veined hearts, cut bare for curious eyes; prophetic utterances, concrete and clear; or some word of pathos or fun from the old friends who have endenizened themselves in everybody's home. You want something, in fact, to lift you out of this crowded, tobacco-stained commonplace, to kindle and chafe and glow in you. (P. 6)

Rejecting this demand, she insists instead on presenting "very common lives . . . such as are swarming in yonder market-place" (pp. 6–7). Later, introducing "the love part of my story," she again details the literary strategies that she rejects: she will give us no fairy tales of "Once upon a time," and no old-fashioned embodiments of virtue and vice. In such traditional accounts, she writes, "The heroine glides into life full-charged with rank, virtues, a name three-syllabled, and a white dress that never needs washing, ready to sail through dangers dire into a triumphant haven of matrimony . . ." (p. 101). Accordingly, Margret's initial physical description is innovative: "There were no reflected lights about her; no gloss on her skin, no glitter in her eyes, no varnish on her soul . . . her hair, the only beauty of the woman, was lustreless brown, lay in unpolished folds of dark shadow" (pp. 22–23). Yet in the final third of the book, her appearance is transformed into that of a stock heroine as Holmes "loosened her hair, and it rolled down about the bright, tearful face, shining in the red fire-light like a mist of tawny gold" (p. 242). After their Christmas Eve reconciliation, Margret even likens herself to a heroine: "You shall go, now, Stephen Holmes,—quick! before your sovereign lady fades, like Cinderella" (p. 243). Similarly, Holmes becomes a traditional patriarchal hero. Not only does he take "his rightful place" as Margret's judge, but she concludes as he does so that she has erred more than he and is "glad to be humbled before him" (p. 233). Holmes later gives his fiancée some standard intructions:

> "I need warmth and freshness and light: my wife shall bring them to me. She shall be no strong-willed reformer, standing alone: a sovereign lady with kind words for the world, who gives her hand only to that man whom she trusts, and keeps her heart and its secrets for me alone." (P. 242)

Even the grasping urban environment of the mill town is transformed into a place "where Santa Claus might have made his headquarters" (p. 205). Later, the discovery of oil on the Howth farm is appropriately likened to the surprises chronicled in the Arabian Nights (p. 255). This discovery of oil, of course, tidies up the only remaining loose end. The spiritual economy of scarcity has already been replaced by one of abundance as romantic love has led to Christian love; now, the material economy of scarcity is replaced by an affluence that transforms Margret into an heiress as wealthy as the abandoned mill owner's daughter.

In addition, other internal evidence hints at the shape of "The Deaf and the Dumb." A caged chicken in the factory seems a useful symbol for the entire novel, up to Holmes's rescue: it speaks to the anti-urban, anti-industrial bias of the narrator and to her determination to find significance in the unromantic commonplace. Emblematizing the economy of scarcity, the caged chicken has, as Dr. Knowles asserts, its own work to do; and Holmes's efforts to rescue it during the fire signal that his values are basically humane (pp. 14, 204). But with Holmes's recovery and Margret's affluence, this symbol loses significance.

The shifts in literary references are equally telling. In the first third of the novel, the narrator describes the account book Margret keeps in the factory, refers to the *Daily Gazette* and the Bible, glances aslant at old Mr. Howth's medieval romance, and defines Miss Hearne's snobbery by her references to "King

Copelia and the Beggar Maid." In the last third, however, completely different literary references appear: in addition to the comments about Cinderella and the Arabian Nights, we are told of Christmas at the Howths that "Dickens himself, the priest of the genial day, would have been contented" (p. 249).

The collapse of the chronological structure of *Margret Howth* further supports the notion that in "The Deaf and the Dumb" Stephen Holmes died in the flames. Consider: the first seven chapters present the events of forty-eight hours. Day one, carefully identified as October 2, 1860, Margret's twentieth birthday and her first day in the mill, is dramatized in chapters 1 and 2.[45] Day two, October 3, is dramatized in chapters 3 through 7. This use of the day as a structural unit recalls the organization of "Life in the Iron Mills"; yet after chapter 7 the temporal pattern breaks. The final four chapters, which account for a third of the book and replace its "gloom" with a "June" perspective, are organized in relation to the passage of a year.[46]

It seems likely that Harding's original gloomy text, after dramatizing the events of October 2 and 3, 1860, presented the events of October 4—Holmes's death in the fire, Lois's beautiful death, Dr. Knowles's abandonment of his dream of a Good Society (shown briefly in chapter 8)—and that the book ended with Margret working among the poor, in Holmes's words, "a strong-willed reformer, standing alone" (p. 242). This scheme certainly would constitute a story that Fields felt "assembled the gloom"; it would also con-

situte a story that Harding could cut, then append
with a sunny new ninety-page conclusion, in the brief
eight-week interval between her request for the
return of her rejected manuscript and her submission
of the revised text that Fields would entitle *Margret
Howth.*

But without Harding's manuscript, it is impossible
to determine the exact shape of "The Deaf and the
Dumb." We can be certain only that after "Life in the
Iron Mills" the young author wrote a serious first
novel voicing the same outrage and dramatizing
many of the same social problems that had distin-
guished her earlier story, that the editor of the most
important literary publication in America rejected
her book as gloomy, and that she then rewrote it to
conform to his demand for a sunnier literature. Yet
the importance of Harding's novel remains: Amazing-
ly, at the outset of the Civil War, this young, middle-
class white woman in Wheeling dramatized the social
problems that would plague the postwar nation. Harding's depiction of the America she had glimpsed in
her earlier story, her portraits of white-collar working women, crazed millgirls, southern medievalists,
communist reformers, acquisitive go-getters, and
alienated African-Americans—characters excluded
from genteel antebellum fiction—are a stunning expression of the effort "to know and to tell the truth,"
an effort William Dean Howells later judged crucial
to the development of a democratic literature.[47]

Years ago, Ann Douglas charged women and clergymen with responsibility for "the feminization of American culture" in the the nineteenth century, but *Margret Howth* presents an important instance in which the leading member of the white male literary establishment required that a nineteenth-century woman writer "feminize" her text.[48] Rebecca Harding Davis was to produce steadily for the commercial press for more than forty years. Damned by dollars and by gender conventions as surely as her creation Margret Howth, rarely would she again overtly treat themes like those that had ignited her early writings of social protest. When she named her first novel "The Deaf and the Dumb," the young writer apparently was referring to the comfortable who are deaf to the dumb cries of the hungry. Read within the context of her work, however, Harding's title signals the deafness of the powerful editor who struck the young writer dumb.

Jean Fagan Yellin

Notes

1. "A Story of To-Day" appeared in the *Atlantic Monthly* 8, 9 (October 1861–March 1862): 471–486, 582–597, 707–718, 40–51, 202–213, 282–298. It was republished as *Margret Howth—A Story of To-Day* by Ticknor and Fields in Boston, 1862. References to *Margret Howth* are to this edition. "Life in the Iron Mills" had appeared in the *Atlantic*

Monthly 7 (April 1861): 430–451; it was republished by The Feminist Press in 1972; my references are to *Life in the Iron Mills and Other Stories,* edited by Tillie Olsen and published in New York by The Feminist Press in 1985; page numbers are designated *LIIM.* I am grateful to librarians at Pace University and the University of Virginia, to Pace University for a summer grant that enabled me to work on this paper, to Rijksuniversiteit Limburg for collegial hospitality, to Kate Schachter and Richard Fabrizio for their expert translations, to Karen Davy for help locating texts, and to Jean Pfaelzer and Rita Gollin for comments on an earlier version.

2. See, for example, Upton Sinclair, *The Jungle* (1906), and Mike Gold, *Jews Without Money* (1930).

3. Arthur Hobson Quinn, *American Fiction: An Historical and Critical Survey* (New York: D. Appleton-Century, 1936), p. 204.

4. Fred L. Pattee, *Dictionary of American Biography,* vol. 5, eds. Allen Johnson and Dumas Malone (New York: Charles Scribner's Sons, 1930), p. 143.

5. Bernard R. Bowron, Jr., "Realism in America," *Comparative Literature* 3 (Summer 1951): 273.

6. James C. Austin, *Fields of the Atlantic Monthly* (San Marino: The Huntington Library, 1953), p. 370.

7. Jean Pfaelzer, "Introduction to 'Marcia' by Rebecca Harding Davis," *Legacy* 4 (Spring 1987): 3. Also see Pfaelzer, "Rebecca Harding Davis: Domesticity, Social Order, and the Industrial Novel, *International Journal of Women's Studies* 4 (1981): 234–244. For connections between Olsen and Rebecca Harding Davis, see Frances M. Malpezzi, "Sisters in Protest: Rebecca Harding Davis and Tillie Olsen," *Re Artes: Liberales* 12 (Spring 1986): 1–9.

8. Biographical information about Rebecca Harding Davis comes from the following sources: Rebecca Harding Davis, *Bits of Gossip* (New York: Houghton, Mifflin & Co., 1904); references in my text are to the edition published at Cam-

bridge: The Riverside Press, 1905, designated *BOG;* Gerald
Langford, *The Richard Harding Davis Years: A Biography
of a Mother and Son* (New York: Holt, Rinehart and
Winston, 1961); Helen Woodward Sheaffer, "Rebecca Harding Davis, Pioneer Realist," Ph.D. diss., University of
Pennsylvania, 1947; William F. Grayburn, "The Major Fiction of Rebecca Harding Davis," Ph.D. diss., Pennsylvania
State University, 1965; and to items in the Rebecca Harding
Davis Collection (#6109), Clifton Waller Barrett Library,
Manuscripts Division, Special Collections Department,
University of Virginia Library. Unless otherwise noted, all
references to correspondence are to items in this collection;
I am grateful for permission to quote from them. I regret
that I have been unable to examine Margret Wyman,
"Women in the Realistic Novel, 1860–1893," Ph.D. diss.,
Radcliffe College, 1950.

9. Langford, p. 4

10. LeMoyn declined; in April 1840, the Liberty party
nominated James G. Birney and Thomas Earle. For Le-
Moyn, see Margaret C. McCullouch, *Fearless Advocate of the
Right: The Life of Francis Julius LeMoyn, M.D., 1789–1879*
(Boston: Christopher Publishing House [1941]). Rebecca
Harding Davis later included Dr. Knowlon in "The Harmonists," *Atlantic Monthly* 8 (May 1866): 529–538.

11. Rebecca Harding to James T. Fields, 26 January 1861.

12. Listing Rebecca Harding Davis's writings, Grayburn
(pp. 413–414)) cites for 1861 "Life in the Iron Mills," *Atlantic Monthly;* "A Story of To-Day," *Atlantic Monthly;* and
"The Murder in the Glenn Ross," *Peterson's Magazine.* For
1862, book publication of *Margret Howth;* in *Atlantic Monthly:* "John Lamar," "David Gaunt," and "Blind Tom"; in
Peterson's: "The Locked Chamber," "The Asbestos Box,"
"A Story of Life Insurance," "My First Case," and "The
Egyptian Beetle." Harding's books, following *Margret
Howth* (1862), are *Waiting for the Verdict* (1868); *Dallas
Galbraith* (1868); *Berrytown, or Kitty's Choice* (1873); *John*

300   MARGRET HOWTH.

Andross (1874); *A Law Unto Herself* (1878); *Natasqua*
(1886); *Kent Hampden* (1892); *Silhouettes of American Life*
(1892); *Mr. Warrick's Daughters* (1896); *Frances Waldeaux*
(1897); *Bits of Gossip* (1904). The obituary is in the *New
York Times*, 30 September 1910.

13. See, for example, Richard Wright, *American Hunger*
(1977).

14. Holmes's hungry eyes, however, betray him; see pp.
133 and 137.

15. Rebecca Harding to James T. Fields, 11 April 1861.

16. Rebecca Harding to "My Dear Jim" [Jim Wilson],
[May, 1861], Baird manuscript, quoted in Sheaffer, p. 36.

17. Rebecca Harding to James T. Fields, 30 July [1861].

18. Rebecca Harding to James T. Fields, 17 August
[1861]. In *Margret Howth*, see, for example, pp. 197–200.
For more on Harding's wartime Virginia, see *BOG*, pp.
109–139.

19. *Pro Aris et Focis: A Plea for Our Altars and Hearths*
(New York: Virtue and Yorston, 1870); the misattribution is
discussed in Philip Eppard, "Rebecca Harding Davis: A
Misattribution," *Papers of the Bibliographical Society of
America* 69 (1975): 265–267; and in Sharon M. Harris,
"Rebecca Harding Davis: A Continuing Misattribution,"
Legacy 5 (Spring 1988): 33–34.

20. For patterns of behavior of female characters in
nineteenth-century women's fiction, see Nina Baym,
*Woman's Fiction: A Guide to Novels by and about Women in
America, 1820–1870* (Ithaca: Cornell University Press,
1978); and see Jane Tompkins, *Sensational Designs* (New
York: Oxford University Press, 1985).

21. For a discussion of the Tragic Mulatto as a True
Woman, see my *Women and Sisters: The Antislavery
Feminists in American Culture* (New Haven: Yale Universi-
ty Press, 1990).

22. One passage, however, where Lois weeps at the sight

of a wedding dress, suggests that she, too, had hoped for marriage.

23. See Harriet Beecher Stowe, *Uncle Tom's Cabin* (1852).

24. See Herman Melville, "Benito Cereno" (1855) and Harriet Beecher Stowe, *Dred* (1856).

25. For James T. Fields, see W. S. Tryon, *Parnassus Corner: A Life of James T. Fields* (Boston: Houghton Mifflin, 1963); for Annie Fields, see Mark A. De W. Howe, *Memories of a Hostess* (Boston: Atlantic Monthly Press, 1922), and Rita Gollin's forthcoming biography; much of the pertinent correspondence is included in Grayburn.

26. Rebecca Harding to James T. Fields, 15 March 1861.

27. Rebecca Harding to James T. Fields, 11 April 1861.

28. Rebecca Harding to James T. Fields, 10 May [1861], from ms. published in Sheaffer, pp. 56–57, and in Austin, pp. 370–371; original manuscript in the Huntington Library, FI 1167.

29. Rebecca Harding to Annie Fields, 20 May [1861]; Annie Fields frequently performed important literary tasks for the *Atlantic*.

30. Rebecca Harding to Annie Fields, 18 June 1861.

31. Rebecca Harding to James T. Fields, 30 July [1861].

32. Rebecca Harding to James T. Fields, 9 August [1861].

33. Rebecca Harding to James T. Fields, 9 August [1861].

34. Rebecca Harding to James T. Fields, 17 August [1861].

35. Rebecca Harding to James T. Fields, 17 September [1861].

36. Rebecca Harding to James T. Fields, 28 September 1861.

37. Rebecca Harding to James T. Fields, 19 November 1861.

38. Rebecca Harding to James T. Fields, 26 November [1861].

39. Rebecca Harding to James T. Fields, n.d. [December 1861].

40. Charles G. Leland, "Sun-shine in Thought," *The Knickerbocker* 19 (April 1862): 320–24.

41. Rebecca Harding to James T. Fields, 6 January [1862].

42. Rebecca Harding to James T. Fields, 4 September [1862]. A projected edition of *Margret Howth and Other Stories* is mentioned in Rebecca Harding to James T. Fields, 27 June [1862]; this letter is published in Grayburn, p. 39.

43. See Grayburn, pp. 159, 204.

44. This is true even though the narrator includes the parenthetical caveat, "a Christian dinner to-day, if we starve the rest of the year!" p. 248.

45. "I wish you would add '1860' to the date of the ledger.—somewhere in the first pages, will you please?" Rebecca Harding to James T. Fields, 17 August [1861].

46. This perspective is so insistent that I can only read Harding's assurances to Fields that her revision will evoke "a perfect day in June" and her plea that he receive her book in "a real July humour" within the context of her narrator's disgust at the mill-owner's daughter, who portrays the month of June in a tableau vivante. Rebecca Harding to James T. Fields, 10 May 1861; 30 July 1861.

47. William Dean Howells, *Criticism and Fiction* (New York: Harper and Brothers, 1891), p. 187; for the commercialization of Rebecca Harding Davis, see James C. Austin, "Success and Failure of Rebecca Harding Davis," *Midcontinent American Studies Journal* 3 (Spring 1962): 44–49.

48. Ann Douglas, *The Femininization of American Culture* (New York: Knopf, 1977).

The Feminist Press at The City University of New York offers alternatives in education and in literature. Founded in 1970, this nonprofit, tax-exempt educational and publishing organization works to eliminate sexual stereotypes in books and schools and to provide literature with a broad vision of human potential.

NEW AND FORTHCOMING BOOKS

Allegra Maud Goldman, a novel by Edith Konecky. Introduction by Tillie Olsen. Afterword by Bella Brodzki. $9.95 paper.

Bamboo Shoots after the Rain: Contemporary Stories by Women Writers of Taiwan, edited by Ann C. Carver and Sung-sheng Yvonne Chang. $35.00 cloth, $14.95 paper.

A Brighter Coming Day: A Frances Ellen Watkins Harper Reader, edited by Frances Smith Foster. $35.00 cloth, $14.95 paper.

The End of This Day's Business, a novel by Katharine Burdekin. Afterword by Daphne Patai. $35.00 cloth, $8.95 paper.

How I Wrote Jubilee *and Other Essays on Life and Literature,* by Margaret Walker. Edited by Maryemma Graham. $35.00 cloth, $9.95 paper.

Journey Toward Freedom: The Story of Sojourner Truth, a biography by Jacqueline Bernard. Introduction by Nell Irvin Painter. $35.00 cloth, $10.95 paper.

Margret Howth, a novel by Rebecca Harding Davis. Afterword by Jean Fagan Yellin. $35.00 cloth, $11.95 paper.

Now in November, a novel by Josephine W. Johnson. Afterword by Nancy Hoffman. $29.95 cloth, $9.95 paper.

On Peace, War, and Gender: The Challenge of Genetic Explanations, Genes and Gender Volume VI, edited by Anne E. Hunter. $35.00 cloth, $15.95 paper.

Quest, a novel by Helen R. Hull. Afterword by Patricia McClelland Miller. $11.95 paper.

Ripening: Selected Work, second edition, by Meridel
Le Sueur. Edited and with an Introduction by Elaine
Hedges. New Afterword by Meridel Le Sueur. $10.95
paper.
*Truth Tales: Contemporary Stories by Women Writers of
India,* selected by Kali for Women. Introduction by
Meena Alexander. $35.00 cloth, $12.95 paper.
Women's Studies International: Nairobi and Beyond,
edited by Aruna Rao. $35.00 cloth, $15.95 paper.
*Women Writing in India: 600 B.C. to the Present. Vol. I:
600 B.C. to the Early Twentieth Century. Vol. II: The
Twentieth Century.* Edited by Susie Tharu and
K. Lalita. Each volume $59.95 cloth, $29.95 paper.

For a free catalog, write to The Feminist Press at The City
University of New York, 311 East 94 Street, New York, NY
10128. Send individual book orders to The Talman Company, Inc., 150 Fifth Avenue, New York, NY 10011. Please
include $2.00 postage and handling for one book, $.75 for
each additional.